MOON CURSED

A WOLF HOLLOW SHIFTERS NOVEL

NIKKI JEFFORD

For my sisters:
Chelsea, I am so proud of you, Little Wolf.
Morgan and Sara, I'll howl alongside you any day.
Kendall, even though you prefer cats over dogs.
Pam and Julie, thanks for letting me steal your brother.

✦ chapter one

TIME WAS IRRELEVANT after the fall of civilization …that is, for everyone besides the witch wolf shifter Elsie.

For Elsie, time meant everything.

Time was running out.

She had three weeks to claim a mate or become the property of a particularly brutish bear shifter in serious need of a shave. Billions of humans had died during the last couple decades, leaving behind billions of amenities—like razor blades. But Brutus was part caveman, and Elsie didn't want his bearded face anywhere near hers.

As the sun began its descent over Balmar Heights, she paced the stone terrace of her father's villa the same way she had every evening since leaving Wolf Hollow. The skirt of her gown billowed against her ankles and whispered over her legs like mist.

Below their mountaintop, the forest stretched on as though the trees knew no boundaries and would never end. On and on they went—oblivious to time. If only she had that kind of luxury.

In three weeks, she'd reach her twentieth year.

1

In three weeks, she'd be mated . . . Would she be claimed by a wolf or a bear?

The plan had been to find a mate among her half-brother's packmates, and Elsie might have succeeded if a young woman from the city hadn't thrown herself on the pack's mercy. Now the woman's cruel brother would send out his men to search for her.

Elsie should have been allowed to remain in the hollow. She could have helped. But Tabor had stubbornly insisted she wait it out at Balmar Heights like some kind of princess sequestered in a stone tower.

She clenched and unclenched her fists. If she didn't love her brother so much she'd curse his name. But she could no more curse him than forsake the air in her lungs. Instead, she whispered a protection spell into the wind. Too many miles separated her from the hollow for the incantation to have any effect, but it brought her comfort. There wasn't much else she could do.

The soft chatter of neighboring families and the clack of plates reached her ears as patio tables were set. Smoky, fishy smells rose from outdoor grills.

Elsie wrinkled her nose.

Her father had gone to check on her friend Sharon, who was about five weeks away from giving birth to her first child. Sharon had been bedridden the past month and would remain so until the birth. Lazarus diligently checked on her every few days and didn't expect to return until dark.

Elsie cast one last wistful look at the dusky forest before drifting away from the balcony's iron railing. If she'd lingered a second longer, she might have been spotted by William. His voice sailed across the lawn.

"Have you seen Elsie?" came his hopeful, boyish pitch.

She backed up slowly, one careful step at a time toward the open doorway to the second story of her father's villa.

"I'm not sure," came the answer from their nearest neighbor, Tanya. "Lazarus left to check on Sharon. I don't know whether Elsie went with him or not."

"I'll see if she's around. Thanks!"

Elsie could just picture the spark in William's eyes—his anticipation of finding her alone. Perhaps sleeping with him when they were sixteen had been a mistake. By now she would have thought he had accepted her fate and moved on. He hadn't.

"Elsie?" he called from the first floor.

She exhaled a sigh through her nostrils and glided toward the stairs, her shoulders slumped. Before she reached the landing, her legs stopped moving, anchoring her to the second floor.

"Elsie? You here?" William's voice snaked around the first floor.

Her mouth opened, but no words emerged.

"Elsie?"

It would be awkward if she answered now after waiting for so long while William went from room to room calling her name.

"Don't see me," she whispered as she moved swiftly away from the landing. It wasn't a spell so much as a plea. There was nothing William could do to help her. He could only make things worse.

She drifted into her father's upper-floor den with its busy oriental rugs, statues, and oil paintings, calming her heartbeat and softening her breath along with the gentle patter inside her chest.

William mounted the stairs. When he reached the top, he stopped. Elsie waited for him to call her name. When he didn't, her heart rate picked up. His silence unnerved her more than the sound of his voice. She felt as though she'd been cornered into a game of hide and seek.

The hairs on the back of her neck rose and her jaw ached as her wolf fought to take possession of her body so she could attack the unwanted intruder. A silent growl reverberated up her throat.

The soft rustle of pant legs moved past her toward the balcony. William would likely check outside first–see if she stood at the railing staring out wistfully as she so often did.

After he passed the den, she slipped into the wide hall and down the stairs, drifting one step at a time to the first floor. She left her father's villa from an arched opening in back, her bare feet brushing against stone until sinking into the soft grass of the yard.

She strode forward, not bothering to duck into the shadows of neighboring villas. When she reached the cobblestones connecting all the homes, a wind gusted up as though to prevent her from reaching the gates and road leading off the mountain. She kept walking, her hair rippling at her back.

A light mist gusted over her bare arms and face

from a large three-tiered fountain splashing water from the center of the wide road. Elsie had never given such extravagances a second thought until spending time in Wolf Hollow. Life in the hollow was much harder, but she'd also felt a keener sense of kinship, community, and space to breathe. Her wolf didn't like walls. The stone pillars flanking the entrance of Balmar Heights loomed toward her as her gown billowed in the rushing wind.

A wizard named Everett stood with his back resting against the wall, smoking from a pipe, watching her approach. Everett was a tall, fit wizard nearly twice her age. His eyes were a deep, penetrating brown that matched the thick hair on his head and tidy scruff over his chin and cheeks.

Puffs of white smoke wafted in the air around him. He straightened as Elsie neared. He pulled the pipe from his mouth to smile.

"Good evening, Lady Wolf."

Elsie laughed and curtsied. "And greetings to the most desired bachelor at Balmar Heights."

Everett's eyebrows jumped. "Most desired?"

"According to more than one witch on this mountain."

Everett's laughter boomed. He lifted his pipe to his lips and sucked in languidly, expelling smoke through his nostrils while holding Elsie in his brown-eyed gaze. He pulled the pipe out of his mouth and pointed it at her.

"Flattery is not going to work on me, Elsie. Lazarus made it clear he doesn't want you running outside the gates on your own."

She smiled playfully.

"Oh, Everett. I know better than to try and use flattery to get past you. I just want to give you something pleasant to think about while I'm away."

The skin around Everett's eyes started to crinkle in confusion as Elsie hit him with her spell. *"Slenti."* With her words, Everett froze in place, pipe pinched between fingers at his side.

He wouldn't be able to move for the better part of an hour; however, he would be able to think. Too bad the spell didn't include a mental fog. Everett's mind already had to be racing with the shock and betrayal of what she'd done.

The number one rule on the mountain was no casting spells on other wizards, but it wasn't as though they could toss her out. Soon enough she'd have to leave them whether or not she liked it.

Elsie drifted to Everett's side.

"I'm truly sorry about this, Everett, but I'm about to jump out of my skin. I'll run, then I'll return like I always do."

She hurried past him and out the gates, pulling her dress over her head and tossing it onto the ground. Crouching naked over the rocky terrain, Elsie shifted.

Wind flowed through her fur as she ran along the mountain, breezing over her nose and down the ridge of her back to her tail. The wizards of Balmar Heights could transform liquid and objects into almost anything they wished, create electricity or fire with a touch, manipulate the weather, and use vast combinations of words to create spells for endless possibilities. But none of them knew the exhilaration of running free.

Elsie could experience the best of both worlds, yet she found herself at war between two lives. Wolf and witch. Both sides of her were equally strong and neither could be suppressed for long.

The high-pitched call of an eagle pierced the air. Elsie dashed down the mountainside, to the next mountain and the next, covering great distances with little effort. When she ran, she felt untouchable, strong, and brave. She felt her place at the top of the food chain.

What need did her wolf have of possessions, clothes, or electricity?

None at all.

She stopped on top of a grassy plateau, lifted her head, and howled, drowning out the hoot of owls. Her powerful call silenced the forest.

Elsie looked over the darkened woods with a satisfied grin. The trees around her seemed to hold their breath—the forest creatures waiting for permission to resume their activities. Before they could, a roar bellowed across the mountain valley and shook the ground beneath Elsie's paws.

The hair on her back lifted and a snarl parted her lips as a massive brown bear charged through the forest straight at her. Brutus. She should have known he'd be lurking nearby, anticipating her need to step outside the gates for a run. She wouldn't allow him to intimidate her. She didn't belong to him yet and hopefully never would—though he couldn't know that, not until she'd succeeded in claiming a more suitable mate.

Growls erupted from Elsie's throat. She flew down the

plateau and around Brutus, snapping at his hairy back.

Brutus spun around and took a swipe at her with his thick claws, but Elsie was already racing around him. Her growls were answered by vicious roars as Brutus spun around again and again to face her. When his paw came within an inch of her muzzle, she jumped back, fangs bared. Brutus charged her. She darted past him, snarling, and bit him from behind, quickly releasing his thick hide to put a good three feet between them before he had a chance to whip around again.

Elsie could run circles around Brutus, but without the help of packmates, she would tire out quickly. She should run, no race back to Balmar Heights but she couldn't stand to give Brutus the satisfaction of chasing her off. These were as much her woods as his.

Her lips lifted over her gums and a snarl rose in her throat. The next time she got around him, she bit him above his back leg.

Brutus roared and jerked around. His mouth opened wide enough to fit her entire head between his jaws.

Elsie sprang back and growled. Brutus charged her, but she darted around him.

Big, lumbering brute. His massive size did not intimidate her in the least.

As soon as she got around him, she pounced to nip him again. But he'd already anticipated her move and spun back in her direction. A thick hairy arm and wide paw swung at her as she closed in. Brutus batted her away as though she weighed no more than a twig. She flew back and crashed against a tree trunk, crying out.

If she'd been in her human form, the blow would have knocked her unconscious and possibly broken a few bones.

While she lay on her side, stunned like one of the unfortunate birds that sometimes hit the villa's windowpane, Brutus shifted. He performed the transformation on two legs, watching her the entire time with dark black eyes that turned brown. His snout receded, ears shrank, and fur turned into hair that covered his head, face, chest, arms, and legs. Buried beneath all the hair was a tall, muscular man with a sharp jaw and stern gaze.

Elsie shifted as Brutus approached. She spoke an incantation as she stood, calling for an invisible barrier between herself and Brutus—one he walked right through. She repeated her words, spreading her arms to strengthen the spell, but Brutus kept coming.

His fishy breath hit her face from half a foot away. Elsie's lashes fluttered as though that would clear the stench from her nostrils. Brutus grinned wide but did not leer at her naked form. He was too busy turning over his right arm to show her the symbols carved into his skin. A curved line cupped his wrist before descending four inches down his arm where it curled into a pentagram. Another line zagged midway through the line. The pattern rose above his skin in a red, angry scar.

"Your father gave this to me. Protection from all sorcery. Your spells won't work on me, Little Witch."

The pride and triumph in his voice made Elsie scowl. Why hadn't her father warned her?

Brutus's smile widened. "Did your father not tell you?"

He lifted his head and let his gaze roam over her body. "Your spells won't save you, and you won't be able to use them against me once we are mated."

"I'll still have my claws," Elsie retorted.

"Mine are bigger," Brutus said.

"I'm faster."

Brutus opened his mouth to respond, but nothing came out. Elsie didn't need magic to shut him up. She could outwit, outrun, and best him any time. Without a ready response, Brutus resorted to a human growl. His arms shot out, trapping her between the tree trunk and his hairy chest and bristling beard. Body tensed; heat flushed over Elsie's skin. Too bad her magic had been smothered, unlike her anger, which wanted to lash out and maim Brutus for his act of dominance. The hairy beast's chest hovered inches from hers. If he groomed himself, he could make himself more pleasing on the eyes, but his wild, unkempt exterior fit his boorish personality spectacularly.

"Once we are mated, you will obey me." He glanced at her breasts and sneered. "I have no desire for a witch, but I will take pleasure in knowing how much it kills your tyrant of a father to think of his sweet little girl warming my cave."

Elsie couldn't hold back a shudder of revulsion and outrage. Brutus's gaze snapped up and he glared into her eyes.

"You will cook my meals, wash my clothes, and tend my fire. Let me be clear: Your purpose is to serve me. I will mate you to seal our claim, but that is all. I am not your father. I will not bring more half-breeds into this world."

Elsie slapped him, but his damned beard got in the way of a satisfying smack. She shoved his chest next. He didn't even budge. Brutus threw his head back and laughed.

Dark energy coiled inside Elsie's stomach.

"Formella lavita!" she screamed, trying to throw him off.

Through his dark beard, Brutus smirked.

"I told you, magic won't work on me."

Elsie ducked down and darted away from him.

"Then I will shift and tear you apart," she snarled.

Brutus turned slowly and folded his arms. "Do that and your brother is dead."

His words hit her like arrowheads. Elsie clutched her chest.

"Did your father not mention that part either?" This time Brutus sighed. He glanced off toward the mountains as though their conversation had begun to bore him. "My father was a shrewd man and a mighty bear shifter—smarter than Lazarus gave him credit. Before he agreed to your father's bargain and returned those little witchlings, he made sure Lazarus would not be tempted to back out. Not only will there be no more births among the wizards of your coven if you do not claim me by your twentieth year, but any child fathered by Lazarus will immediately perish. You. Your brother." The truth behind Brutus's words tore through her chest.

Brutus shrugged, showing how little he cared either way. Whether she was his mate or dead, her father would lose her. But there was one more option. One Brutus couldn't know. The bear shifter's father might have been shrewd, but her father was far more cunning.

Elsie tossed her hair back. "I still have three more weeks."

Three weeks to save herself, her brother, and the future of her coven by claiming a wolf shifter—a mate who would not impede her powers or freedom.

"Enjoy them, because after we mate, I will see to it that you never run wild or leave my cave without permission."

"Or what?" Elsie challenged, unable to resist. "At that point you'll have no more leverage over my father or his people, and I promise you, whatever misery you think to bestow on me will come back at you tenfold."

Brutus grunted dismissively. He turned his arm over, flashing her his marked flesh.

"You make threats because they are all you have left." He rolled his neck and cracked his knuckles. "You will come to me in three weeks, I promise you that." Brutus lumbered away without a backward glance.

Elsie spit out a curse at his retreating form even though it did no good.

Three weeks. She still had three weeks to find a suitable mate. When her father made his oath to Brutus's father, he hadn't specified that his firstborn daughter would have to marry a bear shifter. His exact word had been "shifter."

Elsie had a wolf to claim; a bashful, brawny shifter with beautiful brown eyes and full lips she'd imagined kissing a hundred times. He just didn't know it yet.

chapter two

FULL DARKNESS HAD swallowed the mountain by the time Elsie returned to Balmar Heights. Three lanterns glowed outside the gates. She breathed in the familiar scents of her father, Everett, and William.

As soon as she shifted, Everett and William turned their heads—averting their gazes. William's lantern caught the flush in his cheeks and the silver glow of her father's hair. Lazarus, a tall, dignified, and handsome man in his mid-sixties, straightened his back. He held a lantern in one hand and Elsie's dress in the other, his green eyes staring into hers as she stepped forward to retrieve her gown from him.

As she pulled the long, flowing dress over her head, Lazarus said, "You may return home now."

"But–" William began in protest.

"It's late," came Lazarus's stern voice.

Elsie pulled her dress down in time to catch the sneer William directed at her father. A shiver slid down her arms. Her father saw William as a harmless boy, but size had nothing to do with intention; something malevolent lurked beneath the surface of William's mind. He had never hidden his distaste for her father or his opinion that he could take care of her better than Lazarus. No matter how many times Elsie had snapped at William that she could take care of herself, he'd start up the same conversation the next time he came over. Until she broke up with him.

Luckily, William stormed away without another word, his lantern winking out after he rounded the stone gates.

Her father next turned to Everett and raised his eyebrows.

"Are we good here?"

When Everett turned his gaze from Lazarus to Elsie, she bowed her head, guilt swirling up her body like a sudden storm.

"If it had been anyone else . . ." Everett paused to sigh deeply.

"I'm sorry," Elsie whispered.

"She will never do anything like that again," Lazarus said. He turned to Elsie. "Isn't that right?"

Elsie lifted her head and stared at her father. She wouldn't be around much longer to do much of anything, but she held back the comment. Instead, she nodded.

Everett shrugged. "Well, what's done is done. At least Elsie is back safe."

"Yes," Lazarus said slowly. Elsie could practically hear his unspoken thoughts. *"For now."* He nodded toward the gates. "Let us retire, my dear, and leave Everett to guard his post—" Lazarus cleared his throat, "—without further hindrance." Elsie caught the amusement in his eyes. Just as quickly, he whisked it away with a sweep of the lantern.

She fell into step beside her father, walking in silence down the middle of the road. The cobblestones were cool against Elsie's feet. Soft lights glimmered from villa windows. The fountain no longer splashed water. Solar lights glowed around the borders of yards and lit up the walkways. They had their own set that lit up the way to the terrace of their villa. Her father opened the front door and waited for Elsie to enter before following her inside. Candlelight flickered from pillar holders and glass bowls atop antique side tables and stone shelves against the walls.

Once he'd shut them inside the villa, her father clasped his hands behind his back and paced in front of the door, all the while training his green gaze on Elsie.

"You should have told me you needed to run."

"I always need to run." Elsie's tone was matter-of-fact. She'd never felt a need to sass her father. He'd always tried to understand and nurture her wolf nature—never suppress it.

"This is a volatile time. It would have put my mind at ease to place a protective spell over you before you went out."

Elsie wrinkled her nose, the foul, fishy smell of Brutus's bear breath coming back to her. She narrowed her eyes.

"And what good would that have done me against Brutus?"

Her father stopped pacing to face her, his own eyes turning to slits as though mirroring her expression.

"Did you see him? Did he harm you? Touch you?" Lightning flashed across her father's expanding pupils, which temporarily eclipsed his irises.

Elsie shook her head, lips pursed.

"He made his usual taunts. He has no interest in me. He only wishes to torment you."

Her father's lips lifted over his gums as he hissed disdainfully.

"Foul creature. I would sooner the world end before I allow him to have you. I would have never made such a bargain—" Her father shook his head. The green returned to his eyes as he gazed into the candle flames along the wall. "Lillian was barren. It mattered not to me. She was my forever. I thought we would grow old together."

In the silence that followed, Elsie drifted to her father's side and hugged him. He patted her head, eyes still focused on the candles whose flames whiffed out, pitching them in shadowy darkness.

"I loved your mother, too, and Tabor's. I loved them all so much." Her father's words were hollow and pained Elsie's heart. She couldn't imagine losing one life mate, let alone three. And now, her father would lose her as well. Even if she successfully claimed a wolf, she would have to leave Balmar Heights and the family and friends she'd grown up with. But at least she'd have the freedom to visit.

Elsie pulled away from her father and lifted her chin.

"You did it to save those children. It was the right choice. I *am* part wolf shifter. Why shouldn't I marry another of my kind?" Elsie squared her shoulders.

Her father's jaw tightened. "We have to get you back to Wolf Hollow. There's no time to waste."

Elsie frowned. "What about the human threat?"

"I'll kill those city dwellers myself if I have to." Her father's voice boomed in the foyer. "You will claim a wolf shifter—whichever one you want." He placed his hands on Elsie's shoulders and stared into her face, his voice dropping. "You remember the spell I taught you?"

A cold chill sank into her bones. He was referring to the enchantment. She'd never use it, but her father didn't need to know that. He required hope and peace of mind and she owed him that. Elsie pressed her lips together and nodded.

"Good." He gave her shoulders a squeeze before backing up. "Get a good night's rest. You'll pack whatever gowns and garments you can fit into a backpack tomorrow. We leave the day after for the hollow. Tomorrow will be your last at Balmar Heights. You must say your goodbyes."

THE SCENT OF freshly baked bread tugged Elsie out of sleep the next morning. Her eyes fluttered open as she awoke with her head sunk into a soft pillow on her four-poster bed. She stretched beneath the covers then sat up slowly, stretching again before rolling out of bed in her pink pajama shorts and tank top.

Fresh air wafted in from her open window and morning light teased the edges of the stone walls. Soft, sumptuous rugs covered Elsie's floor and beautiful antique furniture housed her clothes. A wide bookshelf displayed books and baubles in the middle of her room. Without shops to browse, Elsie and her friends were perpetually trading and loaning small statues, figurines and books.

Elsie left her room with a yawn then walked to the kitchen where she found her friends, Mia and Charlotte. A smile lit up her face upon seeing her company.

Mia, who was slicing a round loaf of bread, paused and grinned at Elsie.

"Good morning, sunshine," Mia said.

"Good morning," Elsie returned. "What a pleasant surprise—my two best friends and freshly baked bread."

"Don't forget the jam," Charlotte said, lifting a jar containing purplish contents.

Elsie's smile widened as she rushed up to Charlotte then Mia to give each a tight hug. Then she leaned over the loaf of bread and inhaled deeply, closing her eyes as she sighed.

"You make the best bread, Mia."

Mia held her head high. "It's because I use only the best materials—super-fine grains of sand for the flour. The other witches are always digging up whatever dirt is easiest. That's why their bread is lumpy. I take the time to sift through the soil, which is why my bread is the best in the whole wide world."

Charlotte snorted and rolled her eyes.

"I actually made this jam from *real* ingredients."

"Sand is a real ingredient," Mia countered.

"Well, the two of you could have brought me stale bread and tart blueberries, and I still would be delighted to see you," Elsie said. She glanced at the closed door of her father's room. "Have you seen my father this morning?"

Charlotte nodded. "He left earlier. He instructed us to spend our last morning together with cheer and optimism."

"He told us not to cry," Mia added as she sawed off the last piece of bread.

"Good. No tears allowed," Elsie said. "I know our coven considers me moon cursed, but I believe I am blessed. I have gained a brother and very soon I will claim my life mate."

Elsie grabbed plates and butter knives while Charlotte and Mia brought the bread and jam to the dining table.

Lifting a slice of bread to her mouth, Mia sighed wistfully and said, "If only I could transform one of our wizard boys into a wolf man." She bit into her bread and shot a sly glance in Elsie's direction. "Tell us more about the shifters of Wolf Hollow."

"Yeah, Elsie. Tell us more." Charlotte placed her elbows on the table and sighed dreamily.

Elsie laughed. "Let me guess, you want to hear more about their muscles?"

"Don't stop at muscles," Mia said. "We want the whole nine yards . . . And ten inches."

"Mia!" Charlotte burst out, her cheeks turning rosy.

Mia shrugged and took another bite of bread.

Elsie looked from Mia to Charlotte and grinned.

"The males have muscles as big as boulders." Elsie spread her arms wide over the table. Mia and Charlotte leaned in closer. "Their bodies are gorgeous—large, firm, and tan. I get to see it all when they're naked before and after a shift."

Mia slammed her arms over the table and said, "Take us with you!"

They erupted into laughter, giggling their way through breakfast. Elsie would miss her friends terribly. After polishing off more bread and jam, they followed Elsie up to her room to help her pack.

"You must bring your light blue gown, it brings out the blue in your eyes," Charlotte said, holding up a long silky frock.

"I'll be living in the woods, remember?" Elsie laughed. "I want to fit in. Hand me my floral sundress."

Charlotte returned the blue gown to her closet and grabbed the sundress. Meanwhile, Mia set lacy bras and panties on the bed. When Elsie turned around, she counted seven pairs. She met Mia's eyes and raised a brow.

"What?" Mia asked. "They hardly take up room."

"Shifters don't wear undergarments," Elsie said with a wink.

"Oh my," Charlotte said, fanning her face with her hand.

Mia plucked a sheer red bra from the bed and cupped it around her bosom with a teasing smile. "Then you will definitely stand out—in a good way. Add a little spice to one lucky shifter's life."

Charlotte swatted at Mia. "You are so bad. Thank goodness Lazarus isn't around to overhear."

The three young women shared a look before bursting into laughter.

"What's so funny?" a male voice demanded.

The women stopped laughing abruptly when William stormed inside Elsie's bedroom, scowling from cheek to cheek. His hair was rumpled, as though he'd spent the entire night tossing and turning in a fit of unrest.

Mia drew up, glaring at William. "Ever hear of knocking?"

"I did knock, and when no one answered, I felt it was my duty to come inside and make sure Elsie was okay."

Mia huffed and Charlotte rolled her eyes.

"Perfectly fine and lots to do," Elsie said in a friendly, but firm tone.

William's gaze softened at the sound of her voice. The change in his expression made her stomach twist up and writhe as though infested by snakes. He planted his feet shoulder width apart as though he meant to take root inside her bedchamber.

"I will be saying my goodbyes later this afternoon," Elsie added.

When William made no move to leave, Mia cleared her throat and stared pointedly at the door. But William didn't look that way. His eyes scanned the room. Before Elsie could stand in front of her bed, he noticed the sheer and lacy underthings placed over her covers. William's cheeks filled with color and his eyes expanded as though they might explode. He gasped then stomped over to the bed and pointed at the dainty little pile.

"You're not taking these with you to the hollow, are you?" he demanded.

When he swung around, Elsie felt the full weight of his frown over her.

She placed her hands on her hips. "What I wear, or *don't* wear, is none of your concern, William."

Mia and Charlotte nodded their agreement.

A petulant frown formed over William's lips. "You

shouldn't be packing at all. This is your home. You belong here with us."

"I will be with family," Elsie tried to soothe, but William merely sneered.

"Your brother can't protect you."

"I can protect myself." Elsie lifted her chin, quite done with William's outbursts.

"She's part wolf, remember?" Charlotte said, joining Elsie's side.

"A huntress," Mia added, taking the open spot by Elsie.

William glowered at Elsie's friends, finally backing away.

"You'll find me later?" he asked, gaze boring into Elsie's. She gave a slight nod.

"See you soon, then." Before reaching her bedroom door, William paused and looked back. "Please don't pack those undergarments. It would give those animals the wrong idea." With that, he walked out of her room.

They stood in silence, listening to his footsteps clomp through the foyer. Elsie held her breath as she waited for the front door to open and close. After William shut it roughly, she looked at her friends. They held on for another second before erupting into a fit of giggles.

"What a bore," Charlotte said, once she regained her breath.

Mia rushed over to the bed and patted the small pile of undergarments. "Better put these back. William doesn't approve."

Elsie sighed, feeling the good humor drain from her mind. "Poor William. I wish he'd move on."

"That's the trouble. There's no one to move on to," Mia said. She folded her arms. "We're so limited up here on the mountain. We might as well live on an island."

Charlotte nodded, her lower lip turned over.

"You're so lucky," Mia said to Elsie. "Maybe after you choose a mate you can find one for me."

"And me," Charlotte interjected.

The thought of having her closest friends nearby made Elsie's heart float, but reality made it resettle as surely as fall leaves.

"I don't think you'd enjoy living in the woods without being able to shift."

"So send us males to live at Balmar Heights," Mia said.

"They wouldn't be happy up here behind stone walls," Elsie said.

Mia pursed her lips. How could she understand? Her friends probably thought it was enough for her to go on the occasional run outside the gates, but that wasn't remotely enough. She craved pack life and wilderness. She longed to sleep with the moon above her head and the night stars as her ceiling. She missed her brother and Sasha; she missed the new friend she'd made in Kallie; and her mind had drifted often to Zackary and the kiss they might have shared at the pond. Staying in Wolf Hollow had awakened a new hunger in her that she'd never felt with the wizards at Balmar Heights.

Charlotte returned her attention to Elsie's dresser drawers.

"I don't suppose you want to pack any socks?"

"No need," Elsie replied.

"And the underthings?" Mia asked.

Elsie smiled. "Leave them out."

An hour later, she had her backpack stuffed with two short sundresses; two full-length, comfortable dresses; five pairs of underthings; a shawl; a hairbrush; and a beautiful embossed hardback filled with illustrated fairy tales to gift to the den. When Charlotte had tried to talk her into taking a few pieces of jewelry, Elsie had declined. A sapphire necklace definitely wouldn't help her fit in.

Elsie zipped up her pack and spun around.

"Time to say my goodbyes."

As they left her room, a shout emerged from downstairs.

"Elsie!"

Elsie and her friends rushed to the landing. Looking down, they saw Lisa, Sharon's fifteen-year-old sister, a witch with sun-bleached hair. She gasped in breaths of air at the bottom of the stairs.

"Elsie! Your brother is coming!"

Thank the moon, Elsie thought.

✦ chapter three

ELSIE'S HEART BEAT up her throat with excitement. Did this mean the battle with the humans had ended? She'd worried for the pack's safety every day.

"Tabor's here? Now?" she demanded.

"I saw him coming up the mountain. He's on his way. He's—" Lisa gasped, out of breath.

Mia chuckled. "Breathe, Lisa. Breathe. Has he shifted yet? Is he naked?"

"Mia! He's mated," Charlotte scolded.

"His mate is with him," Lisa said.

Elsie's head jerked in her direction. "Sasha's come with him?"

"I, uh, don't know," Lisa said. "There's a beautiful woman with brown hair coming up the mountain with him."

"They're on foot?" Elsie asked.

"Yes, and partially clothed," Lisa said pointedly to Mia.

That was odd. It didn't make sense for Tabor and Sasha to travel to Balmar Heights on foot when they could cross the distance five times as fast as wolves.

Elsie hurried out of the villa. Mia, Charlotte, and Lisa

followed, chattering behind her as they hurried to keep up.

"Tabor is the cutest guy I've ever seen," Lisa said. "Do you think all the men in the hollow look like him? Well, not like him, but, you know, toned and muscly like that?"

"According to Elsie they do," Charlotte said.

"Oh my gosh. Really?" Lisa said.

They'd all met Tabor briefly when he escorted Elsie to Balmar Heights, but he had only stayed one night—eager to return to his mate and help protect the hollow. What had transpired since he left Elsie here?

Witches and wizards emerged from their villas, joining Elsie and her group on the cobblestone road. They all walked, as though in a parade, toward the gated entrance. Lazarus was already there, greeting Tabor with a clap on the back. Beside them, Sasha kept her eyes trained on the strangers closing in around them as though they meant to challenge rather than greet her. Tabor was shirtless over a pair of torn jeans. A light green dress with faded stains and poorly stitched holes sagged over Sasha's fit frame. They looked like they'd put on the hollow's worst possible clothing before trekking to Balmar Heights.

Unable to hold back any longer, Elsie ran ahead of her friends and launched herself at Sasha. The mistrust melted from her pack sister's eyes as a smile lifted her cheeks. Sasha hugged Elsie in a tight embrace. "We missed you," she said.

"I've been so worried."

"Everything's fine now," Sasha said.

The pureblooded wolf shifter was one of the most fearless females Elsie had ever known and she was proud to call her "sister."

Elsie pulled out of Sasha's arms and regarded her brother for several seconds. He offered her a grin. Whatever annoyance she'd felt at being dumped on the mountain disappeared the moment she saw him back at Balmar Heights, unharmed.

Elsie walked the four steps to her brother and threw her arms around his middle, squeezing tight.

"Good to see you again, sis," Tabor said, rubbing her back.

"Took you long enough," Elsie grumbled. But she couldn't help returning his smile. "What happened?"

Tabor looked around the gathering warily. "Is there someplace we could talk in private?"

"Certainly," Lazarus said in a booming voice. "Make way, everyone. My son and his mate have traveled a long distance. They will rest at my villa. You may all wait outside to say your goodbyes to my daughter."

The crowd murmured as it parted to let their family through. Elsie was no longer the focus of attention. Everyone's eyes latched on to Tabor and Sasha.

Only when Tabor and Sasha were inside Lazarus's villa, away from the crowd, did Tabor share what had happened with the humans.

Tabor sat at the dining table with Lazarus and Elsie, but Sasha paced along the backs of their chairs, eyeing the ceiling, walls, furniture, and appliances mistrustfully. She had taken a quick sip from the glass Elsie offered before setting it down as though it might bite. She folded and unfolded her arms as she paced, ever alert.

Meanwhile, Tabor told them that the first group of humans to approach Wolf Hollow had all been quickly killed. But while the pack was preparing for battle, a second group of humans, led by their leader, Hawk, had snuck in undetected.

Elsie's body tensed the moment she found out that Hawk had gotten his hands on Kallie and tried to use her to bait Wolfrik.

She forgot her own problems the moment she heard her friend had been put in danger. She grasped hold of the water glass in front of her brother. The water inside boiled and steam rose from the surface. Sasha stopped her pacing and stared with wide eyes.

Realizing what she was doing, Elsie yanked her hand back.

"Sorry," she said sheepishly. "I'll get you a fresh glass of water."

Lazarus raised his eyebrows, lips twitching before he pointed a finger at the glass and said, *"Frio degio."* The water abruptly ceased steaming. "It's safe to drink again," Lazarus announced.

Tabor's attention locked onto Elsie, not the water. He leaned over the table and reached his hand for hers, brushing his fingers over hers.

"Kallie's fine. More than fine," he added. "We took care of the humans, including Hawk, and celebrated with a claiming ceremony between Wolfrik and Kallie."

"What? They're mated now?" Elsie's jaw dropped. "And I missed the ceremony?"

"It wasn't much of a ceremony," Sasha offered with a

wry grin, "more of an official claiming."

Elsie's lower lip pouted. "But I missed it."

She wanted to shout with joy that her friend had managed to win over the wild wolf, but she also hated missing out. Kallie had become her closest friend in Wolf Hollow and Elsie hadn't been there to witness her big moment. She felt like she'd been cheated, all because Tabor had insisted on sending her away. She turned her eyes to him and glared.

"You'll be around for the best part—when she gives birth to her first pup," Sasha said.

Once more, Elsie's jaw dropped. "Kallie's pregnant? Really?"

Sasha grinned. She'd managed to stand still for over a minute beside the table. "Really. And that's not all." She looked at Tabor and nodded. They shared a grin.

Tabor cleared his throat. "Elsie, you're going to be an aunt."

"What?" Elsie shrieked. She jumped out of her seat and ran over to Sasha. "You too?"

As Sasha nodded, Elsie threw her arms around her. She squeezed, but not too hard, even though Sasha's stomach was as smooth as the last time she saw her. Elsie drew back, beaming at her in excitement.

Both Sasha and Kallie were pregnant—what wonderful news!

Lazarus stood, too, more gracefully than Elsie. He walked over to Tabor and placed his hand on his shoulder. "Congratulations, son." He stared across the table at Sasha, eyes practically glowing green. "And congratulations to Sasha."

Sasha narrowed her eyes slightly. She'd never hidden her mistrust for Lazarus. Elsie hoped that one day she'd see that Lazarus posed no threat. He was a strong and just leader to his coven, and a protective parent who loved her and Tabor as much as any father could.

"It was nice of you both to deliver the news to us, but why did you walk here?" Elsie asked.

Tabor winced and rubbed the back of his neck. "We have a packmate waiting at the bottom of the mountain to bring up a woman badly wounded. She is human, but not a threat."

Elsie narrowed her eyes. Humans were always a threat, and she didn't want this one in her territory. She had already endangered the Wolf Hollow shifters. The human didn't need to go bringing her bad juju up to Balmar Heights.

"She doesn't belong here," Elsie said. That didn't mean they wouldn't take her in, but she needed to say it.

Tabor pursed his lips. "Aden will be disappointed if you don't take her."

A smile burst over Elsie's cheeks. "Aden is here?" She looked over Tabor's shoulder as though she might catch him striding in all tanned, bulging muscles, and kind smiles. The werewolf was the exact opposite of William—a secure and attractive male who would never smother a female. She thought maybe he'd taken an interest in her when they'd traveled in a small group together to find lost pack members. If it came down to Aden and Zackary, she might have to pick the bolder one of the two. Her stomach sank. Both males were strong, sweet, and thoughtful, but she'd only ever imagined one set of their lips on hers. Zackary, always Zackary. She couldn't explain it. Kallie didn't understand. No one else would if they knew.

"This packmate of yours is unmated?" Lazarus asked hastily, a gleam in his eyes.

He and Elsie were of the same mind. She needed to secure a mate before her time ran out.

"Uh, yeah." Tabor scratched his head and squinted at Lazarus. "Will you take the woman in? He won't bring her up unless we give him the okay."

Lazarus waved his hand impatiently. "Send him up."

Sasha stood rigid, cool gaze on Lazarus the way Elsie used to catch her glowering at pack elders. "Do you not need to discuss it with your people first?" she challenged.

Lazarus faced Sasha with a flirty smirk. Elsie saw her brother in his face, but, from her brother's growl, she could tell he didn't like their father flashing it at his mate.

"The men will be happy for another woman. Perhaps she will turn into one of their forevers." His tone took a seductive lilt that made both Sasha and Tabor narrow their eyes.

Elsie, on the other hand, felt encouraged by this idea. Maybe William could nurse the woman back to health and focus his attentions on someone attainable. She gave Tabor a reassuring smile.

"She will be treated with the utmost care. We have healers, shelter, comfort, and food. I imagine she will never wish to leave once she spends a day at Balmar Heights."

Tabor grunted. "She's been unconscious for days. She might not be lucid enough to appreciate the luxuries you have to offer." Tabor glanced around the kitchen.

Ignoring the censure in Tabor's tone, Lazarus continued to smile. "What better place to wake up than Balmar Heights?"

"You should send Aden up," Elsie said cheerfully. "The human can have my room since I am returning to the hollow with you."

Tabor's gaze softened when he looked at her. "You still want to come back?"

"I've been counting the days." Elsie put her hands on her hips for emphasis.

Her brother's eyes crinkled when he smiled. He turned to Sasha and they carried out a brief whispered conversation in which she caught them arguing over who would shift and call Aden to come up the mountain. Tabor didn't want any of the wizards gawking at Sasha naked, and Sasha didn't want to stand around waiting.

"I'll be quick," Tabor said. When Sasha made a growling sound, his tone tightened. "Stay with my sister." Tabor stormed out before Sasha could object. She glowered at his back instead.

Oh boy, they were both stubborn type-A alphas who never gave in easily. From what Elsie had observed, it fueled the passion between them. They were always sneaking away for personal time in the forest, Tabor's cabin, and Sasha's cave. It gave Elsie a thrill of anticipation to imagine doing the same with a male of her own. Alpha personalities abounded in the pack, regardless of gender. Wolfrik—the last shifter to claim a mate—was most definitely alpha. Raider too. She saw Aden and Zackary more as puppy dogs—cute, sexy ones, who would be loving, loyal, and protective of the female they mated and deadly to everyone else. Elsie didn't want an alpha. Like her brother, she thought of herself as a dominant, take-charge kind of individual. Gender and size had nothing to do with it. All William had ever seen when he looked at her was a sweet, delicate female. He too easily forgot about her bite.

While Sasha waited, she rubbed her arms, glancing frequently at the ceiling as though to make sure it hadn't lowered to crush her.

"We can wait outside," Elsie suggested.

She didn't have to ask twice. Sasha had already started toward the door.

Out on the front patio, Sasha paced, clutching her fingers while casting furtive looks in the direction of the gated entrance.

"Will our wolves be running back to Wolf Hollow?" Elsie asked to take her pack sister's mind off her unease.

Sasha's brown eyes met Elsie's.

"Yeah. Not taking the clothes—they're rags anyway. Heidi's trashed this dress with rabbit guts." Sasha glanced down at the stained dress. "There's no getting the bloodstains out." I could get them out, but I kept that to myself as Sasha continued. "We need a supply run. Since we killed so many humans in the attack, it's probably safe for a time." Sasha pinched the short hem of the dress and wrinkled her nose.

"At least baby clothing doesn't take up much room," Elsie offered with a warm smile.

Sasha went back to pacing. She rubbed the back of

her neck, staring in the direction Tabor had disappeared as though that would bring him back faster.

Lazarus stood so close to Elsie their shoulders nearly touched. "I wonder what kind of powers the baby will have?" he mused, eyes on Sasha.

"Shh," Elsie admonished. "She's spooked enough already." Lowering her voice, she added, "I wonder what they will name the baby."

She was so excited to be an aunt and to hold her little niece or nephew in her arms. Babies were a rarity at Balmar Heights. Early miscarriages were sadly common. Their coven thought they were all cursed, and that once Elsie claimed a shifter, the curse would be broken. It was a relief that Sharon's due date wasn't for another seven weeks. Elsie didn't want to be blamed if something went wrong. She didn't believe she was responsible for the coven's trouble with fertility, but it weighed on her that some did. "Too much power in constant proximity is overwhelming our ability to produce strong, healthy babes—sort of like inbreeding," Lazarus had said. The first group to arrive had managed to breed the first generation of Balmar Heights' witches and wizards. Unfortunately, Lazarus's forever had been barren, but he had no trouble impregnating two wolf shifters after her passing. The rest of the tribe didn't think they should mix with shapeshifters. Elsie doubted they'd have a problem with a human woman, though. Her father had told her it had been common for wizards to breed with humans before the fall.

A flurry of witches and wizards lined the street as Tabor and Aden—carrying a limp woman—made their way to Lazarus's villa. Aden was topless and barefoot like Tabor. He wore gray faded sweatpants that would have been baggy on any other male on the mountain but were too short and strained against Aden's muscled legs.

Sasha stopped pacing and lifted her chest as the males approached. All traces of her former irritation gone.

Aden stood over a half a head taller than Tabor. He towered over everyone, and the muscles of his torso were like chiseled crags in a mountain range. His full head of thick brown hair was always trim and well groomed, despite living in the wild. Elsie wasn't the only female raking her eyes over the striking werewolf as he stepped ever closer. She caught Charlotte and Mia clutching one another as though they might faint without support. Maybe she should have felt a tingle of possessiveness, but she'd always been practical—like her father. She saw Aden as an attractive potential mate. Love and forever feelings would have to come later. Elsie didn't have time to nurture them now.

"Aden!" she called happily, walking toward him once he reached the edge of the yard.

She'd expected to see his dimpled smile, not the strained one he gave her as he cradled the brunette woman's skinny drooping form against his chest.

Elsie's smile faded like twilight. She'd always considered herself skilled at reading body language— observing others had been a favorite pastime of hers growing up. Her peers had preferred gossip and experimenting with their powers, whereas Elsie enjoyed listening in and deciphering facial expressions.

Aden's wrinkled forehead expressed unease, but he didn't dart glances at the gathered wizards the way Sasha did. He kept glancing down at the unconscious woman in his arms. Elsie didn't need to be a soothsayer to predict that no one in the coven had a shot at the human. Not to mention she could cross Aden's name off her extremely short list of potential wolf mates.

Still, she considered the upside. This just made things easier.

Ha! Another voice laughed. *Easier, Elsie? Really? Your brother despises Zackary. Hates him with the blinding hot plasma of the burning sun.*

Well, he should try meeting Brutus. Zackary wouldn't seem so bad if her brother met the big bad bear.

Aden followed them to Elsie's room on the villa's second floor. She removed her backpack from the bed. The clothing, toiletries, and book would have to wait until her father came to visit since she was running back with her packmates.

Tabor pulled the blankets back on the bed then Aden tucked the human in gently.

"She's in a coma," Lazarus said as their small group stood around her. The rest of the coven had been made to wait outside. "We will see that she receives the proper nutrients while we work on healing the trauma to her head."

Aden loomed over the unconscious woman; his arms folded. "Do not force her to wake too soon. It could do more damage."

"My father is an excellent healer," Elsie said.

He only frowned.

"There's nothing else we can do for her," Sasha said from the doorframe. "We should go."

Aden leaned beside the woman. At first, Elsie thought he intended to kiss the human, but his lips were at her ear, whispering. The intimate gesture made her heart ache with longing for a mate who would look at her with such tender devotion. Something must have happened between Aden and this intruder while he guarded her in the southern caves. She'd have to ask Kallie what she knew once she returned to the hollow.

"You must be hungry after your long trek. Stay for a quick bite," Lazarus encouraged.

"We've already been away too long," Sasha said.

Aden was the last to leave Elsie's room. Outside, the coven waited around, chatting animatedly as though they were having a block party. This was the most excitement Balmar Heights had seen in years.

Charlotte and Mia hugged Elsie when she stepped out. This time, her friends had tears in their eyes.

"We will miss you so much. Promise you'll visit after you claim a mate," Mia said urgently.

"Of course." Elsie had to blink back tears gathering in her eyes.

"And bring your mate along for us to meet," Charlotte added.

Elsie's laughter was cut short when William stepped over, stormy-eyed. He had a disapproving frown on his lips that reminded her more of a parent's than a boy her age. There were no tears in William's eyes—not even longing. Tiny yellow sparks tinged his green eyes that usually gleamed with an unsettling mix of hostility and possessiveness. It brought out Elsie's inner wolf instincts, warning her of danger.

Well, she'd be far out of William's sight in a matter of minutes. That knowledge made it easier to paste a smile over her lips.

"I wish you all well," Elsie said, including William in her final goodbye.

His jaw tightened. "I will talk to your father about bringing your clothes since you are unable to carry them with you today."

Elsie lifted her brows. "That's okay. They have extra clothing in Wolf Hollow."

"You should have your own," William said firmly.

Before she could tell him it didn't matter, William stormed away. Elsie felt both relieved and apprehensive. Mia patted her back. "Don't worry. Your father will keep him on the mountain. He doesn't want William mucking up your chances with a mate—none of us do."

"Jeez, he's creepy," Charlotte said, shuddering. She squeezed her eyes closed and reopened them, a smirk forming over her lips. "He's probably going to repack your bag—remove all the lace underthings and replace them with heavy cotton."

Mia nodded and grimaced.

Elsie put the underthings and William out of her mind. Balmar Heights was no longer her home. It was time to return to Wolf Hollow and claim a mate.

chapter four

TREES WHIZZED BY—A kaleidoscope of green, brown, and blue. Sasha led their group through the forest like a thunderstorm streaking across the sky. Elsie's wolf was the smallest, but she had no trouble keeping up. She was just as eager to reach the hollow—more than Tabor and Sasha could possibly realize. Even running there on four legs took a day and half.

Tabor could never know about the curse. She knew he'd try to take on Brutus . . . and likely end up severely wounded. There was nothing her brother could do for her. She had to claim a wolf mate. Only one shifter knew the truth, Elsie's best friend, Kallie.

They reached the hollow's northern border late in the afternoon. Sasha lifted her snout in the air and howled. Tabor and Aden followed suit. Elsie joined them, excitement pulsing through her legs to her paws. Their howls felt like big excited whoops leaving her chest.

A chorus of wolves responded. Sasha took off—a flash of fur through forest. Tabor, Aden, and Elsie pursued her in wild abandon, leaping over fallen logs, tangled roots, and brush. They arced away from the steep bluff at the edge of the den, circling around through thick brush.

Upon reaching the den, Sasha led them to the center of the clearing where they all shifted. Elsie jumped to her feet, spinning around with a gleeful smile at all the activity surrounding her. Not only was she home, but so were the den mates. Rope ladders were being dropped down from treehouses overhead. Shack doors were propped opened and shutters opened. Kindling was gathered and set beside small rock pits in front of individual dwellings. The families with treehouses had stored essential kitchenware, extra clothing, and the like safely above ground for the den mates living in huts. Woven baskets were being lowered with rope to children waiting below to untie the handle and take their family's meager possessions home.

An air of jubilation filled the clearing.

Elsie craned her head around until catching sight of Kallie in her yellow dress, her thick brown hair unbound over her shoulders. Kallie dipped a mug into a bucket of water and poured it into the soil teeming with herbs in circles of stacked stones outside the garden.

"Kallie!" Elsie cried. Her feet pounded over dirt and grass as she raced across the clearing and threw her arms around her friend, squeezing her tight. "Oh my gosh! You're mated and pregnant. You've been busy since I left. I want to hear all about it."

In her excitement, Kallie accidently sloshed water over Elsie. Her eyes crinkled as she laughed and hugged Elsie back. "Sounds like you know everything already."

"Yeah, but I want to know all the details."

Kallie laughed again and gave Elsie a squeeze. "I've missed you, Elsie."

Tabor walked over and tapped Elsie's shoulder. The two females pulled apart. He offered Kallie a smile and a hello before turning his attention back to Elsie. "Sasha, Aden, and I are headed to the glade."

"I'll see you there in a bit," Elsie said.

Tabor flashed a brief smile before joining Sasha and Aden. Backs turned to the den, the three shifters walked out naked. Elsie's eyes followed the movement of their butt cheeks before turning her attention back to Kallie.

"So, Aden's fallen for a human?"

Kallie scowled. "They were humping while he guarded her, but I doubt he has any real feelings for her."

"Hmm." Elsie wasn't convinced, but she left it at that.

Kallie looped her arm around Elsie's, tugging her across the glade. "How much time do you have left?" she whispered.

"Three weeks," Elsie answered.

Kallie worried her lip. "And you can't tell your brother?"

Elsie shook her head. She patted Kallie's arm gently. "Don't worry, friend. I will claim a wolf as a mate before Brutus has a chance to trap me inside his cave forever. Look how quickly you domesticated Wolfrik. My task is easy compared to your feat."

"Some animals can never be tamed." Kallie laughed then pressed a kiss to Elsie's cheek. "Oh, how I've missed you. Let's find you a dress." They walked arm and arm to the den's communal shed, taking their time to allow for Kallie's limp. "Your white dress is still here."

Elsie pulled the familiar gown over her head inside the shed. It was the same long white dress she'd first arrived in.

"There's a big celebration gathering in the glade tonight," Kallie said, grasping her hands. "The entire pack will be there."

They shared squeals of excitement. This homecoming was better than anything Elsie had imagined. She had been afraid the hollow would be somber or on lockdown.

"I'll see you there later, okay?" Kallie gave Elsie a quick hug then resumed watering herbs.

Elsie dashed onto the trail leading to the glade, waiting until she was alone in the woods to slow her steps and speak the word to a spell.

"*Arto ra le* Zackary."

Unfortunately, she didn't have an article of Zackary's clothing to perform a location spell the way she had using Jordan's tank top after the she-wolf had gone missing from the hollow. But Elsie did have feelings for Zackary that could be used to point her in the right direction. She closed her eyes and concentrated on the sound of his voice and his bashful grin every time she had spoken to him. He was a large man. Aden was the biggest in the hollow, but only because he was a werewolf. The largest true shifters in Wolf Hollow were Zackary, Raider, and Wolfrik. In her mind's eye, she brought a mental picture of him to life, repeating the spell.

"*Arto ra le* Zackary."

An invisible string tugged her down the trail. Elsie had nearly reached the glade when it yanked her down a narrow westward path.

LATE-AFTERNOON SUNLIGHT FILTERED in through the canopy of the forest. Even in the shade, it was hot enough to keep the insects away. Zackary did not have the luxury of lazing around, waiting until evening brought cooler temperatures. He raised the ax above his head and brought it down over the fallen tree. The blade bit into the bark with precision and force. He lifted it and struck again.

Sweat sheened over his broad, bare, muscled chest. The only clothes he wore were a pair of snug khaki shorts with the top button undone to allow more room for his bulky hips.

Wiley and Justin sat on the ground, slouched against trees, yapping while Zackary did all the grunt work. They'd taken in two loads of firewood to the glade for the big bonfire celebration Jager had planned to welcome back the hollow's den mates and their families. Until enough wood was chopped for the three of them to carry another load, it made sense for Zackary to do the felling since he was the biggest and strongest.

"You should have seen the human's eyes balloon when I went for his throat. Pissed himself," Justin boasted yet again.

Every time Zack lifted the ax, he caught snippets of his friends' ceaseless narration of the pack's battle with the humans.

Thunk.

"They sound like rabbits when they scream," Wiley

tossed in.

Thunk.

"Hi, Zackary," a sweet, feminine voice broke through the chatter.

Zack lost hold of the ax as he hefted it over his shoulder. It flew back, thwacking a tree trunk behind him.

Elsie laughed. Thankfully, she was at his side rather than behind him.

"I didn't mean to startle you." Her eyes shone with mirth as he turned to face her. Before their eyes could meet, her gaze was traveling down his chest, a gleam of appreciation in her expression as she surveyed his six-pack. Zack had seen females gawk at Raider this way, but never at him. It made his cock stir to life inside shorts with no room to grow. Maybe the pain would help get his head back on straight.

The council could have banished him from Wolf Hollow, instead they'd denied his right to ever claim a mate. He'd accepted his punishment without argument. All females were off limits to Zackary—not that any had ever shown an interest in him, not until Elsie. Tabor's sister. That reminder helped sober him.

"You're back." He tried to sound casual even as his muscles strained with a vainglorious urge to flex the longer she stared at his body.

Elsie's eyes lifted to meet his. She grinned. "I'm back."

Justin and Wiley had gone utterly silent. Zackary didn't have to look at them to know they were staring. At least he didn't have to worry about blushing; his entire face was already flushed from chopping wood. Zackary rubbed his clammy palms together, wanting to blame the sweat of his exertions for losing hold of the ax.

Elsie looked like an angel in her white dress, so out of place among barbarians, like himself, and the pack's she-wolves who could turn vicious in an instant. Elsie was like some long-ago dream of a beautiful time before the world went to shit. Sometimes her kindness felt like a punishment—her attention like torture. It would be easier to avoid that which he could never have. The more she talked to him, the worse it got. The wanting. The desire. The guilt. The ache. The agony.

The need.

Zackary frowned and turned away to retrieve the ax. He gave the handle a yank, releasing it from the tree's bark.

"Well, I just wanted to say hi and see you tonight," Elsie said, still sounding cheerful. She lifted her hand in a cute little wave and spun around. "Hi, guys," she said to Justin and Wiley as she passed.

"Hi," they muttered in unison, avoiding eye contact with her, as though she might put them under a spell if they weren't careful.

Elsie didn't need spells. The moment Zackary first saw her appear with her father in the glade, he'd been enchanted. If she weren't a half witch, every single male shifter in the hollow would be after her. At least now he stood a chance. Zackary scowled at his own stupidity. He had as much chance with Elsie as a rat had with a dove.

Justin and Wiley remained silent a long while. Zackary could practically feel their thoughts turning like stew in the cauldron. They were waiting until Elsie was safely out of earshot. Zackary wasn't any better. He held the ax and stared at the fallen tree as though he'd turned into a caveman who'd never seen a tool before.

Justin was the first to break the silence.

"The witch bitch is back," he said in a low, cruel voice.

Zackary wheeled around and snarled at him. "Don't talk about her that way."

"Uh-oh," Wiley said with a grin. "You've insulted Zack's girlfriend."

"She's not my girlfriend."

Justin and Wiley got to their feet, wearing twin smiles.

"I think he meant hump buddy," Justin said with a gleam in his eyes.

Zackary's growl should have scared Justin instead of making him laugh. Zackary slammed the ax into the fallen log with a violent *thunk*. If he kept the tool in his hand, he might use it as a weapon. Instead, he stormed up to Justin and pushed him against a tree.

"Whoa!" Wiley shouted. When he tried to grab Zackary's arm, Zack shook him off easily. His friends were scrawny and didn't come close to his physical strength or stamina. They both knew it.

"Hey, I was only kidding," Justin said. "What's gotten into you lately?"

Zackary stepped back and huffed with frustration. He gripped his neck with both hands and turned to the fallen tree he needed to finish hacking apart. Pulling in several steadying breaths, he turned slowly to cast a look of stern warning on his friends.

"You weren't there when she helped find Jordan and

David. She really cares about the pack. And she's nice. So be nice back."

Justin and Wiley exchanged a glance then shrugged. "If you say so," Wiley said.

Zackary pulled the ax out of the log and stared down Justin. Their eyes locked. Wiley looked between the two friends and lifted his brows.

Justin released a breathy sigh. "Yeah, okay, so long as she doesn't hex us."

"Maybe don't give her a reason to," Wiley suggested.

Zackary grunted. Elsie seemed too considerate to use magic against the pack. And she really had cared about recovering their missing members when their small group ventured outside the hollow. As awkward as it had been to team up with Tabor, Zackary had liked being part of the rescue group. He only wished they'd caught up to the humans in time to save David. The rough wood handle of the ax dug into his calloused palm as he squeezed it.

"Why don't I take a few swings?" Justin suggested as he sauntered over. The wicked gleam returned to his eyes. "Before you accidently throw it into one of our heads."

Wiley winced.

Zackary rolled his eyes. "I was startled."

"Well, you should watch out," Justin said, tugging the ax out of Zackary's grip.

"Why's that?" Zackary folded his arms over his broad chest, staring Justin down. His friend's face filled with mirth.

"Because that little witch wants to ride your broomstick."

Justin and Wiley howled with laughter as Zackary turned beet red. He could feel his cheeks blazing brighter than the color from his earlier labors. Seeing his face, Wiley doubled over as he erupted into fresh laughter. Justin flipped the ax around, handle pointing toward the sky, and ran his fist up and down the hilt suggestively. Zackary felt a fresh wave of anger and embarrassment.

"Give that back before you cut yourself," he snapped.

As soon as Justin handed the ax over, Zackary began chopping wood with gusto. His friends leaned against a tree watching him and chattering away like a couple of gossipy females.

"Do you think witches ever do it doggy style?" Wiley asked Justin.

"I'm sure they do more than get on their hands and knees," Justin answered. "They probably levitate or something while they're going at it."

Wiley's mouth gaped open. "Do you really think so?"

"For all we know, they're banging up against their ceilings." Justin grunted. "Crazy shit happening on that mountain. You can be certain of that."

Zackary increased his speed, hacking away at the log in double speed. He knew he should reserve his energy, but he had extra to spare. He only wished his friends would return to their banter over the battle rather than speculating as to the mating practices of witches; he didn't want to get hard again.

chapter five

DEN MEMBERS CROWDED the glade talking, eating stew, and drinking mugs of brew old Jager had prepared. While the adults mingled, the kids climbed boulders and trees along the edges of the commotion.

"Who wants to play at the river?" Emerson hollered over the din.

"Me! Me! Me!" the kids cried.

"Then follow me," Emerson said, swinging her arm in a wide arc over her blonde head. She, Gina, Taryn, and Janelle took the hands of smaller kids, leading the way to the river trail. They were followed by several of the single males: Heath, Alec, Carter, and Dylan.

Elsie was still trying to catch up on all the news. As much as she adored Sasha, the pureblooded she-wolf wasn't big on details. Elsie wanted all the gossip she'd missed out on while she'd been away. But first, she offered Raider her condolences on the loss of his father. She hadn't known Garrick well, but her heart went out to the grieving shifter, and to the pack for losing another elder, leaving them with only two.

When Tabor waved Elsie over to his spot in line at the cauldron, she waved back and shook her head. Too much excitement was thrumming through her to eat.

She found Kallie seated on a stump. There was an empty seat beside her that Kallie patted.

"I'm fine standing," Elsie said, bouncing on the balls of her feet.

Kallie chuckled. Wolfrik swaggered over, setting two bowls of stew on the empty log. As soon as his hands were empty, Elsie hugged him.

"Wolfrik! Oh my gosh! Congratulations! You have the best mate in the pack."

Wolfrik's eyes expanded as though he didn't know how to react to Elsie squishing herself against his chest, squeezing his middle while jumping in place. Finally, he chuckled and patted her head. "Can't argue with you there."

"Kallie *is* the best!"

Kallie laughed. "Have you had too much brew?"

Elsie pulled away from Wolfrik and shook her head. "Not a drop."

"So, this is normal behavior?" Wolfrik looked at Kallie when he asked. His mate smirked.

"I'm beginning to think so," she said.

Wolfrik shook his head. "Witches are weird."

"You're weird," Elsie returned.

"You're weirder," Wolfrik countered.

Kallie put her head in her hands and groaned. "I'm getting a mental image of what kind of father Wolfrik's going to be."

Elsie snickered. "He's going to be so much fun."

Kallie grabbed both bowls of stew and looked pointedly at Elsie. "You should sit."

"Yeah, sit," Wolfrik echoed. "Eat."

Elsie looked from the second bowl of stew to Wolfrik, brows furrowing. "But that's your meal."

"Sit with my mate. I can get more." His tone left no room for argument.

Elsie plonked onto the stump beside Kallie as Wolfrik barreled through the crowd toward the cauldron.

"Your mate is bossy," Elsie said with a grin. "I like him," she added.

Chuckling, Kallie handed Elsie a bowl of stew. "I'm quite fond of him myself."

Elsie ground chunks of stew between her teeth and swallowed it down. This batch was extra chewy, reminding her how much she loved the taste and texture of wild game—food that wasn't magicked out of anything else. The wizards at Balmar Heights didn't seem to notice, but she did. She'd been too polite to ever mention anything.

"What's going on with the pairings?" Elsie asked between chewing.

"Shifters were partnered after the battle," Kallie said.

"Who is Zackary with?"

Before Elsie left, the council had paired him with a male from the den while he was on probation. But with the den mates only just returned, he must have been paired up with someone else.

Kallie set her bowl in her lap and pursed her lips, eyeing the treetops in thought. "Hmm. Oh, right. He was paired with Chase. Neither of them looked happy about the arrangement." She grinned with amusement then lifted her bowl to her lips, slurping a thick meaty portion into her mouth.

"Which territory do they have? Who is next to them? What about on the other side?" Elsie fired off questions.

Kallie answered them all patiently before clearing her throat and changing the topic to a different shifter. "Wolfrik is working on the council to rescind the ban the elders put on Aden to take a mate."

Elsie sat up. It felt as though her heart rose in her chest, taking her with it.

"Can you ask Wolfrik to do the same for Zackary?"

In the following silence Elsie turned on the stump to get a closer look at her friend. Kallie's lips were pressed together in a flat line. Seeing Elsie's scrutiny, she sighed. "I wish you didn't like him."

Elsie's hope fizzled as quickly as it had risen. Kallie hadn't witnessed Zackary's dedication to the pack when he insisted on joining the search party to find Jordan and David. Elsie still remembered the rabbit he'd hunted and left for her that first morning of the journey. She knew he'd been the one to leave it for her after listening to her talk about her preference for wild game over fish. She'd smelled him on it after shifting to devour his gift. It was the sweetest thing a male had ever done for her.

Elsie's brows drew together. "You can't keep judging him for past deeds. He's been nothing but considerate and helpful since I arrived. That is the only Zackary that I know."

Kallie twisted her lips to the side and gave a

begrudging nod. "I'll talk to Wolfrik. Can I tell him about your   situation?"

"As long as he can keep it secret."

"Don't worry. He's not in the habit of information sharing so much as gathering."

They went back to eating their stew.

Wolfrik's swift return made Elsie suspect he'd cut in line. He sat on the ground beside Kallie alternating between a glower when he looked into the crowd and a contented smile whenever he glanced at his mate.

Taking a closer look at him, Elsie noticed a new scar above his right thigh—bright red and circular.

Elsie gasped. "What happened?"

When Wolfrik squinted at her, she pointed at the welt on his side.

"Oh, that." Wolfrik shrugged. "Got shot during the fight with the humans. I've got another one in my back thigh."

Kallie clutched a hand against her heart, her lips frowning at the memory.

"Did someone get the bullets out?" Elsie asked.

"They're out. I'm fine." Wolfrik tilted his bowl back, chowing down on his stew.

Elsie frowned and resumed eating hers slowly. Yet again, she wished she had been present for the battle. Once she was mated, Tabor couldn't send her away at the first hint of danger. She'd finally become a full-fledged member of the pack.

Upon finishing her dinner, Elsie bid her friends goodbye. She had arrangements to make before everyone headed off to sleep.

BALMY EARLY MORNINGS were Zackary's favorite time to labor. The end-of-summer heat could be some of the most brutal, and he'd been assigned the northwestern field where trees and shade were sparse. Thick rows of blackberry bushes teemed with ripened fruit.

Fingers stained dark purplish-blue, Zackary attempted to pluck berries from their thorny bushes delicately. With his thick hands, berry picking didn't come easily. He held a basket in one hand while pulling berries with the other. Some of the den mates had constructed little wood crates that could be filled with berries and stacked inside the basket so they didn't all smoosh together.

At the opposite end of the row, Chase cursed then sucked on his finger. So far, the shifter with the slimmer fingers was the one always poking himself on thorns. Chase kept his basket on the ground beside his feet, which seemed like a whole lot of unnecessary bending, but Zackary figured the male could complete the task however he chose. They'd only been patrol partners for a few days and didn't spend much of it conversing.

Their territory was one of the closest sections to the glade, which served as part of their border to the east. It meant an easy walk at the beginning and end of duty. Their northern border was the Sakhir River. It glinted in the background, casting a sense of serenity over the field.

When Zackary had first started his new duties, he'd been bored out of his skull. But he'd quickly adapted, going into a focused trancelike state as he worked methodically, removing ripe blackberries from the bushes.

Chase hissed, yanking his arm back. "Damn fucking thorns!"

Maybe if Chase hadn't drunk so much of Jager's brew the night before, he wouldn't be poking his fingers like a clodhopper. Zackary kept his comment to himself and his attention on his task. As with his friends, it was clear that he'd be the one pulling most of the weight in this partnership. He didn't mind. Working hard helped him feel deserving of a place in the pack. It still wasn't enough, but it helped. A little.

"Greetings, friend!" Hudson called out, strolling in from his neighboring territory.

He popped over briefly a couple times a day to say hello to his friend–singular–the greeting never included Zackary.

He didn't bother looking over, not until Chase asked, "No fair. You get a third partner, Huds. Hey, Elsie. Where's Rosalie?"

"Good morning," Elsie said sweetly.

The sharp tip of a thorn stabbed into Zackary's thumb, instantly stinging his rough skin. Blood beaded to the surface. He rubbed his fingers together, smearing the blood rather than sucking his damn thumb like Chase.

"Not exactly," Hudson said as he and Elsie walked over. Chase jogged up to them, leaving his basket on the ground. Zackary remained standing in a sideways position, unsure whether to continue berry picking or act as though he was part of the conversation.

Elsie threaded her fingers in front of her. The white

dress clung to her petite frame. Hudson looked at her before explaining, "Elsie and Aden were paired together last night and assigned the eastern hunting grounds. Elsie traded partners with Rosalie and now she's trading with you so that I can patrol with my buddy." Hudson smiled big.

"I'd rather pick berries than hunt animals," Elsie tossed in.

Pick berries with him? Become his partner?

Everything inside Zackary stilled. He felt like a goddamned rabbit freezing up at the hint of danger, hoping it would pass him by if he didn't make any sudden movements.

Chase laughed. "Right, sounds great, but you can't just go around trading partners."

"Why not?" Elsie asked.

"Jager would have a shit fit for one thing."

"So, don't tell him."

Chase's next chuckle came out devious. "I didn't realize you were such a little rebel."

"Never judge a shifter by her size. Do we have ourselves a trade?"

"Done!" Chase said happily.

Zackary's jaw tightened. He still hadn't moved, hadn't spoken. No one asked for his consent. That was how it had always been. *Just a dumb mutt.* That was what his father had always called him.

"Some shifters are meant to lead, others to obey. You're soft in the head, just like your mother," Vallen had reminded Zackary often. *"No female will ever want you. Keep your mouth shut, do as you're told, and don't*

embarrass me or I'll run you out of Wolf Hollow myself."

The day a rabid wolf bit Vallen had been the best day of Zackary's life. He thought he'd have to endure his father's insults and fists for the remainder of his natural life. Vallen had made sure to hit him in private, but there were shifters who had suspected. None of them had spoken up—not once. No one cared about a dumb mutt. That rabid wolf had done him a huge favor. Too bad it hadn't killed Vallen in the process.

Chase took off with Hudson, not bothering to tell Zackary goodbye. Unholy rage rose up his bare chest straight into his head. His mouth opened, the word "no" rising up his throat. It didn't make it past his lips. Obedience was too ingrained in him. He didn't need his father around to flatten him under his callused heel. He would do what he was told, what others decided, because that was the only way he knew how to exist.

Zackary returned to picking berries, being mindful of the thorns. Just because he'd been cornered into this situation didn't mean he'd tear his fingers up in frustration.

"You're upset," Elsie said, sounding confused.

Zackary picked another berry before turning to face Elsie, his basket at his side. He started out his mornings in khaki shorts before taking them off in the midday heat. Now he wouldn't be able to work nude in the sweltering sun.

Elsie's brows pinched together. She looked hurt. Zackary wished he could find the right words to tell her she should stay away from him. As much as he liked her, he'd accepted the council's punishment, banning him from ever claiming a mate. He didn't deserve a female, and if he couldn't have a mate, he didn't want anything else. Secretly, Zackary was the kind of romantic fool who only wanted to lay with the female he meant to claim.

"You shouldn't mess around with Jager's pairings," he told Elsie now.

The hollow had a system. Besides, he didn't want Elsie to get in trouble. She was their newest pack member and part witch. The pack was already wary of half-breeds. Though he did admire her audacity. Unlike Zackary, Elsie wasn't one to keep her head down. Isn't that why he'd noticed her in the first place? She hadn't scorned him either.

Only because she didn't know any better. Not yet.

Elsie frowned. "I would rather pick berries, but if you don't want me for your partner, then I will trade back."

When she started away, the "no" that had been lodged inside the back of Zackary's throat made it out. Elsie stopped and turned, facing him with a question in her eyes.

"Rosalie will make a fuss if you trade back now. Her complaints could easily get back to Jager, and I don't want him giving you any grief."

"So, you're just looking out for me?" There was a hopeful lift to Elsie's voice, but her lips still formed a flat line.

If he truly had her best interests at heart, he'd send her straight back to Aden.

Grrr, the thought of her spending her days running around with the werewolf burned and darkened the inside of his chest like charred deer meat.

Rather than answer her question, Zackary handed

Elsie his basket.

"You said you wanted to pick berries. Watch out for the thorns."

Zackary walked over to Chase's basket, picking it up with a grunt. Chase had only filled one small wood crate with berries. Slacker. Setting to work, he waited for Elsie to start up her usual banter. Instead, she worked in silence, and the longer it went on, the more uneasy Zackary felt. He snuck sideways glances at her—ones she did not return. Her concentration had turned to the task. Unlike Chase, she removed berries rapidly, without cussing.

Zackary inched his way toward her, taking his time so as not to be obvious. He cleared his throat softly, trying to keep her from hearing the nervous vibration of his throat.

"You had a safe journey back to Wolf Hollow?" He kept his eyes on the berries and the tips of his fingers removing them from the bush.

"We ran straight home," Elsie answered.

Home. She'd called the hollow home. It shouldn't matter to Zackary, but it did. His stupid heart hammered with happiness when he thought of Elsie choosing the pack over her coven. Even if he couldn't be with her, at least she'd be a packmate. That was better than nothing, right? Sure, what about when she wised up, turned her sights elsewhere, and claimed a mate?

Dark liquid burst between Zackary's fingers as he squished an unfortunate berry into purple mash.

"What's it like at Balmar Heights? I've never known anything besides Wolf Hollow."

"What's it like?" Elsie repeated. "How much time have

you got?"

He could hear the smile in her tone. It made Zackary feel lightheaded.

"All day," he said.

And like that, Elsie lit up. She spent the rest of the morning telling him about life on the mountain among the magically gifted. Zackary asked questions, but mostly he listened raptly to a way of life so different from everything he'd ever known. Despite the differences, it turned out wizards and witches had the same squabbles and drama that came with group living. When Elsie told him about two witches who didn't speak to one another for an entire year after one accidently ruined the other's favorite sweater, he found himself chuckling alongside her. All the while, they picked berries, filling the baskets in no time at all.

Elsie followed Zackary to a tree, setting her full basket beside his in the shade.

"That was easy," she said. "Now what?"

"Now we keep an eye out. This patrol area isn't very large. The berries will all get eaten tonight and we'll pick a fresh batch tomorrow." He looked at Elsie's white dress and grimaced. The stains were a dead giveaway. "You might want to find some darker clothes to wear."

Elsie looked down as though noticing the stains for the first time. She shrugged.

"Good thing we're by a river." A smile radiated over her face. She headed to the Sakhir, Zackary following behind her slowly, wading in behind her. When Elsie pulled her dress up her legs, he turned around to give her privacy. "Does my nudity make you uncomfortable?"

Elsie asked curiously.

Naked females had always made him wary. He feared his body would react and he would be ridiculed and rejected.

"I do not wish to . . . offend you."

"Offend me?" Elsie asked.

Zackary's cheeks burned. There was no way he could explain without sounding like a horny mongrel. He did not want to scare her off with an erection. Females did not have to worry about such things. They didn't have dicks that stretched and expanded like a third leg for everyone to see. He could hide his feelings, but not his desires. It made him feel exposed in a way that was as frightening as fuck.

"Is there a lot of nudity at Balmar Heights?" Zackary asked, staring at the blackberry bushes in the distance. The cool water flowing around his ankles felt refreshing. He tried to concentrate on that rather than think of Elsie behind him. Had she removed the dress entirely?

She laughed at his question. "Not publicly. Definitely not. Shifter life sounds barbaric to them."

Had she felt lonely growing up as the only outsider in the community? Elsie seemed like the kind of female who could handle anything, but it still angered Zackary to think of her being treated as different. Mostly, he was infuriated at himself for being such a prick to Tabor. He'd taken his own insecurities out on a half-breed. Real courageous of him. His jaw tightened as self-loathing sliced through him colder than the Sakhir in winter.

"I'm rinsing my dress off. I'll tell you when I'm finished."

Zackary bent down to submerge his hands in the water. He rubbed his palms together in the current then swished his fingers around, but the stains stubbornly clung to his skin. There was no way Elsie would get them out of her white dress. Zackary cupped water into his palms and lifted them to his lips, scooping up several more handfuls of water to drink.

"Do you mind taking my dress and laying it in the field to dry? I'll put on my fur in the meantime." The damp dress appeared at Zackary's side when Elsie held it out. Forehead wrinkled, he took it, staring over the white fabric. There wasn't a single stain or trace of discoloring. When he turned to question Elsie, he found her staring up in wolf form. Her lips formed a mischievous grin and her tail wagged. Sloshing back to shore, Zackary crossed the field going from tree to tree until he found a good branch to hang the dress from. The one he selected had two twigs that slipped under the sleeves. Elsie followed him around, sitting on her hind legs to watch. Finished with the dress, he offered her a grin.

"Might as well avoid grass stains."

Elsie's tail swished side to side over the ground. Zackary took a seat beneath the shade looking out over the field and the lazy flow of the Sakhir. When Elsie moved to his side and sat, he found his hand in her fur stroking down her back. Together, they surveyed the small territory, listening to the various bird warbles and calls. Zackary's hand moved higher, his fingers running over Elsie's head in a gentle caress.

"You're good company," he remarked, lowering his

hand to his lap. When Elsie nudged his arm with her nose, he chuckled and resumed petting her. "Okay."

Zackary barely registered the time slipping away until Elsie gave a *wuff* right before Hudson and Chase entered the field. They talked the whole way over until stepping into the shade.

"Time to switch back," Hudson said, addressing the wolf at Zackary's side.

When she stood up, Zackary did the same.

"Turn around," he growled at Hudson and Chase.

Hudson's gaze cut up to Zackary. He narrowed his eyes. "What about you?" he challenged.

Zackary glowered back. "I'm turning around too."

Hudson didn't move until Chase elbowed him. "Huds, be a gentleman . . . for Elsie's sake."

"Elsie wants to be treated like a member of the pack—not some squeamish human prude."

Zackary folded his arms across his broad chest. "That doesn't mean you have to gape at her while she shifts and dresses."

Hudson took a step toward him. "I'm not gaping. Why is she in wolf form, anyway? Got tired of talking to you, I suppose."

With a snarl, Zackary started toward Hudson, stretching his arms out to grab the mongrel by the shoulders and shake him.

The sound of barking stopped him in his tracks. Elsie ran around them and barked again. Chase laughed. "I don't think she likes the two of you fighting."

"We're not fighting; we're arguing. Unless you were

coming over here to take a swing at me." Hudson sneered at Zackary.

What would be the fun in that? Zackary thought. *I could snap you in half like a twig.*

He kept the comment to himself, smiling menacingly instead.

The fur receded on Elsie as she began her shift. This time, Zackary didn't have to say anything, all three males turned their backs to her, each of them going silent as they stared into the field. None of them spoke until Elsie's cheerful voice said, "You can turn around now."

When they did, she was standing in her white dress.

As though on cue, the gong clanged through the hollow, sounding extra loud so near the glade.

"Dinner bell," Chase announced.

Elsie took off with Hudson, leaving Zackary to watch after them until they disappeared. Chase picked up one of the baskets full of berries and waited for Zackary to do the same before heading over to the glade. Tonight, the pack would enjoy fresh fruit after supper. Tomorrow, the little wood crates would be empty and he'd get another opportunity to fill them with Elsie.

It turned out he didn't have to wait until tomorrow to spend more time with the beautiful witch shifter. After setting the berries out on a crude wood table in the glade, Zackary spotted Elsie sitting on a log with Justin and Wiley. Heart pounding in his chest, he hurried over.

✦ chapter six

ELSIE HADN'T BEEN talking to Justin for long before calling bull. "Hold up. You're telling me you killed two humans at once. How is that even possible?"

"Yeah, Justin. How is that even possible?" Wiley said, kicking his friend's ankle.

Elsie laughed. It was the kind of warm sound that made both boys grin. They'd looked mistrustful when she first approached. All it had taken to get through their defenses was to ask for a recap of their battle against the humans. They'd loved it even more after Elsie had groaned and said she wished she could have been there. It was the truth. She really could have taken down two humans at once—more like ten. But she *hadn't* been there that fateful day so she decided to be nice and let the guys recount their moment of glory.

Suddenly, Zackary loomed over them, gritting his teeth. "What's going on over here?"

"Hey, Zack," Wiley said, missing the dark look in his friend's eyes.

Elsie smiled up at him. "We were waiting for you."

She held her arm up. Zackary stared at it for a couple seconds before understanding flashed in his eyes. He took her hand and helped her up. There was warmth and strength in his grip that sizzled through her veins. It reminded her of the steady stroke of his fingers through her fur that afternoon. She wanted to know what his hands felt like over her entire body.

The moment she was on her feet, he dropped her hand as though it was a flaming branch and jerked his head around, searching the glade. Elsie headed to the line that had formed behind the cauldron, Wiley jogging alongside her.

"Have you ever heard a gunshot?" he asked eagerly.

"No. Is it really loud?"

"Louder than thunder," Justin said, hurrying to her other side.

"Deafening," Wiley tossed in.

Elsie shuddered. Humans and their weapons made her stomach twist.

"What happened to the guns?" she asked with a grimace.

Justin and Wiley looked at one another.

"That's a really good question," Justin said, scratching the back of his head. "I'm pretty sure they were gathered up, but I don't know where they were stored."

"The council probably knows," Elsie said. She hoped they'd destroyed the weapons. What use did wolf shifters have of such devices? Their animals could hunt and protect them. Wizards had a similar advantage with their powers that provided every advantage they required to survive and thrive. She liked to think of a world without guns or weapons of any kind. Like her father, Elsie believed civilization was better off returning to simpler times when people lived in small communities and were caretakers of the earth. She had no desire to live a life so far removed from nature that she wasn't even aware of the moon cycles taking place above the lights of some long-ago city, or the rooftops of a subdivision.

As the line inched toward the cauldron, Justin and Wiley continued their chatter while Zackary searched the crowd.

When Elsie placed her hand on his shoulder he stilled and met her eyes with his deep brown gaze.

"Tabor isn't coming to dinner. He told me he and Sasha needed some private time after patrol."

Elsie studied Zackary's face to see how he would react. She figured he'd either relax a little or stare ahead awkwardly. He did neither. He looked directly into her eyes with a heated stare that licked down her spine. The longer he gazed at her, the hotter the flames burned and spread through her belly to her thighs.

Standing this close to Zackary's broad sun-kissed chest fortified how very large he was. Hard, toned muscles covered every inch of his torso as densely as fur covered his wolf form. Something feral glinted in Zackary's earth-brown eyes, a color as rich as the soil beneath her toes.

How could she have ever thought of him as a puppy? Zackary was all man, and all beast. He'd crush her. Rather than being frightened, the thought sent a jolt of excitement that struck her body like lightning.

Elsie's nipples hardened to stone. She bunched the

fabric of her dress at her thighs, tamping down the urge to caress her breasts. Everything she'd done with William had been spurred on by curiosity, never desire. Never had her body ached as it did now to be claimed by this big, beautiful shifter standing before her.

As though beckoned by her reaction, his eyes traveled down her neck to her breasts and the sharp points jabbing through the fabric. There was no pattern on her dress to hide her arousal. Zackary's nostrils flared the moment he noticed. His eyes latched to her chest.

Justin and Wiley moved forward with the line, but Elsie stood transfixed, as though a spell had taken hold of her. In that moment, she didn't care about her impending deadline with Brutus. Curse be damned, she wanted Zackary for herself. If his stare could stir up this kind of hunger in her, what would mating with him do to her?

She could hardly wait to find out. She had little time left to wait as it was. Seventeen days. Sixteen tomorrow.

After they dished up stew, Elsie returned to the log with the guys. Her body's awareness of Zackary seated at her side distracted her from the banter between Justin and Wiley. Zackary didn't talk much either. She wondered if he shared her fantasy of sneaking off for a little private time of their own. Elsie didn't know where they would go. Not counting Jager's crude hut, Tabor was the only shifter outside the den with a cabin. He'd inherited the place from his deceased mother. There was a communal cabin, but the place seemed too public, even though Elsie had learned that if the curtains were drawn over the windows, it meant it was in use.

Deciding tonight wasn't the night, Elsie excused herself to spend the remainder of dinner with Kallie and Wolfrik. When it was time to sleep, she joined Lacy, Maureen, and Jolene on a mossy patch of earth beside the glade.

"You traded with Rosalie, didn't you?" Jolene asked. She was about two inches taller than her friends with an oval face and fine, wispy brown hair. When Elsie nodded, she said, "That means your new patrol area is next to mine."

Well, not exactly since Elsie had traded again, but close enough.

The three friends had warm smiles. Of all the female groups in the hollow, Elsie found them the most approachable.

"I'm on meal duty . . . well, obviously." Lacy smiled sheepishly, and her friends giggled.

"I had meal duty last patrol cycle," Maureen said.

"Maybe I'll get assigned to the glade during the next pairings," Jolene said. "Jager seems to like us to serve food."

The females chuckled again, clearly unbothered by the placement. Elsie wrinkled her nose, not at all keen on breakfast and dinner duty. Luckily, she didn't have to worry about preparing pack meals. She'd be mated to Zackary before Jager, or anyone else, ever had a chance to place her at the cauldron.

Following words of good night, the females undressed then shifted into wolf form and curled together in a fluffy group. Elsie had never had trouble making friends at Balmar Heights. She figured it wouldn't hurt to get closer to other she-wolves, especially now that Kallie had a mate and pup on the way. Sleeping in fur was a new experience since coming to Wolf Hollow. Elsie found she preferred it to snoozing in human form. There were no nagging thoughts to keep her awake, or worries sneaking into her mind early in the morning. Her wolf had the ability to settle into a deep, contented slumber unplagued by cursed outcomes. The nightmares had started after returning to Balmar Heights. Early every morning, she'd found herself trapped in a cave with no way out. In the hollow, her sleep was always restful—another indication that she was home.

ELSIE GOT DRESSED alongside Lacy, Maureen, and Jolene the next morning before strolling with them into the glade to line up for breakfast.

Tabor and Sasha were already seated on a log eating porridge. Elsie joined them after dishing up and watched shifters as they entered the glade. Rosalie sauntered in wearing a short halter dress that showed off the swells of her boobs. Low-cut tops amused Elsie when packmates were constantly removing garments to shift. It didn't matter what any of them wore, they all got naked every day. There was no mystery in that department. Some shifters were more private than others, like Zackary who was always trying to shield himself from her. Elsie had caught a brief flash of him the day he joined her and Kallie swimming in the pond. Like the rest of him, he was well endowed.

Warmth crept up Elsie's neck. She swallowed down the mushy porridge, all too aware of the damp heat blooming between her legs. She had a naughty mind filled with carnal desires that would have shocked most of her coven. No matter what she did or said, they always saw a sweet girl. Well, Elsie was no longer a girl, and it was possible to be both naughty and nice. Her fantasies no longer centered on candlelit bedrooms and touching beneath covers. Now she envisioned herself naked beneath the moonlight, coupling with Zackary against the earth. This desire burned in her belly, fluttering around like a moth trapped behind a villa window. Once inside her head, Elsie couldn't let it out. Every time she saw Zackary her thoughts turned delirious. Good thing she was skilled at hiding what went on inside her wayward mind.

Elsie mashed more porridge between her teeth and swallowed it down.

Rosalie was met by her friends Olivia and Camilla. As they walked by, Rosalie winked at Elsie, who waved. Tabor frowned at the exchange.

"Making new friends?"

"I consider all my packmates friends."

Sasha beamed at her while Tabor pursed his lips.

"Be careful," he said. "Not everyone is friendly toward our kind. If anyone ever bothers you, let me know immediately."

Elsie set her bowl in her lap and sat up straight. "I'm not worried, and I can handle things myself."

"Elsie . . ." Tabor sighed and gripped the back of his neck.

"I think Elsie is fitting in just fine," Sasha said.

The pureblooded she-wolf really was the best pack sister. Even if Sasha wasn't mated to her brother, Elsie would have adored her. Sasha had a worldly, kind, and commanding way about her. It was as clear as a cloudless sky that she loved her pack and would do anything for them. She was the most selfless being Elsie had ever known. Was Elsie willing to make any sacrifice necessary to save the coven she'd grown up in? If there was no other option, would she give herself over to Brutus?

Recalling their recent encounter in the forest made Elsie squeeze her eyes closed and shudder. Zackary was big, but Brutus was even bigger. The muscular bear shifter, however, did not excite her in the least. The thought of the hairy beast lazing around naked inside his cave made the porridge churn inside her stomach.

Elsie needed to make her move soon, but not so fast that she scared Zackary off. William had not appreciated her forwardness. He'd said it wasn't ladylike.

I'm not a lady. I'm a wolf and a witch, Elsie grumbled to herself.

Their bodies were made for mating, but William had acted all weird about it, ruining the experience. He'd never wanted to try anything different, either. Always beneath covers. Always on top, bumping into her in a rush to come and get it over with before things got "out of control." He'd never given Elsie an orgasm—not even close. He probably considered it unseemly for a woman to climax. She was glad to be rid of him.

Unable to finish her porridge, Elsie stood up—her movement drawing her brother's attention. He stared at her with keen eyes, the same green as their father's.

"You're partners with Aden?" he asked.

Elsie glanced across the glade to where Rosalie stood beside Aden, playing with the ends of her long brown hair. She chewed on her lip and returned her attention to Tabor.

"I switched partners with Rosalie."

"Switched?" Sasha's forehead wrinkled as though she'd never heard of such a wild notion.

Aden had been open to switching, but he said he wouldn't lie if anyone asked. It hadn't taken much convincing, not when Aden still appeared preoccupied with the human he'd left behind at Balmar Heights. Elsie had fed him the same story she shared now.

"I didn't want to be on hunting duty."

Tabor leaned forward, green gaze locked on hers. "Who is your new partner?"

"Hudson."

Tabor relaxed on the log and nodded. This time, Sasha frowned.

"You can't just switch like that. Jager paired you and Aden together."

"Sasha leave it," Tabor said. "The old man barely leaves his hut. What difference does it make?"

Sasha jerked sideways and glared at him.

Uh-oh. Elsie didn't want to be the cause of a fight between them. But she had to stay the course. She took a step backward.

"So, anyway. I'm headed off to duty. Will I see the two of you at dinner?"

"Yes," Sasha said at the same time Tabor said, "No."

"Um, okay. So maybe?" Elsie spun around, leaving the mated pair to work things out.

WHEN ELSIE AND Hudson entered the small field by the river, Chase and Zackary stood waiting with smiles.

The boys were soon gone, leaving Elsie alone with Zackary. She walked over to the baskets and looked down. Finding them empty, she grinned.

"You waited for me."

Zackary gave an amused grunt. "It didn't seem fair for me to get a head start."

Elsie's eyes lit up. "Oh, so this is a race to see who can fill their basket first."

"Um, no. That's not what I meant." Zackary rubbed his jaw.

She could see he hadn't intended it as competition, but Elsie's pulse quickened in anticipation. She scooped up a basket.

"If I win, I want a kiss."

Zackary's lips parted, and his eyes went to her mouth.

She'd tried to get one out of him at the pond last moon cycle before Jack and Kallie put a stop to it. They'd meant well, she supposed, but she should be free to make her own decisions. There was no one to stop them today.

Zackary looked around as though expecting a packmate to storm in and pull them apart. Early morning sunlight tickled the blades of grass in the quiet field. There wasn't so much as a breeze whispering at them to take caution. Birds whistled merry encouragement, darting low across the field before disappearing into the bushes.

"What do you want if you win?" she asked before he

could object to her terms.

Zackary's large fingers slid from his jaw to his chin as he studied her. He didn't seem particularly scared. What would he ask for? What if he wanted the same reward? Would that mean she could kiss him now? Elsie bounced on the balls of her feet, impatient for his answer.

"If I win . . ." Zackary's smile faltered.

"Yes?" Elsie coaxed, standing on her toes.

Zackary lowered his arms, a mask of confusion settling over his face.

"If I win, you tell me why you want to kiss me."

"That's it?" Elsie asked, disappointed. "That's the reward you choose if you win?"

Zackary nodded.

"I can tell you right now, you know."

"No," he said quickly. "A bet is a bet." He grabbed his basket and began plucking blackberries with a determination that made Elsie's heart sink. It looked like he wanted to win so he wouldn't have to kiss her.

That sobering thought took the fun out of the task. A weight pressed against Elsie as she picked berries, deep in thought. Beside her, Zackary emptied the bushes of their burden with quick efficiency. Every time she looked over, her stomach hollowed out a little more. She was getting such mixed signals from the burly shifter. One moment he seemed to only have eyes for her, the next she felt like a pest he wanted to avoid.

The sun lifted above their heads. Soon, Zackary was two wooden crates ahead of Elsie. She wasn't racing him, though, not when he so obviously wished to avoid her lips. It wasn't even midday yet when Zackary set his basket down and announced, "Done."

The triumph in his voice hurt worse than thorns piercing through flesh.

Elsie set her own basket down. She still had one more layer of crates to fill up the top.

"Congratulations," she said, unable to mask her pout.

"So?" Zackary asked, placing his hands on his broad hips. The khaki shorts he wore were unbuttoned and partially unzipped. There was just too much of him to fit inside his clothes. He should take them off and work naked. But he didn't want to *offend* her. He didn't want to kiss her, either, and that really did offend Elsie.

"Why do you want to kiss me?"

Elsie glared at him. Zackary cocked his head, looking taken aback. It was humiliating enough that he'd rushed to beat her so he wouldn't have to kiss her. Answering his question would only make it worse.

But a bet was a bet.

Elsie stared at him for several seconds before looking into the sky. "Because you're the most beautiful male I've ever seen. You're attractive and thoughtful and . . . Ugh. I didn't realize how difficult this was going to be." She kept her head tilted up, mindful of the sun. She didn't need her eyes watering on top of everything else. "I'm drawn to you, but the feeling obviously isn't mutual so—"

Zackary was on her so fast it was as though he'd shifted and lunged in beast form. But it wasn't a furry wolf who gathered her into his muscular arms. His grasp was surprisingly gentle, as though she was one of the berries he didn't wish to crush. Because of that tenderness, she wasn't prepared for the blistering force of his mouth claiming hers. He didn't just kiss her, he commanded her lips, forcing them apart with his own. A possessive growl rose from Zackary's throat and entered her mouth, vibrating down to her core. She moaned in answer. It was as though she'd never been kissed until now. It felt as though his mouth was mating hers, more so when his tongue pushed between her teeth and swirled inside.

Elsie never thought she'd be the kind of female who went weak in the knees, but she found herself clinging to Zackary for support.

Slick heat seeped between her legs and her nipples prickled.

His kiss was exquisite. Absolutely exquisite.

Her fingers itched to yank down his tight shorts, lift up her dress, and join their bodies against the open field.

Zackary's searing lips continued without pause while his hands held her against him. He kissed her until they were both panting then pulled away and stepped back, leaving Elsie swaying on her feet. They stared at one another speechless. Elsie's heart thrummed inside her chest. Her entire body felt alive. Her mind was screaming with joy because she knew now without a shadow of a doubt that Zackary was more than just her savior, he was the mate she'd always wanted.

Sunlight streaked over Zackary's ripped torso as he got his breathing under control.

"I guess we both got what we wanted out of that bet," he said. His voice was smooth, not winded at all.

Elsie smiled. "And I didn't even fill my basket."

"I'll help you."

Working together, it didn't take long to top off the berries. As with the day before, they set the baskets beneath the shade of a tree. Elsie bent down and grabbed one, offering it to Zackary to eat from her raised fingers. His eyes glinted at her before he closed in and took the berry from between her fingers with his teeth. Elsie shivered, the quakes sending her body back into reaction mode.

Hesitantly, Zackary lifted his hand and ran his thick thumb over her nipple. It tightened on contact. Elsie took in a sharp breath. Zackary touched her other nipple, leaning forward to watch it press against the white polyester. Deep in concentration, he rubbed circles around each bud, working them into hard points that he stroked into obedience like a fire he refused to let burn down. All she could do was rasp for breath, which only seemed to fascinate Zackary more. He leaned closer with a slow smile that spread up his cheeks.

When she tried to run her hands down his chest, he gently pushed her arms aside and continued touching her. When Elsie went for Zackary's groin, he captured her wrist, keeping her hand out of reach. Then he took her lips with his while his hands lingered over her breasts. Kisses hotter than sunbeams scorched Elsie's lips.

Just when it felt as though her mouth would blister, Zackary let up and touched her nose with his.

"Are you thirsty?" he asked huskily.

"Parched," Elsie answered.

He curled his fingers around hers and, holding hands,

they walked to the river. Wading in, they cupped handfuls of cool, fresh water and watched one another drink with an intimacy that curled inside Elsie's belly like a soft tail.

"So, your mother was a wolf?" Zackary asked, making Elsie laugh at the change in conversation.

She rubbed her elbows and grinned at him. She'd always considered him handsome, but after the kissing and touching, she found him downright scrumptious. Zackary's abs rippled with muscles that descended into a wide V to his groin. With his shorts partially opened, she was able to follow the triangle to a patch of wiry brown hair—not entirely hidden. Elsie's throat went dry. She bent down and scooped up more river water. After she took another drink and stood, Zackary raised his brows.

"Yes, my mother was a wolf."

"But she didn't want you to grow up in her pack?"

"She wanted to live with my father. They were madly in love." She locked eyes with Zackary and widened her smile.

"What happened?"

"She died when I was a baby—natural causes."

"I'm sorry."

"I still have my father, which is more than most shifters in Wolf Hollow have." Elsie considered herself lucky.

Zackary's frown deepened. "He doesn't mind you living in the wild?"

"He's never wanted me to suppress who I am. He understands that I'm part wolf with animalistic needs." With a wicked grin, Elsie scooped water from the river and flung it at Zackary. He looked way too serious. Maybe if she got his shorts wet, he'd take them off.

Smirking, he pranced out of the river, and out of reach. Elsie trailed him back to the shade beneath the trees. Zackary sat on the ground. Elsie sat beside him.

"Can we kiss again?" she asked.

Elsie liked the confident smile that puckered his lips. She liked that he didn't hesitate to pull her into his lap and turn her around so that she straddled him. Once his lips were on hers, Elsie closed her eyes and took in all the sensations his mouth brought to life inside her body.

She tried again to touch his shaft, finally giving up when it became clear Zackary had no intention of giving her access—at least not today. Tomorrow might be a different story. Once they mated, Elsie had no doubt Zackary would insist on claiming her as his life mate. He was an honorable male. He'd owned up to his mistakes and volunteered his help the moment packmates went missing. He would claim her and treat her with tender loving care.

She could already imagine Brutus's roar of outrage echoing inside his cave. Wizards would triumph over bears yet again.

Elsie pushed that thought aside as Zackary thrust his tongue inside her mouth. She wrapped her hands around his neck and pushed her breasts against his chest, kissing him until her lips were puffy and swollen.

✦ chapter seven

ZACKARY WAS SO screwed. Totally fucked.

Elsie's moans had nearly made him explode inside his shorts. The way her nipples speared through her dress at his touch made his teeth ache to nip her sensitive flesh and turn her gasps into cries of release. At this rate, they'd be humping like rabbits the next day. His face flushed with equal parts terror and hunger.

"You lucky dog," Justin crowed as they sat on a cluster of stumps with their bowls of stew near a small bonfire.

"Shut up," Zackary hissed, staring across the glade at Tabor.

The half-shifter sat alone at the moment, scanning the crowd.

If Tabor knew Zackary had touched his sister, he'd kill him. Or, if not murder, he'd shrink his dick or make it disappear altogether.

Zackary needed his dick more than ever . . . to stick inside Tabor's sister.

He sneered at his own crude thoughts.

"Do you think Elsie has a sister?" Wiley asked while

chewing his food.

"Well, we know she has a brother." Justin jabbed Zackary with his elbow. His friend's grin was way too gleeful. "Can I have Elsie after Tabor kills you?"

Zackary's nostrils flared right before he grabbed Justin's neck.

"I said keep it down, unless you really do want me to die." He released Justin's neck as suddenly as he'd grasped him. No harm done. Zackary knew how to hold back his strength—unlike Wolfrik, whose temper had only recently been reined in after claiming and impregnating a mate.

"Don't be a prick," Wiley admonished Justin. "We're rooting for you, Zack. We'll refer to you-know-who as Annabelle."

"Annabelle?" Zackary quirked a brow.

"Wiley's invisible girlfriend." Justin snorted.

"Not true," Wiley said.

"She the one you jack off to every morning?" Justin asked.

Zackary grumbled. "We are not calling her Annabelle."

"What are we calling her then?" Wiley stuffed more stew into his mouth, chewing loud.

"Nothing. No names. Just don't even talk about it, okay?" Zackary tried eating, but the only hunger he felt was for the she-wolf whose name he couldn't say out loud.

Justin set his half-empty bowl on the ground and leaned forward on his knees. "Come on, dude. You have to tell us something."

Wiley swallowed a big chunk of stew. "Yeah, don't be a prick."

Zackary snorted. "Now *I'm* the prick?"

Wiley ran his tongue over his lips before smacking them. "We're your best friends. You can't go popping your cherry and not tell us about it."

"Nothing got popped."

Zackary put his face in his hands and groaned. He should have never told his friends about the trade Elsie arranged. But if he hadn't, she might have, and the pair of them would have given him an even harder time. Either way, they'd be hounding him every spare second until the new pairings. Would Elsie find a way to switch partners again? The thought sent a thrill of pleasure through him. He wished he could just claim her as a mate so they wouldn't have to sneak around. But that was never happening. Not so long as Tabor breathed.

"You should be careful, though," Justin said.

Zackary lowered his hands. "Why's that?" he asked, even though he knew the answer.

He and Tabor had years of bad history together. That alone would have been enough to ensure Zackary was the last male Tabor would ever allow to claim Elsie.

Then Zackary had done the unforgiveable and helped Garrick abduct Tabor. Garrick had made Zackary believe they were dumping him at the gates of Balmar Heights to be with his own kind. The elder had lied, revealing he had no intention of taking Tabor to his father's people—he meant to leave him for the humans to imprison. The whole ordeal had made Zackary sick to his stomach. He would have rather left Garrick behind in that pit outside the wasteland, but the elder had bullied and threatened him the entire way. Zackary still hadn't been able to let it go—couldn't have lived with himself if he hadn't gone straight to Sasha to tell her what happened. But it would never be enough to make up for what he'd done. Tabor had every right to hate him until the end of time. If only Zackary could go back and do things differently.

"Once a mongrel, always a mongrel," Vallen's cruel voice clawed through his mind.

When Justin didn't answer right away, Zackary sighed. "Tabor's going to kill me. You don't need to remind me."

Justin laughed. "No. Well, I mean that too. But I was thinking more along the lines of breeding."

"What the fuck are you talking about?" Zackary snapped.

"Um, hello? She's part witch. She doesn't need a full moon to get pregnant."

Zackary's eyes stretched in their sockets. He'd never considered that. Well, he'd never considered he'd find a female willing to sleep with him, especially not one as lovely and kind as Elsie.

"Witch pups," Justin mouthed, smirking when Zackary's mouth hung open.

"Shit," Wiley said, staring into his empty bowl of stew.

"Yup. If our boy here blows his load inside you-know-who, there's gonna be a little Zack Junior on the way."

Friend or not, Justin really needed to wipe the smirk off his face.

Wiley leaned in and lowered his voice. "But maybe if that happened, you-know-who's brother couldn't you-know-what because the council would protect our friend here. They wouldn't allow a family to be broken up that way."

Justin considered Zackary with a sideways look. "Maybe."

He barely heard him over the thundering of his heart as it pounded in his eardrums. Now he truly was terrified, and it had nothing to do with Tabor. Zackary would make a terrible father. Disastrous. He knew nothing of childrearing. He'd had no siblings and spent no time in the den. Not to mention, he'd had the worst role model in the pack.

His breathing became ragged, on the verge of a panic attack. They'd only kissed, he reminded himself. Thank goodness he'd stopped things before going too far. They hadn't mated.

The council had forbidden him from taking a mate, anyway.

They didn't say anything about breeding, a wicked voice whispered in his ear.

He gritted his teeth. Same thing. Worse. He wasn't such a scoundrel as to impregnate a female without being free to claim her as a mate.

I'm not a complete mongrel, no thanks to you, Father.

It wasn't until the next afternoon that Zackary wished he'd never thought of the bastard. Even in his madness, the vicious beast always seemed to find his way back to the hollow. It was as though Vallen intended to terrorize his son for the remainder of his life.

"**D**ID YOU LEAVE behind close friends?" Zackary asked Elsie as they picked berries the following day.

Elsie nodded as she reached deeper into the bush,

her movements mindful of the thorns. With no bet to spur them on, they worked side by side carefully.

"My two closest friends are Charlotte and Mia. I promised I'd keep in contact and visit when I can. They'd love to see Wolf Hollow . . . especially the males." Elsie looked over and winked in her cute way.

Zackary chuckled. "Don't tell that to Wiley and Justin unless you want to be hounded every day."

"Ha. Too bad my friends aren't part shifter like me. I doubt anyone from Balmar Heights could hack living in the woods for long, not when they have so many comforts on the mountain."

Zackary's fingers hovered above a ripe berry. "And you don't miss them—the comforts, I mean?"

Looking over at him with a reassuring smile, Elsie said, "They were nice, but not necessary . . . not for me. But I have an advantage over my coven." She rubbed her lips together, looking thoughtful. "It's funny to say I'm half witch and half wolf. When I'm in wolf form, I am full wolf, you know what I mean? And I have the same powers as the rest of the coven. So really, I'm not half anything—I'm double." Her wide grin was infectious.

Unlike Tabor, Elsie's self-confidence came across as attractive rather than superior. Maybe it had to do with her being female, but Zackary believed it was more than that. She was someone who looked for the good in others rather than jump straight into defense. Elsie wasn't just whole or double, she was everything Zackary could have ever wanted.

Too bad he could never have her.

Why? He snarled at himself in silence.

Because of Tabor. Because of the council. Because of the real reason . . .

He was unworthy of love.

Mood darkening, he squished the next couple berries, shoving them in his mouth so they wouldn't go to waste. Even the sweet, sun-warmed blackberries tasted bitter on his tongue.

Luckily, Elsie kept her focus on the berries—and thorns—and didn't notice Zackary frowning.

What would happen if he pushed her away? Would she find another male to kiss and touch?

Zackary huffed in a sharp breath. He glared into the bushes. Elsie looked over.

"Is everything all right?"

No, things were far from okay, but he couldn't tell her that. The thought of another shifter laying his grubby mitts on Elsie cleaved his chest in half. Zackary knew he didn't deserve her, but Mother Moon help him, he couldn't let her go.

Gripping the basket against his side, he asked the question that had been weighing on him all night.

"Do witches require a full moon to get pregnant?" His cheeks heated, but he didn't care. From the corner of his eyes he saw Elsie pause and turn toward him.

"No. We do not need a full moon to procreate," she answered slowly. "We use spells to avoid pregnancy . . . unless we're trying for a baby."

Zackary resumed berry picking, all too aware of Elsie watching him. After several seconds had passed, she faced the bush and began filling her basket.

"Do you want children?" Elsie asked in a serious voice.

"I am not allowed a mate," Zackary answered gruffly. Elsie might not know. She wasn't present for his punishment.

"The council seems a lot more lenient these days," Elsie remarked. "And you didn't answer the question."

Zackary's fingers curled around the next berry, squishing yet another one. His hands were too big, too meaty to hold something as delicate as a baby.

"I would not make a good father." He held his breath, waiting for Elsie to contradict his statement. Wisely, she remained quiet. Good. Maybe she was beginning to see reason. Zackary still couldn't figure out why she'd sought his attentions in the first place. She said she found him attractive. Pity for her.

They finished picking berries in silence. By the time they were done, Zackary had worked himself into a foul mood. Like burnt stew, there was no coming back. Nothing to salvage.

After setting his basket in the shade, Zackary turned around, preparing to suggest Elsie spend the remainder of the afternoon elsewhere.

What he found left him momentarily speechless.

Elsie pulled her white gown over her head and dropped it into a heap on the ground. Subtle, perky breasts pointed at him from above a flat belly and narrow hips. She had smooth, long legs. Perhaps the witches of Balmar Heights were in the regular habit of hair removal. Maybe it was magic. Despite being petite, those legs were long enough to wrap around Zackary's broad hips.

"Oust nada, yayo jur egun. Diena ou tagos. Araw des voda ferus," she whispered.

Zackary swallowed. "What are you doing?"

Bright blue eyes stared back at him. "That was a spell to prevent pregnancy. It lasts for a full day."

Zackary's groin throbbed, nearly popping out of his shorts. His chest rose and fell rapidly, arms starting to shake.

How could she stand there so calmly offering herself to him? Someone needed to warn her. Protect her.

Zackary wanted to be the one to protect her. He also wanted to mate her—spread her open and bury his cock deep inside her. He'd never been with a female, but living with the pack, he'd seen enough over the years to understand the fundamentals. There were shifters who weren't shy about fucking in front of the community, especially during the full moon celebration. Dance partners would pull one another to the ground and go at it right there in front of the bonfire with the drums beating in the background.

He knew the actions, could see them playing out inside his head.

His unruly cock wanted to thrust inside her and pump out seed until her cunt was spilling over, marking this female as his.

How could Zackary do something so indecent to Elsie?

He wanted to protect her. He also wanted to fuck her. He couldn't do both, not unless he claimed her. But he couldn't do that either.

Zackary raked his stubby nails through his scalp and groaned.

"Moon above, Elsie. I want to. I want to so bad, but we can't." He squeezed his eyes closed. When he dared reopen them, he did a double take to see that Elsie was once more dressed.

She smiled, but it looked forced. "That's okay. I was being too frisky. I didn't mean to make you uncomfortable." She lowered her head, eyes on the ground as though she'd done something wrong.

Anguish howled up Zackary's throat, but it didn't make it past his lips. He didn't want Elsie to feel bad on his account. He wished she could understand that he wasn't worth it, that he was trying to do the decent thing even though it killed him.

"Can I kiss you?"

Elsie's lashes lifted and her eyes flashed as she frowned. "Do you *want* to kiss me?"

She had no idea how hopeless he was when it came to her. He stepped up to her and stared into her blazing eyes. Pushing some of her hair over her shoulder, he whispered into her ear, "I want *everything* with you."

Then his lips claimed hers in a punishing kiss to demonstrate just how much he wanted her. Elsie clawed at his back, as though expressing her unspoken frustration. She couldn't hurt him if she tried. His muscles were thick as hide.

Elsie kissed back with an intensity that wasn't there yesterday. He wasn't sure whether he wanted her to calm down or keep going in this wound up way. Maneuvering her onto the grass, Zackary pulled her on top and lay back, guiding her head against his to continue the kiss.

He loved the taste of her mouth, as fresh as forest air. He wondered if that, too, was magic. It made him want to suck her in like oxygen. He wanted every last breath. To consume her, then revive her, and repeat the process all over again.

When her hand reached for his groin, he didn't stop her. Elsie yanked his shorts down then wrapped her delicate fingers around his thick, engorged shaft and stroked up and down. When Zackary groaned, she thrust her tongue inside his mouth. She worked his cock faster. The pleasure was blinding. Blood rushed through his shaft and his balls tightened. Elsie's hand was tight around him, pumping him so good. When she gripped the foreskin around the tip and pulled it over the head, he felt as though he might die of euphoria.

Zackary's hand shot out, grabbing her by the wrist right before he exploded. His thick fingers tightened on her slim ones as they pumped his cock several more times in unison, releasing warm spurts of cum. His body shuddered with release, cock still standing on end, coated in his pleasure.

Blissed out on his back, Zackary knew he was done for. They still had the entire afternoon together. He'd recover and, when he did, he'd do the unforgiveable and mate her. He'd do anything for her—even if it meant damning himself.

✦ chapter eight

VICTORY AT LAST. Elsie had finally managed to get Zackary's shorts off.

After bringing him release, he'd pulled the tight pair of khakis free before heading to the river to rinse off. He crouched in the water, the current flowing over his shaft, washing away his seed. Elsie couldn't take her eyes off him. She kept her dress on because it seemed to make him more comfortable. She'd feared she'd scared him off for good when she removed it earlier. It had hurt when he turned her down, but she suspected it had less to do with his feelings for her and more to do with his inner demons. She hoped he'd get over it soon and claim her. His orgasm had been a promising start. She smiled to herself. What need of enchantments did she have? Relationships simply took patience, love, and time.

Time was the problem. She was down to fifteen days.

Zackary sat in the river, submerged from the neck down. His eyes drifted closed, a contented smile on his lips. His pleasure brought Elsie joy. Despite everything, she couldn't help feeling like they were meant for each other.

She pulled her dress above her knees then sat on the edge of the river and stretched her legs in the cool water. Arms propped behind her back, she lifted her head to the sky and closed her eyes, bathing her face in sunshine.

She loved that they could spend time together without having to speak and still feel comfortable. She wouldn't have minded lazing around all afternoon.

Water splashed with the sound of Zackary standing. Elsie lowered her face away from the sun and opened her eyes, taking in the sight of river water dripping down Zackary's muscular chest, thighs, and legs. It clung to the dark patch of hair above his cock.

He waded into the shallows, up to his ankles, and faced her. Pulse racing, Elsie stared at his naked body, transfixed. Zackary kept still, not meeting her gaze. His thoughts looked miles away from the hollow as water dripped off him and he began to dry off in the heat of the sun. As he dried, his cock hardened, growing thick and long.

Once his body was no longer damp, Zackary stepped onto the shore, eyes now locked on Elsie's. She scrambled up the bank using her wrists and feet, not making it far before Zackary planted a foot on either side of her, staring down with a firm set of his jaw.

"I'm a mongrel, Elsie. A big, dumb brute. Tell me to get lost. Say it quick before I do something you regret."

Knots jerked inside her stomach to hear him say such awful things about himself.

"Stay," Elsie commanded, enraged by his words. They hurt her, too, because he was none of those horrible things, and she cared about him.

His nostrils flared. He dove down, his great big body looming over hers, blocking out the sun.

Elsie's breath quickened. Chills of anticipation rippled over her skin. Her nipples tightened. Thick arms were propped on either side of her, Zackary still holding back, despite calling himself a brute. Ironic, when he took such care not to crush her.

He dipped his head to her chest, nipping one hard peak through the fabric of her dress.

A gasp of pleasure blasted up her throat.

Wetting the material over her breast with his tongue, Zackary bit down gently and tugged.

Elsie bit her tongue to keep from crying out as pleasure and pain shot through her. She was afraid he might stop if he thought he'd hurt her. She grabbed the back of his head, holding him to her breast so he'd keep going. A deep, smug chuckle shook Zackary's shoulders, helping her relax until he repeated the torture on her other nipple.

Sweet moon above! It was like there was a string connecting her breast to her core. Her inner thighs dampened with the slick heat of her desire.

Zackary pulled her dress above her hips, coarse fingers skimming her thighs. They traveled to her center and glided across Elsie's arousal. Zackary's finger slipped inside her easily. His face brightened, a look of pleased fascination entering his eyes. He pushed his finger in deeper then added a second one after feeling how wet she was. Both fingers slicked through her in pleasurable strokes.

Closing her eyes, Elsie pictured him spreading her open and joining their bodies. She imagined them grinding together until reaching their climax, and Zackary emptying inside her. Being filled with his seed would be like a claiming of sorts. She was so close to breaking her curse and discovering happiness in the process. Perhaps it had been a blessing. If she hadn't been cursed, her father would have wanted her to stay at Balmar Heights. He never would have gone to such lengths to seek out Tabor and ask him to take Elsie in. She would have never met Zackary. Big, beautiful Zackary whose fingers slipped out of her and spread her legs apart as he positioned himself.

He held his cock in one hand. The tip was slick, weeping to have her the same way she slicked in readiness to take him in.

Zackary inched closer, bare chest rising and falling, eyes intent on their joining. The head of his cock pressed between Elsie's legs. He sank into her slowly, his brows furrowed and mouth parting, concern followed by surprise flickering over his eyes.

Had he thought he wouldn't fit?

Her body took him in, one slick inch at a time, filling her until they were fully joined.

Elsie's lashes fluttered closed, and a sigh of pure ecstasy wafted from her lips.

But before Zackary could rock his hips to begin their mating, a howl crashed over the hollow soon followed by frantic snarls.

A VICIOUS GROWL AROSE, one he would have recognized anywhere. Even before a rabid wolf bit Vallen, his snarls had always set Zackary's teeth on edge. Angry. Always angry and out for blood, Vallen had reveled in the hunt. When he wasn't hunting, he'd gotten his kicks by hitting his son. At least he'd spared Zack's mother from his brutality. She'd been too frail to handle Vallen's brute force, but it hadn't spared her from his cruel tongue. Long before the vulhena attacked the pack's elders, she'd wasted away in Vallen's shadow.

It was an ill omen that he'd resurfaced the moment Zackary joined with a female.

He jerked his hips back, pulling out of Elsie abruptly as the sound of angry wolves erupted across the hollow.

He felt like he'd entered heaven only to be ripped back to hell.

"Stay here. Don't shift," Zackary said frantically, scrambling to all fours.

Before Elsie could say anything, he shifted and took off running westward past the blackberry bushes. Dirt flew behind Zackary's paws as he raced in an arc near the Forest of the Ancestors. He blasted through Hudson's neighboring territory—no shifters to be seen—streaking into the western hunting grounds and the horror that awaited.

The howling had moved to the southwest, traveling deeper into the forest. The scent of wolves clung to the earth, along with a body, bleeding over the dirt. Zackary ran past it, taking off after the group pursuing Vallen. He snarled in fury, claws digging into the trail. He could smell the bastard's rank scent in the air, growing stronger then fading, taunting him. Zackary changed his course, feeling as though he was being jerked around in different directions. This was his home, his territory, and yet he felt like he'd entered an ever-changing maze that was baiting him and screwing with his mind.

He headed toward the falls, spurred on by the howls of his packmates. Keeping along the western border of Wolf Hollow, Zackary ran steadily for what felt like hours before reaching the bluff.

A dozen packmates stood near the ledge, voices raised, and arms jerking angrily. Zackary shifted then pushed off the ground and hurried over, staring across the valley below. There was no movement. No wolf. Only wide-open space.

Vallen had gotten away. He always got away.

NIGHT HAD FALLEN by the time a large gathering collected in the glade.

Zackary returned with the small group that had run after Vallen before reaching a seeming dead end at the bluff.

Jolene was dead, her human body ripped apart three feet from a tree she had likely run toward in a failed attempt to climb to safety. Her body had been moved to the communal cabin and shut inside to await burial beneath a tree in the Forest of the Ancestors, close to where she'd been patrolling.

Jolene's patrol partner, Patrick, had been bitten while in wolf form. While nearby patrol wolves pursued Vallen,

Patrick had managed to run away before anyone could stop him.

Lacy and Maureen sat huddled together crying on a log, Elsie beside them with her head bent and sad blue eyes unblinking as she stared at the ground.

A large log collapsed into the bonfire that had been lit, causing sparks to erupt.

Bow and quiver in hand, Tabor stomped over to where old Jager sat, slumped on a log.

"It's time to put this mad wolf down once and for all," Tabor announced to the crowd.

This was met with instant encouragement.

"We're not losing any more of our packmates to that rabid beast!" An angry chorus went up.

"I volunteer to go after him," Tabor continued.

Not that long ago, packmates had sneered and resented him for his powers. Now they cheered like he was their damn hero.

"I'll go with you." Sasha stepped over to his side, chin lifted.

"I will too," Raider said, less enthused. He towered above the crowd; arms folded over his bare chest. His mate, Jordan, stood by him frowning.

Aden lifted his hand briefly. Whenever there was danger, he volunteered. Zackary would, too, since it was his damn dad who'd gotten more of their packmates. Before he could offer, Rosalie yelped. "We can't have all the big males leaving us unprotected."

"I'll stay in the hollow," Wolfrik said, putting his arm around his mate, Kallie.

Jager nodded then looked at Sasha. "In your condition, you should stay, Sasha."

The pureblooded female snarled. "Vallen got away from me once before. I won't let him get away again."

"We should break up into two hunting parties," Raider said. "One group needs to go after Patrick."

"What if they try to bite you?" Rosalie squealed.

"We'll bring guns," Sasha said. "I think this situation warrants their use."

"Yes. Take them," Jager said. "I don't want anyone else getting hurt."

"I can go after Patrick," Aden said.

Jager rocked slightly in place, scratching the back of his wrinkled hand.

"Yes. Good," the elder said. "Raider can stay here in case either of the mad wolves double back."

"Take Ford with you." Raider looked at his burly cousin who had come over from the den. Ford nodded once.

"I'll join one of the tracking parties," Emerson said, sweeping her long blonde hair over her shoulder to fall down her back.

"You should stay," Ford said.

Emerson rolled her eyes. "Believe it or not, I can handle a gun."

"Zackary will join Sasha and me." Tabor's sharp voice gave him a jolt. Green eyes glittered at him through the dark. The half-shifter sounded excited at the prospect of hunting Vallen down and making Zackary watch. Well, he could preen all he wanted. Zackary wanted the mad wolf gone as much as everyone else.

Eventually, Jager retired, his limp more pronounced than usual when he left the glade. None of the single shifters slept that night. It was a lasting kind of torture that dragged on with conversations whispering around him between muffled sobs.

Justin and Wiley joined Zackary sitting beneath a tree, their faces grim.

"Sorry, man," Justin said, tapping him once on the shoulder.

"Yeah, sorry," Wiley said.

Zackary clenched his jaw. He wished they wouldn't apologize. He would not mourn Vallen. If Tabor wanted to make the kill shot, he could have at it. Maybe Zackary should confess that he'd mounted Tabor's sister after he was done dealing with the rabid wolf—let him take a shot at him too. He probably deserved an arrow through the heart or a bullet to the brain. While he'd been defiling the delicate female, Vallen had closed in on Jolene and Patrick. If that wasn't a sign that he shouldn't have touched Elsie, he didn't know what was.

"What kind of female would ever want a mangy mutt like you on her back or your grubby hands pawing her?" Vallen had jeered at him. *"You better learn to jerk yourself off, because that's the only action you'll ever get in Wolf Hollow."*

Was he still a virgin? Their joining seemed too brief to count. But they had joined. The howls had been several seconds too late to stop them.

Had Elsie been a virgin? Somehow, he doubted that. The half-shifter acted like she knew what she was doing.

She even had a spell to block pregnancy.

How many wizards had she slept with?

Zackary shook his head violently. It wasn't any of his concern. She'd probably been curious, that's all. She wanted to compare wizards to wolves. If that was the case, she should have picked someone more experienced than him.

He gnashed his teeth, glowering into the flames of the bonfire, a low growl humming from his throat.

Wiley gave him a light pat on the back, mistaking his affliction for the nasty issue of his father.

When the first traces of morning light finally appeared on the horizon, Lacy and Carter poured dry grains from baskets into the cauldron and added river water for porridge.

After all the chatter that had gone on past midnight, everyone stumbled into line, yawning.

Zackary didn't have much of an appetite, but he filled his bowl and made sure to eat everything inside, knowing he might be gone for a while. Vallen was a tricky bastard. He'd evaded every single hunting party to go after him in the past. Sasha had been intent on ending him after he'd bitten Chase's sister, Rebecca. The pureblooded female had disappeared for a couple days, giving her elders and the entire pack a scare. In the confusion, her scent had gone cold, leaving them to worry that like Wolfrik, at the time, she might not return. She'd returned in a fit of frustration that Vallen had run her ragged before vanishing into the wasteland. Who knew how far the mad wolf would lead them?

After eating, Sasha beckoned Zackary, along with the second hunting party, to follow her along one of the wooded paths.

"Two guns and one lead wolf per group," Sasha said.

"I'll sniff out Patrick. Even if he managed to bite, it wouldn't affect me," Aden reminded them. Being a werewolf had its advantages. He was bigger than the largest wolf shifter. Stronger. Faster. Like wolf shifters, he could transform at any time, and he could even walk on two legs in his beast's form.

"I can sniff out Vallen," Zackary offered. "I know his scent better than anyone."

Tabor scoffed. "No kidding."

"Let's just get this over with as safely and swiftly as we can," Sasha said. She led them to the tall caves she'd been known to sleep in alone before shacking up with Tabor. "Wait for us out here," she said at the entrance.

Sasha and Tabor disappeared inside, leaving Emerson pacing near the opening. Ford leaned against a large boulder; arms folded over a snug navy T-shirt.

As uncomfortable as it was becoming part of Tabor's and Sasha's trio, Zackary felt relieved to get away before Jolene's Sky Ceremony. Listening to her friends cry was too much to bear. He felt somehow responsible just by sharing the same blood as his father. He couldn't wait to be free of him once and for all.

Sasha and Tabor returned with two backpacks. Sasha held one up.

"This contains two guns and extra ammunition we removed from the humans. Practice firing a few rounds *after* you're out of the hollow. We don't want to distress packmates any more than they already are."

Ford hurried over and snatched the pack, making Emerson's lips draw back as she hissed. With a triumphant lift of his head, Ford slipped his arms through the straps. Emerson tossed her golden mane over her shoulder, pasting a smile over her lips.

"Such a gentleman to carry the pack for me," she said in a teasing tone, batting her lashes in exaggeration.

The snap of a twig made everyone whirl around, but there was no danger from the two females who jogged over.

Zackary's heart lurched to see Elsie. For a moment, he thought she was going to run up to him, but she stopped short and glanced at Tabor, biting down on her lower lip. Gina, who had run in with her, kept going until she'd reached Emerson. The redhead threw her arms around Emerson's neck. "Promise you'll be careful."

"We're the ones with the guns and the werewolf," Emerson spoke with unabashed confidence, jutting her chin up.

Gina hugged her tighter. "Promise me."

"I promise." Emerson rubbed her nose against Gina's, flashing her a toothy smile. Pretty soon they were kissing with no signs of letting up.

It made Zackary's stomach tighten with longing, wishing he could hug and kiss Elsie in front of pack members. This definitely was not the right crowd, not unless he wanted Tabor to use him as target practice.

"Be safe," Elsie said softly.

Tabor's face softened, bringing up old ugly feelings toward the half-shifter. He was the biggest obstacle standing between Zackary and the female he'd been drawn to from the very moment she appeared in Wolf Hollow.

"Sorry to have to leave you alone so soon." Tabor gave Elsie a pat on the shoulder—a fucking pat like she was a damn dog.

But Elsie wasn't looking at her brother; her blue eyes stared directly at Zackary.

"You be careful, too, Zackary."

His heart stuttered at the concern and affection in her tone. Sasha pressed her lips together and looked at him with sharp interest, but Tabor didn't seem to notice anything out of the ordinary, huffing, "Don't worry about him."

Elsie's gaze remained on Zackary. He could have sworn he heard her voice inside his head, echoing Gina's words.

Promise me.

He nodded once.

I'll be back soon, he thought.

Maybe he was crazy, but the next words in his head sounded so much like her.

Hurry up.

AFTER SEEING OFF the two hunting parties, Elsie took Gina's hand, squeezing it in hers as they returned to the glade. Gina gripped her tightly. They spoke no words. They didn't need to. Words weren't necessary to express their worry for loved ones headed out into the wilds beyond Wolf Hollow's territory to hunt down rabid wolves.

The shock of it had yet to subside. Elsie had spent the previous night sleeping side by side with Jolene and her friends. The she-wolf had been so friendly and sweet. Elsie had only just begun to get to know Jolene, and now she was gone. And then there was poor Patrick, turned rabid. Elsie hadn't had an opportunity to speak to him at all.

A long procession of packmates was already making their way to the Forest of the Ancestors. Den mates filtered in, crossing the glade in a solemn march to the burial. Elsie and Gina followed them, still clasping hands.

Once they reached the forest, Gina tugged Elsie over to her friends Taryn and Janelle.

The temperature dropped beneath the dense canopy, blocking out the light. A hole about as deep and wide as a person had been dug beneath one of the trees. A shifter named Heath held Jolene's naked body in his arms. The blood had been cleaned from her body and her light brown hair brushed into a silky shine.

Standing on her tiptoes, Elsie could see the gouges in Jolene's skin where she'd been clawed and ripped open. Such things did not make her squeamish, only sad that a packmate had suffered and perished.

Elsie had been so intent on her impending claim that she'd never stopped to consider a worse alternative—not living long enough to have a mate. As a witch and wolf, she'd always felt invincible. Seeing Jolene's mangled body lowered into the earth didn't change that. Elsie had two advantages over humans, and yet her fate had been determined before she'd ever been born.

As Heath lowered Jolene's body into the earth, Maureen and Lacy choked out sobs. The pack's oldest member, Jager, stood slumped to one side in front of the hole in the ground. He made an effort to straighten, though Elsie could see that his health was deteriorating. The elder hunched all the time, whether he was seated or standing, and his response time had slowed considerably. Even thinking seemed to tire his mind. Today's stress and sorrow certainly didn't help.

Everyone quieted to allow him to speak.

"It is with great sorrow that we send Jolene off to the sky realm. A kindhearted and dutiful female, she was loved by all her packmates." The females in the group sniffled. "It is with heavy hearts that we must say goodbye much too soon. This is a sad, sad day in Wolf Hollow." His voice cracked slightly. "A very sad day. Today, we lay Jolene's body to rest in the Forest of the Ancestors where she returns to our spirit pack. As in life, she is not alone. We send her to her family and to the packmates awaiting her in the afterlife where we shall all meet up one day." He blinked several times. "May she run forever free."

"May she run forever free," the rest of the pack murmured.

Packmates took turns throwing dirt into the hole, covering Jolene's body little by little. When Elsie made it over with a handful of soil, only Jolene's arm poked through. Bits of soil spilled from Elsie's fist as she looked down, heart sinking past her feet. Packmates tossed earth in around her. It took Elsie a moment to loosen her fingers over the pit.

That evening, Heath, Alec, and Maureen brought their drums to the glade and beat out a hypnotic melody after dinner. Some of the den mates stuck around, sprawled out on the grass or sitting on logs listening. Most of the mothers had left to tuck in their kids.

Elsie sat with her legs crossed in the grass beside Gina, Janelle, and Taryn. Taryn kept glancing over at Chase with a sad frown. Zadie and Nudara stood beside the drummers and began to sing. The olive-skinned sisters had beautiful voices. Their melody filled the clearing and Elsie's soul. They all stayed up late until, one by one, packmates undressed then shifted into wolf form, remaining in the glade, where they all slept in one big group.

Sitting in human form over the grass, Elsie looked around at the wolves curled into balls, resting against their packmates. The scene around her was one of unity and strength. It was beautiful. Magical. Even in the face of tragedy. She'd never seen so many wolves together in one place—the glade blanketed in fur beneath the night sky.

She pulled her dress over her head and folded it gently before setting it on a patch of grass beside her.

Elsie didn't shift immediately. She remained crouched on the ground, stripped bare beneath the stars and moon. Inside her chest, her heart howled for Zackary. Tears pricked her eyes as she remembered him leaving the hollow, and she suddenly felt selfish. She hadn't shed a tear for Jolene, but here she was blinking the wetness from her eyes over a packmate who would return.

Surrounded by an entire pack of wolves, she felt so alone.

Isolation was preferable to a life mated to Brutus. Zackary needed to come back soon.

She only had two weeks left.

✦ chapter nine

BREAKFAST WAS A somber affair the following morning. Everyone spoke in hushed whispers, as though it was rude to enjoy too much life in the face of Jolene's death. Hudson insisted on staying with Elsie during day duties. Assuring him for the tenth time that she was more than fine on her own and could always howl if she needed help had done nothing to convince him. He and Chase talked about trading off every other day until Zackary returned.

She clenched her teeth. At this rate, by the end of the day her entire jaw would ache.

How many days would Zackary be gone? How much precious time would she lose? If he took too long . . . She didn't want to think it. If her father were there, he'd tell her she had to find an alternative, preferably several, in case Zackary didn't make it back in time.

Her heart erupted into flames at the thought of being with anyone other than Zackary. She didn't want to kiss another shifter, let alone claim one who wasn't her big, beautiful, sexy wolf.

He had to hurry back. He just had to.

"You okay?" Hudson asked, brows furrowed as they took the empty baskets to the blackberry bushes.

He probably thought she was shaken up about Jolene. She was, but her deeper anguish was purely selfish. It wasn't just her impending deadline. An emptiness had filled her chest the moment Zackary left the hollow. An unfamiliar feeling. She'd lived with her father her whole life and loved him unconditionally, yet her heart did not ache over their separation. When Tabor had insisted she return to Balmar Heights until the threat of the humans passed, she hadn't missed her brother this way.

With Zackary, a piece of her soul was missing.

"I don't suppose things like this happen at Balmar Heights," Hudson said as he picked his first berry of the day. "I can't imagine you have rabid wolves and vulhena running up the mountain to attack."

"No, we don't," Elsie answered.

"Your own little utopia above the clouds," Hudson remarked.

"We have problems with bear shifters."

"Bear shifters?" Hudson looked over; eyes wide with curiosity.

"They don't want us up there on the mountain, even though we don't bother them." Elsie ground her teeth. Her gums were already aching.

"Have they ever killed any of your clan?"

"No, but they once stole two of our children."

Hudson snarled and nearly dropped his basket. "Bastards," he said.

Elsie nodded. "They really are a bunch of brutes." One in particular.

The thought of claiming the mangy beast sent spirals of disgust coiling through Elsie's stomach. Given the chance, Brutus would not be gentle with her—not like Zackary in the least. He'd bring her nothing but pain and punishment. Such a life sounded worse than death. Elsie shuddered.

"Chase's sister, Rebecca, was killed by a rabid wolf." Hudson kept his attention on the berries he picked one by one with great care. "I was going to claim her for my mate," he said softly.

"I'm sorry." Elsie looked over, watching the deliberate way Hudson selected the ripest of the berries. He was slow, but they had plenty of time.

Hudson cleared his throat. "Yup. Becks and I agreed we'd become mates, and Chase planned to claim my sister Taryn. It all seemed so bloody perfect at the time." Hudson set a berry in his basket then ran a hand through his hair with a sigh.

Elsie's movements slowed. She couldn't imagine losing her intended mate or a sibling. She didn't want to, but suddenly she was thinking about how the three shifters who meant the most to her were all together outside of Wolf Hollow's protective borders.

Fear came like punches to the gut. The more she thought about it, the more it hurt.

Tabor was a powerful wizard, she reminded herself. Sasha and Zackary were strong too. Super strong.

But time, not strength, remained the real enemy. Every

day that passed hollowed out Elsie's heart a little more and left her jaw aching in the evening. Just like they'd decided, Hudson and Chase took turns partnering with her. Hudson was the more talkative one. Chase ate more berries than he put in the basket, which took him the entire day to fill up with all the breaks he took in between to rest in the shade of the tree. Elsie didn't care what his methods were. She just wanted Zackary to hurry back, especially since Aden, Emerson, and Ford had returned home successful, carrying Patrick's dead wolf body, to be burned in the glade with another, slightly different, cleansing Sky Ceremony.

While packmates chanted "run forever free," Elsie's mind screamed, "run back to me, Zackary. Please return soon."

She hoped that wherever he was, he was safe. And she prayed to mother earth, moon, sun, and sky that he came home before it was too late.

With the scent of burnt flesh and fur stinking the air, Elsie slipped away to the Sakhir River, walking along its bank. The smoke didn't reach here, as though the current was capable of pushing away the smoldering rabid wolf. When the river became shallow, Elsie lifted her dress above her knees and walked upstream.

She stared down at her bare feet slicing through the water, surefooted over the submerged rocks beneath her toes. Her heart ached as she approached the spot where she had lain with Zackary. She yearned to sit there now as though she could summon him back.

Elsie took a step toward land, stopping when the hairs

on the back of her neck rose.

"Elsie," came a loud whisper.

She jerked her head around.

William stood on the opposite side of the Sakhir, his eyes intent on hers. Elsie's heart jackhammered inside her chest. He felt more like a threat than a friend. She waded across, releasing the hem of her dress as she charged straight up to the wizard.

"What are you doing here?" she demanded.

William lifted onto his booted toes and looked over her shoulder. Seeming satisfied that no packmates were around to bother them, he returned his attention to her. His eyes seemed to glow manically when he grinned.

"I've figured it out, Elsie."

"Figured what out?" she asked, frowning.

"Another loophole that doesn't involve you giving yourself over to one of the wolves." His upper lip drew back before relaxing back into a pleased smile. "I'll show you."

As William started for the woods, Elsie's feet remained rooted to the spot. She looked over her shoulder. She'd already stepped off Wolf Hollow territory; she didn't want to go any further.

When he saw that she did not follow, William stopped and frowned.

"It's right in here." He nodded at some bushes then walked around them.

A dull pain entered Elsie's fingers as her wolf's claws prickled below the surface. She tried to soothe her inner wolf before storming around the bushes to see what William was up to. He stood beside a large backpack and duffel bag.

"Clothes and supplies for both of us," he announced, lifting his chin.

Elsie gaped at him. Did he want her to run away with him? Had he lost his mind?

"Those won't do me any good if I'm dead, and I'll die if I don't claim a shifter," she reminded him in a clipped tone.

If he suggested that it was better for her to live a shortened life with him than claim a shifter, she was going to have to throttle him before sending him back to Balmar Heights.

William nodded. "Yes, exactly. Right after you claim Brutus, I'll kill him. The bargain will be fulfilled, and we'll be free to run away together. We'll find another gated community far from the suburbs where we can start our own coven."

A wave of nausea rolled through Elsie's stomach.

"Brutus is immune to our magic," she stammered. That wasn't the real issue, but her head and tummy spun in anxious circles.

William dove down to the duffel bag, yanked the zipper open, and pulled a rifle off the top. He stood holding it, head lifted, and lips grinning.

"I'll put a bullet in his skull just as soon as he's bitten you and the claim is made."

Fury raged through her like thunder. Did William mean to hide himself while Brutus mated her then cap him once the bear shifter pulled out? Or maybe he meant to off the beast while he was still straddling her.

Her stomach recoiled.

WILLIAM DISGUSTED HER, and her hatred of Brutus did not extend to cold-blooded murder.

"No," she said firmly. She stared into the trees beside him, unable to look at him. "This is my home now. Balmar Heights is your home. I can't leave my brother or father."

"Your father?" William hissed in disdain.

When Elsie looked over, William's eyebrows pinched together, and wrinkles formed grooves in his forehead. He set the rifle on top of the duffel with a scowl.

Elsie straightened her back. "I know I can't live at Balmar Heights any longer, but I still plan to visit often . . . after I claim a wolf shifter. It's what my father wants, and it's what I want."

"Lazarus," William sneered.

She narrowed her eyes at his hostility.

"Let me tell you about—" before William could finish his sentence, Wolfrik stormed in naked, seeming to appear from behind the trees.

William gave a girly shriek and went for the rifle, but Wolfrik beat him to it, snatching the weapon then holding it behind his back. He flashed William a menacing look of challenge, as though daring him to try wrestling the rifle from his hands.

"Who do we have here?" Wolfrik drawled. He spread his legs wide. Elsie tried not to look between them—she really did. The whole male nudity thing was still a novelty to her.

Lips pouting, William turned to Elsie.

"Is this your intended mate?" he demanded.

Elsie put her hand over her mouth to cover a laugh. The hilarity quickly passed, replaced with annoyance.

"Wolfrik is a friend. Besides, he already has a mate."

William's eyes pinched together when he scowled.

"And who is this boy who has wandered in from the woods?" Wolfrik grinned wolfishly. The angry scars across his chest were bright red in the sunlight.

William stomped his boot on the ground. "I am not a boy; I am a powerful wizard. Want me to demonstrate?"

"No," Elsie snapped. "Wolfrik is only looking out for me, same as you." Grumbling, William set his snarling glare on her. Maybe that hadn't been the best comparison. Elsie sighed. "I'm not yours to worry about, William. Go home."

Smirking, Wolfrik's eyebrows jumped. "Bye, bye, Willy. Thanks for stopping by and bringing us a gift." He brought the rifle to his chest and stroked the barrel.

"That's mine. Give it back." William took a step toward Wolfrik.

The pureblooded male smiled with all his teeth on display, looking eager for a fight.

"Wouldn't want you to hurt anyone . . . or, more likely, yourself. These things aren't meant for boys," Wolfrik taunted.

William clenched his teeth. His fingers twitched. Elsie recognized the signs of a wizard about to lose control. She could stop him if she had to, but she'd rather he leave her and her packmates alone.

"William! Go home!" she yelled. Her own magic crackled through her veins. It stung beneath the surface of her skin. Unlike Wolfrik, she wasn't itching for a fight. No matter how frustrating, William was still a member of her coven. She knew it wasn't easy wanting someone who didn't want him back, especially when it was slim pickings on the mountain. "Please," she said, voice softening. "I'll be all right. I promise. I appreciate your concern, but you need to let me handle this, and you need to get back to Balmar Heights. The coven will be worried. My father will wonder where you've gone."

The storm clouds in William's eyes swirled, fading slightly as Elsie locked her gaze on his and tried to send him calming thoughts.

With a frown, William grabbed the open duffel bag and thrust it in front of Elsie.

"I brought you clothes," he said moodily.

"Thank you," she said, taking it. She didn't want the garments he'd picked out, but taking the duffel bag felt like the quickest way to get William going.

He grabbed the backpack and looked at Wolfrik, who hadn't stopped smirking.

Casting one more petulant frown Elsie's way, William locked eyes with her.

"If you knew the truth about your father, you wouldn't be so eager to obey him."

The prickly sensation returned to Elsie's fingers.

William nodded dismissively before slipping on his backpack and heading into the woods.

"Watch out for wild animals," Wolfrik called after him.

Elsie winced, afraid William would turn around and work some foul magic. She had half a mind to smack the pureblood for not keeping his trap closed. All she wanted was for William to leave and stay away.

She turned a glowering look on Wolfrik, who shrugged and lowered the rifle until one end touched the earth.

"There are a lot of things out there that would like to make a tasty meal out of a boy."

"He'll be fine. He's a wizard," Elsie said gruffly. She just hoped that she wouldn't have to worry about him sneaking back to the hollow.

There was only one male who could truly save her.

BONE-DRY DIRT DUSTED Zackary's nose as he sniffed the cracked earth leading in the direction of a decrepit subdivision. Instinct reared up, urging him to turn around and go back to the safety of the woods. He had yet to catch sight of the bastard but already felt like the old wolf was taunting him. The path Vallen left had meandered through the hollow, circling back across the southern border at one point. For a while, it had seemed he meant to race eastward through the woods before backtracking yet again. Every time the trail jerked in a new direction Zackary fought back a snarl. He couldn't even run with Tabor and Sasha following on two legs. Tabor wasn't making things easier with his ceaseless grumbling.

Now it appeared Vallen had dashed into the abandoned   subdivision.

Every bone in Zackary's body tightened with dread.

"Stop," Sasha said, not sounding happy at all.

Zackary stopped, but only because it was Sasha, not

Tabor issuing the command. Anytime Tabor tried to order Zackary's wolf, he pretended he didn't understand.

"I need you to shift, Zackary," Sasha said.

At first, it felt good as his fur receded. A scathing sun glared down on them. It felt entirely different than the one over the hollow. It didn't take the sun long to form beads of sweat along his hairline as he stood naked.

Sasha chewed on her lower lip, pupils darting to the subdivision. "He's in there?" she asked.

"His scent leads that way." Zackary frowned, following her gaze to the maze of cement-cracked streets, rusted cars, and decrepit homes with overgrown lawns.

"Fucking awesome," Tabor grumbled, gripping the bow he'd brought with him. A quiver filled with arrows rested against his back, strapped across his chest. Sasha wore the backpack.

"You should keep to this form," Sasha said to Zackary. "There are too many places to hide. Vallen could jump out and bite you before we have a chance to shoot him."

"And what a tragedy that would be," Tabor said under his breath. When Sasha glared at him, he coughed and said, "Kidding."

They both knew he wasn't. Zackary was reminded, yet again, that Tabor would never allow him to claim Elsie, even if the council amended his punishment. He should stop torturing himself with hope. He should have never touched her. He didn't know how to come back from that.

Instead, he returned his focus to the problem at hand.

"Let's go in, put Vallen down, and get out of here," Sasha said. As she took the first steps toward the subdivision, her entire body tensed.

Tabor jogged ahead of her. Their small group moved swiftly to the outskirts, all talk ceasing. When the first home loomed about twenty paces ahead, Sasha pulled off the backpack. She handed Zackary a fully loaded gun before grabbing one for herself. They'd all practiced firing after crossing the Manama River into neutral territory.

Sasha had terrible aim, but Tabor's was spot on with both a firearm and arrow. If he ever decided to turn either of his weapons on Zackary, he'd be dead before he had a chance to defend himself. Weapons didn't really matter, anyway; Tabor could cast a spell over him as easily.

At least Zackary had decent aim with the gun, which he was rather proud of given he'd never handled a firearm until that moment. He'd shot inside the circle Sasha had drawn on a tree with charcoal from the fire pit on the edge of the border where Aden and Wolfrik had guarded the human.

The gun felt heavier than he remembered. Maybe it was the thought of shooting Vallen. He wanted him dead. Hell, he'd wanted the bastard to die before he went mad. That didn't make killing his father any easier. Sick dread knifed Zackary in the gut. He had a duty to protect his pack . . . to protect Elsie. Vallen had killed a female very close to where they were posted. What if that had been Elsie patrolling the western hunting grounds?

Zackary's grip on the gun tightened. All he had to do was think about Elsie to give himself the motivation he needed to shoot Vallen. He could do this. He could do anything for her. His female.

He gritted his teeth. He had to stop thinking of Elsie that way. He'd penetrated her, but he hadn't mated her. Not properly. Not even close. But moon above, for one fleeting moment he'd known such bliss. Being that close to ecstasy would torment him the rest of his days. The least he could do was ensure her safety in Wolf Hollow. Vallen could not be allowed to live.

"We stick together," Sasha whispered.

Zackary nodded. Tabor pulled an arrow from his quiver and threaded it in the bow, keeping the arrow's tip pointed at the ground as they entered the subdivision.

Sasha led them down the middle of the street, trampling weeds that flourished between cracks in the pavement. Not that far in, she held her hand up then pointed at a pile of wolf shit in the middle of the road. Its stink rose in the sun. Sasha bent down, inhaling the pile up close before standing again.

"Maybe a day old," she noted.

Tabor huffed. "So, he probably passed through already."

"Maybe." She didn't sound convinced.

As they crept deeper into the subdivision, they came across a similar pile of crap. This one stunk a lot more than the first heap. Sasha's frown deepened as she studied it.

"This is much fresher, maybe a couple hours old." She turned her head from side to side, scanning the abandoned homes with their broken-out windows and partially open doors. Paint faded and peeled from every structure. Rotten wood teemed with eager ant colonies.

"Maybe I should shift to sniff him out," Zackary offered.

"No. It's too risky in here," Sasha said. She kept her eyes on the houses, ever watchful.

He didn't deserve her concern, but that didn't make him appreciate it any less. Reaching an intersection, they stopped in the middle, studying their options.

"What do you think, Zackary?" Sasha asked.

He looked to either side then forward. Vallen seemed to enjoy leading them in circles, having them curve around and change directions. He also liked to run long stretches at a time. Zackary could see him luring them deeper into the subdivision, away from the open expanse of the wasteland.

"I think we should continue straight."

Sasha nodded, leading them down the road. She kept her gun pointed in front of her. Zackary held his at his side. He was ready to lift the weapon in a heartbeat and shoot Vallen dead. The bastard didn't deserve a Sky Ceremony with the pack. Even fire wouldn't cleanse his black soul. It probably wouldn't be difficult to convince Sasha to leave his rotting corpse behind for scavengers to pick apart.

They advanced cautiously. With the thick tangle of weeds and rubble, they stumbled across a gift Vallen had left for them: a decomposed human arm had been laid out over a patch of pavement as though waving at them. The tissue had shriveled up over bony fingers and turned greenish. Maggots crawled over the rotten flesh, which smelled like putrid fruit. Bile rose in Zackary's throat, but Sasha studied the dismembered arm with her usual calm deliberation.

"Based on decomposition, I'd guess it's at least a few

days old," she noted.

Tabor's nose wrinkled and his tongue lurched out in disgust. "What the hell?" He wheezed.

A pit of unease formed in Zackary's stomach. "He's messing with our minds," he said, scanning the seemingly silent streets.

Tabor scoffed. "Vallen's mad. He's the one with the messed-up mind."

Zackary mashed his lips together, jaw clenched painfully. What he didn't say was that Vallen had been a nasty, violent madman to begin with. Maybe his wolf had built up a certain level of tolerance that made him more calculating than crazy.

The thought was terrifying.

"I don't like this," Sasha said.

Zackary turned to Tabor. "Can't you do magic to locate him?"

His sister had managed to lead them to Jordan and David after humans abducted them. Elsie's skills had been nothing short of miraculous.

"Oh, so now you're okay with magic," Tabor grumbled. "I'm not familiar with locator spells and even if I was, I'd need an article of his clothing, which—obviously—is no longer something he has need of."

"Could you use some of his scat?" Zackary raised his brows, hiding his grin at the prospect of Tabor scooping up a handful of Vallen's rank shit.

Tabor scowled. Guess he didn't appreciate the suggestion overly much. But before the wizard shifter could object, angry hissing went up in the house to their left. Three raccoons ran out the door and down the steps, skittering along the outer wall toward the back.

Zackary's heart hammered up his throat. He held his breath, listening. Despite the risk, he would have felt calmer in wolf form. His senses were dulled on two legs. There was no sniffing the air to detect whether Vallen was in the vicinity.

Sasha faced the house the raccoons had vacated, gun aimed at the partially open front door. Zackary questioned how well aimed. She nodded her chin at the now silent house.

Tabor's lips drew back. "We can't get too close. We need Vallen to come out in the open."

"We can't stand out here in the baking sun either," Sasha said. "Do you know any spells that might help our situation?"

Zackary, along with the rest of the pack, had been forced to make their peace with Tabor being part wizard. It had made him nervous before. No one should have the power to harm packmates in unnatural ways. Zackary had once gotten a dose of Tabor's magic when the half shifter had cast a spell that lifted him right off his feet and sent him flying backward onto the ground. To be fair, Zackary had been coming at him with a switchblade after threatening to cut out his tongue. He hadn't intended to go through with it. He'd only wanted to scare Tabor after watching him strut around making his usual insults and threats. He'd always been too damn cocky and never tried to make friends with other shifters, not counting running off to the den to be coddled by Heidi.

Now that Zackary had begrudgingly accepted Tabor's power, he had to agree with Sasha that this would be a good time to use his advantage.

The half wizard stared at the house with a frown. "I could send him flying back or knock him unconscious, but I still need him out in the open."

"He won't make things that easy," Zackary said.

Tabor scowled. "He might not even be here. He might be halfway to the city by now."

"Then what scared those raccoons?" Sasha hissed.

"Us?" Tabor's brows lifted.

She shook her head. "He's still here. I can feel it in my bones." She looked at Zackary for confirmation. He wasn't entirely sure, but there was no denying the hairs prickling the back of his neck.

"I'll go first," Zackary said.

Jaw tight, he stepped over the cracked pavement leading to the half-open door. Typically if creatures were running away from a place, it was a good idea to do the same. Sasha and Tabor followed close behind. No one spoke as they reached the sunken stone steps leading to a small square of pavement in front of the door, which leaned inward as though it had been left propped open for them.

Zackary's heart pounded like one of the drums during full moon ceremonies. It beat inside his ears. To calm himself, he visualized what he would do if Vallen were waiting inside. Zack was a big man. Maybe he could tackle Vallen and crush him with his body. He'd no doubt get bitten and clawed, but his wounds would heal.

One last time, he thought.

Once Vallen was dead he could never hurt him again.

Shaking off the dread, Zackary bounded up the stairs and shoved the door against the inner wall of the house. Sasha and Tabor ran in after him.

Furniture had been knocked over and stuffing torn out of the upholstery in a large living space to the right. Rugs, pillows, decorations, magazines, and lampshades were strewn all over the floor. Zackary didn't need to be in wolf form to pick up the putrid smell of urine and feces. How many animals had used this spot as their dumping ground?

A quick scan of the living room produced no snarling wolf foaming at the mouth. Zackary glanced up a set of stairs leading up. Seeing nothing on the landing above, he bounded down a hall leading to the back of the house.

Sunlight filtered in through a dirty window above a rusted sink. The cupboards were all open and empty—same with the drawers. An oval wood table was set up beside the kitchen, but there were no chairs.

Zackary turned away. There was nowhere to hide in this space.

A vicious snarl and a scream pierced his ears. Zackary ran with thundering steps back to the living space where he found a crazed wolf on top of Tabor, fangs sank into the shifter's shoulder. Sasha pointed her gun at the pair, causing Zackary's heart to seize. She was as likely to kill her mate as Vallen. All he could think about was Elsie breaking down into tears if her brother died.

"Wait!" Zackary bellowed as Sasha fired.

Fuck! He couldn't tell where the bullet had landed.

Vallen gave a growl, jaw still clamped over Tabor's shoulder, unwilling to relinquish his prey.

This time Sasha didn't try aiming for the pair. She lifted the gun, firing again. A crash of glass followed. Vallen growled louder. Sasha fired again then grabbed an overturned plant pot off the ground and threw it at Vallen, striking him in the back with better precision than the bullets.

Vallen released Tabor with an ungodly snarl, his muzzle jerking in Sasha's direction.

"Come get me, Vallen," she seethed, raising the gun.

Free from Vallen's fangs, Tabor's hands shot up. Before he could get a grip on the mad wolf, Vallen snatched Tabor's hand in his jaws and clamped down. Tabor shrieked. Zackary's heart lurched as he heard the sickening crunch of bones.

Zackary launched himself at the mad wolf, punching him on the side of his head before jabbing his thick arm under Vallen's throat to get him into a chokehold. Vallen released Tabor's hand and darted forward before Zackary could get him in his full grip.

The ear-splitting crack of the gun thundered through the room as Sasha took another shot at Vallen. He flew out the front door on four paws.

"Damn it!" Sasha said, scowling at the door.

"I'll go," Zackary said. Not waiting for her consent, he crashed across the living room and out the door into the glaring sun. He spotted Vallen loping down the middle of the old road.

Zackary got onto his hands and knees, ignoring the rough pavement scorching his bare skin. Shifting was a dumb idea, but it was his only chance of catching up to Vallen. Once he'd shifted into his fur, he took off in his father's direction, quickly picking up his scent. Soon, Zackary had the rabid wolf in his sights.

Vallen sprang over the pavement as though this was all a great game he enjoyed. The mad wolf didn't try to lose Zackary behind houses or cars. He kept on running like a maniac on a marathon to the ends of the Earth.

Zackary was so intent on catching up that he didn't pay attention to his surroundings. It surprised him when cement turned to soil and the decrepit structures disappeared into an open expanse they'd entered between the small town and the city in the distance.

They raced across the wasteland, Zackary's wolf intent on one thing—killing Vallen.

Baked earth crumbled beneath his paws. Searing heat made saliva drip from his lips.

When Vallen stopped suddenly, Zackary slowed to a trot, the hair along the ridge of his back rising. Vallen snapped and snarled at him viciously.

A jumble of hostility entered Zackary's animalistic mind—all of it originating from Vallen.

No good stupid mutt boy. Too big. Dangerous. Teach him his place. Obey. Mangy mongrel. Hot sun. Squirrels. Stars. Sun. Shade. Water. Kill. Obey. Dumb mutt following me. Kill first before he kills me.

Zackary growled. Rage flooded his wolf's body.

A howl rose up from the direction of the suburbs he'd

left behind. Zackary stopped growling, his ears twitching at Sasha's call for him to return.

Vallen made several snarling sounds that sounded like wicked laughter.

Sasha's next howl was more demanding. She wanted an answer.

Zackary's lips drew up as he stared his father down. Vallen was in his sights. He couldn't turn around now. He just couldn't.

Vallen's wolf lips lifted into a cruel smile. His eyes gleamed when he gave a low snarl before turning and racing away.

Indecision rooted Zackary in place, especially when Sasha howled a third time. He lifted his head and bellowed a reply.

Get back here, Sasha's next howl demanded.

Zackary pawed the dirt, snarling in frustration. A beetle paused in its tracks, holding very still as Zackary's nostrils flared over the ground.

Dust clouds rose in the distance as Vallen made his escape, dashing toward the city. Maybe whatever humans were left would put him down. With a final huff, Zackary lifted his head and howled back to Sasha.

He'd used up a lot of energy going after Vallen and hadn't realized how far he'd traveled. The way back felt longer and hotter. His temper flared on repeat.

Back in the suburb, he sniffed out Sasha and Tabor in a neighborhood several blocks from the home where Vallen had attacked. Tabor followed Sasha around in his wolf form, which had no injuries since he hadn't panicked and partially shifted while under attack. Zackary imagined his human wounds were bad, though. He'd likely wait until they returned to the hollow to work on healing himself. Hopefully his human hand wasn't mangled permanently.

Zackary called to his human side, commanding his fur to recede and limbs to thicken and elongate. Once a man again, he got to his feet and blinked several times, taking in Sasha's movements. She set a stuffed black duffel bag on the cracked sidewalk.

"I had to leave this behind on the last supply run," she explained, intent on the bag. "Aden, Jack, and Farley left similar bags. We'll carry back as much as we can." She moved swiftly to a house across the street.

As Zackary jogged up to her side, Tabor growled. Ignoring the wolf, Zackary hurried his pace to keep up with Sasha.

"I had Vallen in sight. I could have kept after him."

"No," Sasha said firmly. She hurried into the shade beneath the decayed awning of the house before stopping to stare directly into Zackary's eyes. "It's not safe for you to go after him alone, especially not in wolf form."

Zackary felt a tingling of appreciation that she cared what happened to him, but he still wasn't convinced Sasha had made the right call.

"Is Tabor okay?" he asked her, not looking at the wolf.

Sasha pursed her lips and stole a quick glance at her four-legged mate. Her gaze lifted back to Zackary. "Vallen took us by surprise. We didn't hear so much as a snarl before he leapt out from behind an overturned sofa. I think he was crouched down waiting. Fortunately, Tabor was standing in front of me." Sasha placed her hand on her belly and sighed. "I hate to admit it, but Jager was right. I should not have gone after Vallen in my condition." The eager glance she aimed down the road made it look like she still longed to track down the rabid wolf. She moistened her lips. "Which direction did he head?"

"Toward the city."

"It would have been no use pursuing him then. Not worth the risk." Sasha pushed her way into the house, returning a moment later with a large backpack and a strained smile. "At least our trip won't be a total waste. Packmates will be thrilled to have new clothes to pick from."

She went back inside, disappearing for several minutes before returning with a white discolored square plastic box. A faded red symbol marked the top of the box with words no longer legible—not that Zackary would have been able to read them even if they'd been freshly printed.

Shame fell over Zackary's mind like a thick shadow. Most of his packmates had been taught to read by their parents. Vallen hadn't bothered. Big surprise. His mother had sung him the alphabet song when he was a boy and written out the letters in the dirt with a stick. Fat lot of good that did without learning how to arrange them into actual words. And it had peeved him that the letter of his name came last. Always last.

Sasha pried the lid open in front of him.

"Medical supplies," she announced.

They both lowered their heads to look inside. Zackary recognized the roll of gauze. He'd seen it used on injured friends growing up. There were other instruments and materials he wasn't familiar with. One was a small, thin finger-length piece of metal. Jager and Palmer would be able to identify its uses.

Sasha crouched beside the backpack and unfastened the top. She emptied the contents of the box and tried to stuff them into the backpack, but it was already too full. Sasha pulled clothes out, sifting through them quickly. She tossed aside a bright red shirt. Next she lifted what looked like a dress, extra thin with lace on top and along the hem. "Farley," Sasha said with a snort and an eye roll. "I told him no bringing home useless gifts for his mate." She flung the scrap onto the scorched lawn.

Appearing satisfied with what she'd discarded, Sasha stuffed the medical supplies into the backpack.

A low growl rumbled through Tabor's throat. It was his intent glare at the road that made Zackary and Sasha go still.

Ever so quietly, Sasha removed her hands from the supply backpack before pulling hers off and reaching in. She handed Zackary a gun before taking the second firearm.

A bark sounded from the overgrown shrubbery across the street. Tabor barked back and flicked his tail. A tail wag would have indicated packmates approaching, but the low growl communicated mistrust, though not fear. He didn't snarl in warning.

Tabor stood his ground in front of Sasha. She and Zackary held their weapons ready. Some time passed before a male voice yelled from across the street, hidden from view.

"My brother and I are wolf shifters. It's just the two of us come to see if you need help. We heard some frantic howls earlier."

Sasha's lips curled back. "How about you and your brother step out where we can see you?"

"How about you lower your firearms?" The next voice sounded sarcastic and gruff. If Zackary had to guess, he'd say that it wasn't from the male who had spoken first. Both males had accents Zackary was not familiar with.

Sasha lowered her gun, nodding at Zackary to do the same. He mirrored her movements, keeping it gripped at his side.

"They're lowered," she called.

They waited until, several moments later, two light brown males emerged naked from the brush. They were muscular and slightly above average height. One had thick dark wavy hair that reached his shoulders. Both had scruff along their cheek bones and chins, along with faint mustaches.

The one with shoulder-length hair smiled and lifted his hand. "Hola amigos!"

chapter ten

DESPITE THE FRIENDLY smiles on the males, Zackary tensed, not liking the way they swaggered forward. Tabor gave another low growl. The males stopped about six feet away.

"Where did you come from? What are you doing in this area?" Sasha asked.

The one with the shorter hair snorted. "*Hola* to you too." He looked Sasha up and down, which made Tabor snarl.

The one with the shoulder-length hair placed a hand on his chest, still smiling. "I am Diego, and this is my brother Rafael. We've traveled from the south."

"Where's the rest of your pack?" Sasha asked.

Rafael jutted his chin and flexed. "We have no pack. We're nomads. Purebloods. We run free."

Sasha's expression softened. "Oh," she said, voice lifting. "I'm a pureblood as well."

The brothers shared a loaded stare before returning their attention to Sasha with renewed interest. Tabor started toward them, snarling.

"Tabor!" Sasha snapped.

He stopped in his tracks but didn't stop growling at the men.

"Was your packmate hurt?" Diego asked, nodding at Tabor.

"Tabor is my mate, and yes, his human form is wounded."

"Mate," Diego repeated. He looked at Rafael, who shrugged. Diego returned his attention to Sasha. "Are there more purebloods in your pack?"

"One male, also mated."

"That's it?" Diego scrubbed his jaw.

Sasha narrowed her eyes. "Why?"

Rafael jutted his chin forward. "What's with the backpacks? You three on a camping trip?"

"We were hunting down a rabid wolf who has killed several pack members over the years and turned a few mad," Sasha said, pulling at her hair. "Unfortunately, he harmed my mate and got away."

"So, you're headed back to your pack?" Diego asked.

"Yes."

"Can we join you? We won't stay long."

Sasha stared at the brothers for several moments, never once turning to Zackary. He didn't expect her to. She was a pureblood and a council member—used to making decisions on her own. Zackary didn't want these strangers in Wolf Hollow, even though they were fellow wolf shifters. But it wasn't his call.

"Why are you interested in other purebloods?" Sasha asked.

Rafael grunted. "My brother has decided he's ready for a mate. We prefer to migrate and have been searching for a pureblooded female who can give him pups, not squalling babies who would make us vulnerable and slow us down."

Zackary had never seen it with his own eyes, but he'd been told that a pureblooded female, impregnated by a pureblooded male, was the only kind of wolf shifter who birthed pups in wolf form. Once pregnant, the female couldn't shift out of her wolf form until after the birth of her pureblooded pups. Even then, she was likely to remain in fur during the first year when her pups remained animals before having the ability to shift to skin. Their instincts were sharp, their minds and bodies stronger than the average shifter. Purebloods had been surviving in the wild before the fall of civilization. They preferred living off the land and sleeping beneath the stars.

Non-pureblooded wolf shifters, on the other hand, were stuck in skin until their twelfth year, when they were first able to make the shift from human to wolf.

Sasha pursed her lips in thought. "As far as I know, Hailey from the Glenn Meadows pack is still unmated. She and her brother Hector are the only younger unmated purebloods left in this area. They are located a five-day run from Wolf Hollow."

"Wolf Hollow is your pack?" Rafael asked.

"Yes, we're headed home now. You can help carry bags."

Rafael frowned. "What's in them?"

"Clothing."

"Why bother?"

"It's the way of our pack."

"It's the way of humans," Rafael said, staring at Sasha in her dress.

"We are part human," Sasha retorted.

Diego placed his hand on Rafael's shoulder. "*Hermano*," he coaxed.

Rafael rolled his eyes before turning back to Sasha. "Anything else you want us to carry? Some paintings perhaps to hang on your trees?" At Sasha's snarl, Rafael winked. Even though she wasn't his mate, it set Zackary's teeth on edge. He didn't want these purebloods sniffing around the females of Wolf Hollow. He especially didn't want him winking at Elsie or teasing her or making her smile or even looking in her direction. Zackary didn't know how to flirt, and this pureblood clearly did.

Rafael swung his gaze at Zackary and smirked. "What about you, *hombre*? Do you not wear clothes? Is it only the females in your pack? You tell them to cover up or some shit?"

Diego folded his arms and narrowed his eyes at Zackary.

Sasha gave an exasperated huff. "He's naked because he left the hollow in wolf form to sniff out the rabid one." She glanced from side to side. "We've lingered in the suburbs too long. Grab the bags and let's get a move on it."

Rafael looked Sasha up and down again. "We didn't catch your name."

"Sasha," she said. "Now let's go."

She lifted her head and whizzed past them. Tabor

stayed behind, keeping a sharp eye on the brothers.

Rafael leaned close to his brother and said, "*Si*, she's a pureblooded female all right. Bossy."

"Shush," Diego scolded.

"You sure you want to add something like that to our dynamic?"

"Strong women don't scare me." Diego gave Rafael a playful shove.

Their chuckles died off when they noticed Zackary glaring at them.

"Like Sasha said, it's time to go," he said grabbing the large backpack off the ground.

"I can take that." Diego pulled the backpack out of Zackary's arms before he could answer. He was the friendlier of the two brothers, but that didn't make Zackary like him any more. "What is your name, *hombre*?"

"Zackary."

Diego put his muscled arms through the straps of the backpack and gave his shoulder-length hair a shake, grinning. He looked good and he knew it. Both brothers were way too pretty . . . attractive in the way females appreciated. They were tall, toned, and muscular. Just the right size, unlike Zackary who was too big and bulky, according to his father.

"You'd make a female cry in pain before ever coming close to giving her pleasure."

"You have a mate waiting for you back home?" Diego spoke over Vallen's voice in his head.

Zackary gritted his teeth. "No," he answered gruffly before crossing the street to grab the duffel bag Sasha had left on the ground.

Rafael had already snatched it up. He followed Sasha around, a joking lilt to his voice. "What about those wind chimes?" He pointed at rusted metal tubes dangling from the sunken overhang of a house. "Want me to grab those for you, Sasha?"

Zackary was surprised when Sasha laughed. Shaking her head, she turned to Zackary.

"There should be another bag in that house there." She nodded at a home with broken windows and a faded blue door.

Zackary jogged over, relieved to find a backpack near the door. Bringing in fresh supplies would make the pack happy, but Zackary would have rather returned with news of Vallen's demise.

Once they'd loaded up, Sasha led the way out of the suburbs. Rafael walked beside her, talking incessantly while Tabor prowled behind him, ears often flattening against his head. Diego tried to make conversation with Zackary, but his short responses soon had the pureblood joining Sasha and Rafael.

The brothers chattered on about their adventures across the continent while Sasha asked questions about all they'd encountered. The brothers ate up her attention, not shutting up for one damn second. Their voices droned on like a swarm of mosquitoes following the group incessantly. But Sasha appeared to delight in their company. Zackary had never heard her laugh so many times. He glanced at Tabor, who had his eyes on Rafael as though waiting for a reason to attack him.

"What does Hailey of Glenn Meadows look like?" Diego asked.

"I've never met her, only her brother," Sasha answered.

Rafael gave a loud whistle. "Is her brother the overly protective type?"

Sasha grunted. "You can decide for yourself."

Zackary wished the brothers would head straight to Glenn Meadows rather than Wolf Hollow—even though they were helping carry supplies. They exuded confidence and never ran out of conversation. They made him feel dull in comparison.

When they'd left the subdivision, blue sky stretched over their heads as far as the eye could see. But the late summer tugged on the sun, dragging the glowing sphere behind the mountains before they reached the base of the first hill.

Sasha looked up. "We need to hurry if we want to make it to the Manama River before dark."

Somehow, Rafael still managed to blather on as Sasha set a grueling pace up the mountain.

"What's the best game around here?"

"Deer," Sasha said.

"Remember that bison we took down in Yosemite?" Rafael asked his brother.

"Yosemite?" Sasha asked.

"Used to be a game park in an area known as California," Diego supplied.

"Now the whole continent is one big park." Rafael laughed.

Yet again, Sasha surprised Zackary with her easy

chuckle. "What's a bison?" she asked next.

"A great big beast with horns and a wooly pelt," Rafael's voice boomed. He walked close to Sasha, brushing shoulders with her. Tabor issued a warning growl and Rafael pulled away, but not nearly far enough in Zackary's opinion. "Think of a cow but much bigger and wilder."

Sasha snorted. "The two of you took down one of these beasts on your own?"

"*Si.*" Rafael puffed up his chest. "If you like, we can take care of dinner tonight. My brother and I are excellent hunters."

"So are we," Sasha retorted.

"But you have been so kind to invite us to your home. You must allow us to show our appreciation."

"Fine," Sasha said.

They reached the summit, traveling faster downhill. Being on foot with backpacks and duffels slowed their progress, but they made it to the Manama River and got a fire started before all traces of daylight fled the skies. They set the bags in a pile outside the caves. Zackary gathered more kindling for the fire while Tabor paced around the small camp.

Rafael and Diego shifted and ran into the woods to go after dinner. Zackary breathed easier the moment they were gone. He crouched beside the fire, feeding in sticks carefully one at a time, stealing glances at Sasha. She'd brought out a metal grill and large knife from one of the caves and was whittling the tips of four sticks into sharp points. The night felt thick with silence. Sasha had seemed so at ease with the pureblooded brothers even though she'd just met them. It made Zackary feel like the outsider, intruding on another pack. He wanted to tell Sasha that he didn't trust them. That he wasn't happy to bring them home. But it wasn't his place. Instead, he glowered moodily into the flames, poking another stick into the base of the fire.

"Don't worry," Sasha said, breaking the silence. "They won't be with us long. Diego is looking for a mate. If he and Hailey don't claim one another, he and Rafael will continue north for a bit or possibly try their luck heading east. They're only passing through."

Zackary bobbed his head, gaze still on the fire. "The one named Rafael shows too much interest in you." He clamped his mouth shut the moment he'd spoken the words.

"It's not your place to caution a pureblooded council member," he silently chided himself.

But Sasha did not chastise him for speaking out of turn. He snuck a glance up to find her studying him in her unsettling way.

"They have not been around other shifters for a long time," she spoke in a kind and patient voice. "They hunger for conversation. Diego hungers for companionship; Rafael does not, which is why he boasts to me. He knows that I am taken and therefore safe to tease without fear of a claim." She set the whittled sticks on the ground with the knife and beckoned Tabor to her side. Once seated beside her, Sasha ran her fingers through Tabor's fur in gentle strokes. An involuntary shiver ran through Zackary, recalling Elsie's fur against his fingers when he'd caressed her wolf.

Sasha looked over her shoulder into the dark woods, taking in the quiet. She returned her attention to Zackary. "Rafael would not act friendly around an unmated pureblood like Hailey. I imagine he would want to keep far away from her. There has always been pressure on purebloods to mate with one another. But Rafael will not have such worries with other females. I imagine he will want to find a willing she-wolf to give him her back before he and Diego leave Wolf Hollow."

Zackary's snarl caused Sasha's and Tabor's heads to jerk in his direction. Sasha's hand stilled on Tabor's back.

"Is there a female who concerns you?" she challenged.

Zackary glanced at Tabor. The wizard shifter could still understand their conversation in wolf form. Shoulders sagging, Zackary shook his head bitterly.

Sasha and Tabor couldn't know his feelings for Elsie

A triumphant howl echoed in the distance. Tabor's ears perked up and his tail twitched. The crackle of the fire was the only sound for some time until Rafael and Diego ambled in carrying a dead deer. They wore great big smiles.

Show-offs, Zackary thought moodily. Yet again, he wished they could leave these arrogant purebloods out here in the forest. What if one female wasn't enough to satiate Rafael's wild needs? What if he took a liking to Elsie?

A roar rose up Zackary's throat. He held it in but couldn't mask the look of murder he cast at the posturing pureblood who placed a foot on the deer carcass while recounting the hunt through the dark woods. If the bastard tried to flirt with Elsie, Zackary would cut out his tongue.

He still had that rusty switchblade hidden near the glade buried beneath a patch of soil at the base of a tree.

Sasha placed the grill over the large rocks forming a circle around the fire. Diego walked over and stared into the flames.

"Wouldn't it be easier if we all shifted to eat? Your mate's already in his fur." He nodded at Tabor whose lips drew back.

"She is afraid to get naked in front of us," Rafael said in challenge.

"I have no such fear," Sasha said. "I do worry about you, though. My mate has shown restraint, but if he catches you staring at my breasts, I doubt he'll remain calm."

"Stare at your breasts," Rafael scoffed a little too loud.

Sasha smirked. "You probably haven't seen a pair in a long time. I wouldn't blame you for looking, but my mate will."

"Let's just carve this thing up and cook it." Diego tucked his hair behind his ears then held his palm open. Sasha picked up the knife and handed it to him.

Diego set to work skinning the animal, handing off chunks as he did. Zackary was quick to make himself useful, setting meat on the grill to cook. Sasha set a raw hunk of flesh in front of Tabor in wolf form who devoured the meat as though it was his last meal. Once the grill was covered and air filled with the scent of roasting meat, Sasha handed out wood spears. They allowed the meat to cook longer before turning the chunks over, poking at them to check the inside.

After filling their stomachs, they settled in for the

night. Once Rafael and Diego shifted into wolf form, Sasha and Zackary did the same.

Sasha was the first to rouse at morning light and shift from wolf to human. In another couple months, or less, she wouldn't be able to shift out of her human form until after she gave birth. Since she had not mated another pureblood, her children would be born in human form and remain that way until he or she was twelve. The council had tried to convince her to claim Hector from Glenn Meadows, but Sasha had refused after falling for Tabor.

By the time the pureblooded brothers and Zackary shifted, Sasha was back in her dress, tapping her foot over the earth.

"I'm still full from last night," she announced. "Is everyone else ready?"

Rafael stretched his arms high over his head and yawned, seemingly unconcerned about the morning wood he brandished in plain sight.

"We're ready," Diego answered.

Rafael lowered his arms and smirked. "We're always ready."

Huffing, Zackary grabbed a duffel bag and started toward the glade, only slowing his steps to remain with the group. Now that he was on his home turf, he just wanted to get back to his friends, duties . . . and Elsie. As much as he'd itched to go after Vallen, he hated leaving her behind. He didn't doubt her power and strength, but pack life was still new to her and she was extremely trusting. A young packmate named Sydney had recently betrayed her own sisters—nearly killing them. Every tribe had some bad apples. Hell, Zackary was one of them. But he'd cut off his own hand before he ever hurt Elsie. Who had she eaten meals with while he, Tabor, and Sasha were gone? Wiley and Justin? Hudson and Chase? Anger spiked through his brain. Everyone in the pack had speculated that Hudson and Chase were sharing Jordan before she claimed Raider. What if they decided they were ready for a new threesome?

Zackary had been gone five whole days. Normally, he didn't count. But ever since Elsie had told him to be safe, he'd taken note of the sun's rise and fall. It had taken only one day of berry picking for her lips to land on his. He'd left her with Chase for five times as many. The mongrel had better have kept his mitts off and his back turned if Elsie had removed her dress to wash.

Damn Vallen to the pits of hell for ever returning. They'd failed to kill him—only wasting time and bringing unwanted strangers back with them.

On two feet, it took their group half a day to reach Jager's hut near the glade. Tabor called out to packmates along the way. Zackary couldn't understand wolf cries with his human ears the way he could pick out words while in wolf form. He did know that Tabor was communicating their status, and that of their guests, so that patrol partners wouldn't panic when they picked up the scent of new wolves.

Jager sat on a stump outside his hut when they arrived. The moment he saw the outsiders, he tried to jump to his feet and stumbled in the process. Brows furrowed, he straightened as best he could.

Sasha set down her bag and walked over to the old man.

"This is our elder, Jager," she said. "Jager, Rafael and Diego are purebloods we came across in the suburbs. They helped carry back supplies. I invited them to stay in Wolf Hollow before continuing to Glenn Meadows."

"Sit," Jager commanded. He nodded at the stumps set around his fire pit, which was dormant during the hot days.

Rafael pulled the backpack off, dropping it on the ground, while Diego set his by Sasha's. Zackary continued holding his duffel, unsure if Jager had meant to include him in the order to sit. The elder turned his attention to the brothers.

"You are friends with the Glenn Meadows shifters?" Jager asked.

"Never met them before." Rafael sat with his legs spread wide on the stump.

Damn pureblood was making himself right at home.

Diego cleared his throat. "I am looking to claim a female, preferably a pureblood. Sasha told me there's one in Glenn Meadows."

Jager rubbed his chin. "Hailey, yes, though she could very well be mated by now. I will send one of our wolves to fetch a report. It's been too long since our packs have communicated. In the meantime, you must make yourselves at home in Wolf Hollow. We will prepare a great feast and entertainment tonight."

Diego looked at Rafael, who shrugged. "We're in no hurry."

"Excellent," Jager said as Zackary thought, "Shit."

146

✦ chapter eleven

EXCITEMENT BUZZED THROUGH the hollow as news of unmated pureblooded male guests passed urgently between shifters. But it wasn't word of the brothers that made Elsie's heart leap and pound. It was the return of Zackary.

However, it was news of her brother's injury that sent her sprinting to the den's medical shed.

"Tabor!" Elsie cried as she entered the shed.

Seated on the edge of the table wearing jeans, but no shirt, Tabor looked up and flashed Elsie a smile.

"Don't worry, I'm fine."

Sasha and Kallie stood on either side of him. There was a bloody cloth and package wrappings from the old world on the table. Tabor lifted his hand with two finger splints and bandages securing two sets of his fingers together. His thumb was his only free finger. Puncture marks left red marks on his bare shoulder.

"Vallen got the jump on me, but we were able to get clothes and more medical supplies from the suburb," Tabor explained calmly.

Heart racing, she hurried over and threw her arms around his neck, mindful of his injured shoulder and hand. Her coven and packmates were like family, but she only had one brother. Tabor meant the whole world to her. She'd give herself to Brutus in a heartbeat to save him, if that was the only option. Hopefully it wouldn't have to come to that. Now that Zackary had returned, it shouldn't.

Starting tomorrow, she was down to eight days. Nearly the last week.

She needed to complete what she'd started. And she needed to do it soon.

"Elsie, why don't you stay with your brother while I attend a quick council meeting." Sasha strode up to Tabor and kissed him on the lips, her eyes softening when she gazed at him. "I am relieved you are well, my love. You scared me so bad. Don't ever do that again."

Tabor touched her cheek. "He didn't get to you. That's all that matters."

They kissed one more time, then Sasha backed up, eyes still locked with Tabor's.

Kallie pulled her hair over her shoulder and smiled warmly.

"I can stay, as well, since Wolfrik will be at the meeting."

After Sasha left, and Tabor convinced Elsie he wasn't suffering, she made him recount every part of their journey, ending with the tan-skinned purebloods they'd brought back to the hollow.

"Rafael and Diego," Tabor supplied.

"What are they like?" Kallie asked.

Huffing, Tabor shrugged. "Typical male purebloods.

Cocky. Boastful." He shrugged again then lifted his injured hand and looked over his fingers.

"Handsome?" Kallie asked, leaning forward as she gripped the table to keep her balance.

Tabor lowered his hand, a shine entering his eyes.

"Looking to upgrade from Wolfrik?" he teased.

"I thought Elsie might be interested." Kallie gave her a hopeful smile.

The gleam left Tabor's eyes and his faint smile was replaced with a frown. He looked at Elsie.

"The brothers are only passing through. They live like nomads. No sense of community. I hope you will stay away from them."

"Don't worry," Elsie said. "I'm not interested in cocky purebloods."

"You haven't met them yet," Kallie said. "Maybe one, or both, of them would be ready to settle down with the right she-wolf."

"Settle down?" Tabor asked, scratching his head with his good hand. He looked at Elsie closer. "You're not thinking about finding a mate, are you? You're still so young."

Dear, brother, if only he knew.

"I will be twenty in nine days," Elsie said softly.

Kallie's eyes widened. She knew what that meant. Elsie appreciated her friend keeping her secret. If Tabor were to find out, it would only put him in danger. Confronting Brutus would surely end in more than broken fingers.

"Young," Tabor repeated. "I know there have been several claimings since you arrived," he glanced at Kallie briefly, "but don't feel rushed. These things take time."

Time. There was that cursed word again. Elsie merely nodded.

"Don't worry, brother. You don't have to worry about me vying for these males' attention."

"You are wise not to. Remember, they are merely passing through," Tabor said.

Peter poked his head in, interrupting any further discussion about the pureblooded males. He invited them all to sit outside his hut and wait for their mates to return from council. Peter and his wife, Heidi, had kindly taken Elsie in when she first arrived in Wolf Hollow. Their children, Amy and Eric, were cute and energetic. They'd all made Elsie feel instantly at home. As much as she adored their family, she'd been happy to gain her independence and join the single shifters in the glade.

Sasha didn't take long to return; she came rushing back ahead of Wolfrik and Heidi.

"There is to be entertainment along with the feast tonight," she said a bit breathlessly. "I'm helping organize the dance. Emerson is selecting females and meeting me at the communal cabin. I must go." She spun on her heel, heading away as Wolfrik and Heidi walked into sight at the edge of the den.

Elsie scrambled to her feet and took off after Sasha. "I'll come with you!" She jogged to Sasha's side and waved to Wolfrik and Heidi as they passed.

Sasha set a brisk pace across the trail connecting the den and the glade. Filled with boundless energy, Elsie kept up without losing her breath, though Sasha was the one to speak.

"Jager hopes to entice the brothers to remain in Wolf Hollow long enough for one, or both, to claim a mate among our females."

Elsie's eyes expanded. "But Tabor said one brother wants to find a pureblood and the other isn't interested in a mate at all."

"That is what they say, but we must still try. We've lost too many pack members. Our continued survival hinges on breeding. Shifters from outside would strengthen our pack, especially purebloods—no matter who they mate with." Sasha zoomed past trees, arms swinging at her sides.

Elsie wasn't a pureblood, but she was a powerful witch and an outsider as well. Mating with Zackary would help make the pack stronger. Not only would she avoid her fate with Brutus, she could help Wolf Hollow more than these purebloods who were merely passing through. Elsie was here to stay.

Despite jogging the entire way, Emerson had beaten Sasha to the communal cabin where seven chattering females giggled and flipped their hair. It was impossible not to get caught up in the excitement. Gina smiled and waved when she saw Elsie. Elsie grinned and waved back.

"Diego is mine," Camilla announced to the group.

Elsie fought back a grin as the large-breasted female entered the center of the group, hands on her hips. It was nice to see Camilla pep up after weeks of pouting about losing Raider to her sister Jordan.

Rosalie dove into the middle with her. "Good," she said. "Because I want Rafael. He's not looking for a pureblood." She lifted her nose in triumph.

Camilla rolled her eyes. "He's not looking for any kind of commitment. At least Diego wants a mate. That's over half the battle." She flipped her hair over her shoulder.

"Ladies, simmer down and listen up," Emerson said. The group quieted and turned to face the blonde shifter. "Tonight's dance is special. There will be no males joining you in performance. Same opening. Shake those lovely curves around the bonfire. Make it sexy."

"Please." Camilla snorted, tossing her hair back then brushing it back over her shoulder, ready to flip again.

"Zadie and Nudara are on vocals." The olive-skinned sisters grinned in acknowledgment. "Heath and Alec are ready with drums."

"What about Maureen?" Sasha asked.

Elsie wasn't surprised to see Maureen and Lacy missing from their gathering. They were still mourning their friend.

"Maureen has agreed to play as well," Emerson said, all business. Sasha nodded, looking pleased. Emerson looked over the remaining women, all except Gina, who stood near her side. "We need five dancers. That's Camilla, Rosalie, Olivia, Janelle, and Taryn."

Camilla and Rosalie looked at one another and squealed in delight.

"Count me out," Taryn said moodily, folding her arms over her bosom.

Emerson narrowed her eyes at the brunette shifter.

Living in the hollow meant hearing all the gossip, and it was no secret that Taryn was having trouble letting go of Chase.

"We need five," Emerson said in a slow, firm voice.

Taryn stared her down, head-on. "Then you do it, *Em*." Her voice rose in challenge.

Gina shot her friend a hurt look, but Taryn was too busy glowering at Emerson to notice. Eyes wide with alarm, their other close friend, Janelle, looked around quickly. She scanned the faces, passing over Elsie's, before returning an instant later.

"How about Elsie?" Janelle asked eagerly. "Elsie's never had an opportunity to perform."

Elsie's heart gave a jolt. She wasn't typically shy, but performing in front of a group wasn't the same as socializing. Watching the females dance around the bonfire in their deer-skin skirts and fur bikinis had been fascinating entertainment . . . as a member of the audience. Elsie wasn't keen to be part of the spectacle. Before she could stutter a response, Emerson jumped in.

"She doesn't know the dance."

"But she's watched it before." Janelle turned to Elsie, begging her with large rounded eyes.

Sasha's brows rose as she turned to face Elsie. "You don't have to," she said gently.

"I don't think Tabor would like that," Rosalie said to Olivia.

Sasha chewed on her lower lip before turning to Emerson. "I can do it. I know the steps well."

"Because Tabor would really enjoy watching his pregnant mate shake her boobs and booty for all the males." With a snort and roll of her eyes, Emerson tossed her blonde hair back. Camilla lifted her hand to her mouth and snickered.

"I mean, I can give it a try," Elsie said. She wanted to be seen as a pack member, not just Tabor's half-sister who had appeared seemingly out of nowhere then left and then returned. Performing in the dance would demonstrate her acceptance of pack customs. She darted a glance at Camilla, Rosalie, Olivia, and Janelle. Hmm. If anyone ought to help her, it should be Janelle for volunteering her in the first place. Elsie locked gazes with Janelle. The shifter smiled sheepishly.

Rosalie sauntered to her side and grinned mischievously.

"Don't worry, Elsie. We'll keep the males distracted."

Not *all* of them, Elsie thought as she smiled back.

Emerson clapped her hands. "Time to prepare."

Camilla, Rosalie, and Olivia rushed into the cabin, returning with large woven baskets. One was filled with the costumes, the other hairbrushes and ties. Sasha grabbed a brush then returned to Elsie.

"I'll do your hair."

"I can do it," Janelle offered. "We could take turns."

Making no move to relinquish the brush, Sasha stared Janelle down. "I've got it," she said firmly.

Lips forming a pout, Janelle joined the three giggling friends beside the baskets. As Gina stared at the trail to the communal gathering area, her frowning lips and furrowed brow indicated that Taryn had taken off in the direction of the glade. Zadie and Nudara joined her, the three of them following the trail as they left.

Sasha moved behind Elsie and ran the brush gently through her long brown hair.

"Thanks for doing this," she said. "The gaps around the bonfire are too wide without at least five performers. We don't have as many single females as we used to." She continued brushing Elsie's hair with careful strokes.

In front of them, the other females did the same. Olivia had paired up with Janelle and was already weaving the light brunette's hair into two long braids. She then pinned them against the back of her head.

Sasha grasped hair ties and pins. She parted Elsie's hair down the middle with her finger then started the first braid.

"I don't think you will be dancing alone for too long. The rest of us will join in shortly after you begin. I already spoke to Raider about it. We want to get the whole pack involved. This isn't just for our guests. It's for all of us."

Soft, furry warmth filled Elsie's chest. She waited for Sasha to secure the first braid before turning and kissing her on the cheek. The pureblood's lips puffed out into a surprised smile.

"What was that for?"

"For being so sweet and caring." Elsie turned back around so that Sasha could pin her second braid.

It took Sasha a moment to resume fixing her hair. Sasha was in alpha mode so much of the time that Elsie doubted she received much affection from anyone other than her mate. She hoped the pureblood knew that Tabor wasn't the only one who loved and appreciated her.

Hair pinned in place, it was time to undress before

putting on the skimpy costumes. Elsie didn't mind doing this with their small group. Sasha helped tie the strings of the fur bikini securely around Elsie's neck and back.

The smell of fire and roasted meat wafted in through the trees. It was amusing to observe the chatter die down as the females lifted their noses to the air and inhaled. Shortly after the delicious scent floated in, Gina, Zadie, and Nudara returned, along with Maureen and Lacy, carrying bowls of cooked game. They handed them out for a dinner break.

"Is everyone else gathered in the glade?" Sasha asked.

"They're all eating," Gina said.

"And drinking," Zadie added.

"Good." Sasha plucked a thick piece of meat from her bowl and put it in her mouth.

Elsie chewed her food slowly, her stomach swirling with anticipation. She didn't want to perform. She wanted to return to the glade with the other females and find Zackary. She wanted to throw her arms around him and hug him tight. She'd missed the large, attractive male so much. Standing around knowing he was nearby gnawed away at her limited patience. Even if time wasn't running out, she would have wanted nothing more than to run to him that second. She'd pictured the set line of his jaw and intensity of his brown eyes, always so serious. She loved his soft, rounded ears, and firm yet gentle lips. He had no idea how handsome he was. The entire pack was blind to it, probably because he didn't swagger around all flirty or aggressive. It was a shame they didn't see the beautiful man Elsie did.

Camilla suddenly burst into laughter, Rosalie giggling so hard, tears leaked from the corners of her eyes. Their bowls of food shook in their hands.

Hmm. Maybe it was a relief the other females hadn't noticed Zackary. Elsie liked having him to herself. If Charlotte and Mia had been there, they would have been eating up Zackary with their eyes day and night. Elsie chuckled softly to herself. She missed her friends. She had yet to form the kind of close, teasing relationship she'd had back at Balmar Heights. Sasha and Kallie were beloved friends, but they were mated. It was different.

Elsie swallowed a piece of meat, the trees going blurry as her mind wandered.

In eight days, she would be mated. She'd been so intent on outwitting Brutus that she'd barely taken time to consider that no matter what, her life of independence was about to end.

Would she and Zackary be good together? Would they make one another happy? Would Zackary feel betrayed if he ever found out about the curse?

She feared his ego was more fragile then he let on. He could never know the truth.

✦ chapter twelve

SEATED ON A log around the bonfire, Zackary chomped down on the bits of roasted meat, eyes roving the clearing.

"I don't mind having guests in the hollow if it means feasting, drinking, and dancing females," Justin said, wiggling his eyebrows.

Wiley slurped moonshine from a mug, swallowed, and belched. He immediately gulped down more.

Seeing single females emerge from the woods with empty bowls made Zackary's frown deepen. He had yet to catch sight of Elsie. She was probably in the den eating with Heidi's family. It was hard to remain patient when he hadn't seen her in five days, but he knew she'd wander in eventually. He had no right to search her out, even though it was what he wanted to do more than anything.

Mashing a chunk of meat between his teeth, Zackary swallowed it, gaze still roving the glade.

"Did the two of you eat with Elsie while I was away?"

Justin took a swig from Wiley's mug before answering. "Don't worry, Zack. She ate with the females."

"Yeah. We wouldn't allow another male to move in on your female while you were gone," Wiley piped in.

"She's not my female." But he liked the sound of that.

Justin jutted his chin. "So, what? You'd let one of these mongrels mate with her?" Zackary's snarl made Justin chuckle. "Didn't think so."

Wiley grabbed his mug back from Justin. Lifting it in front of his face, he flashed a crooked smile. "If a female like Elsie wanted me, I'd claim her before she changed her mind."

"She and Zack should wait to have pups, though, so they don't have to move into the den. We still want to hang out with our buddy."

"And Elsie," Wiley said.

Justin shrugged. "Yeah, I guess she's cool."

Laughing, Wiley took another sip of brew then laughed some more. "Sure, you guess."

Zackary ran a hand over his cropped hair and sighed. "Maybe the two of you should just eat your food and stop planning my life."

"I don't know," Wiley said thoughtfully. "Justin and I think you need a push. Elsie seems to be the one taking all the initiative."

Justin leaned into Zackary. "You playing hard to get or something?"

"Har har." Zackary rolled his eyes.

Wiley nudged Justin with his elbow. "Hey, maybe if Elsie hangs out with us, more females will do the same."

"Yeah, sure. That will happen," Justin said sarcastically. But Zackary didn't miss the gleam in his eyes.

When Wiley offered Zackary his mug, he gave a grunt of refusal.

On the log beside them, two couples from the den were slurping down the moonshine and laughing. He wondered how den mates decided who got to come over for the festivities, and who stayed behind to watch the pack's young. Maybe they had some kind of rotation system. Would he and Elsie be part of that soon?

He almost slapped his forehead for thinking something so stupid. Despite the teasing from his friends, and regardless of his feelings, the moon would turn as green as the trees before Zackary claimed Elsie. If he asked permission, Tabor would run him out of the hollow. He was as sure of that fact as the rising sun each morning. At least he could comfort himself knowing Tabor wouldn't want Elsie with any male. He glanced at Maureen settling in front of her drum beside Alec and Heath. Hopefully Elsie would stay single for many years like other females in the pack. Perhaps if enough time passed, Tabor's hatred of Zackary would ease.

Sure. Yeah, right. Never happening.

The wizard shifter was surrounded by packmates asking questions about the hunt that led to the suburbs. No one approached Zackary for information, which was just as well. Making conversation had never come easy for him. Not like Tabor, blabbing on to Hudson, Chase, Zadie, and Nudara. And not like the hollow's latest intruders, Rafael and Diego. The purebloods stood sipping from mugs with Ford, Raider, and Jordan. At least they were wearing jeans and T-shirts. Someone must have lent them clothes from the hollow's stash—or maybe they'd helped themselves to garments from the duffels and backpacks they'd helped carry. The brothers, and males speaking to them, all postured—chests puffed out, chins lifted, and teeth glinting in the firelight when they grinned.

Drumbeats sounded, lowering the chatter in the glade.

Sasha walked in from the woods. As soon as she spotted the pureblooded brothers, she marched over and spoke to the group. They moved to a log near the bonfire where Wolfrik sat with his legs stretched out. Reaching him, Wolfrik spread an arm in welcome. The brothers sat. Raider and Jordan went to a nearby log where the female sat on her mate's lap. He threaded his arms around her middle and held her against him. Zackary felt a tightening in his gut, wishing hard that he could do the same with Elsie. Where was she? It wasn't like her to stay away from the festivities.

Darkness claimed the sky. The drumbeats grew faster in the night. Shifters were taking seats on logs or simply sitting cross-legged on the grass. The fire blazed and sparked. A fresh wave of chatter died off when five masked females emerged from the forest shadows. They moved with the music's rhythm, crouched like savages sneaking up on enemies.

Zackary had watched them file in during full moon celebrations, but tonight they entered from multiple directions as though surrounding an enemy camp. The performance was always captivating, and not for the obvious reason of females dancing provocatively in skimpy outfits. The drumbeat was hypnotic, and the women seemed a lot less human in their two-legged forms as they prowled over to the bonfire and shook their hips, pitching forward and pulling back before repeating the motions. Their arms lifted to the skies, raising like flames rippling toward the stars.

All of it—the music, the dancing, the fire—put everyone in the glade into a temporary trance.

Zadie and Nudara stood near the bonfire and began to sing along to the music. Their words sounded like chants. Wiley bobbed his head to the beat.

There were no male performers running in to join the females that evening. Instead, couples got up and started to dance near the fire. Raider and Jordan, and Emerson and Gina were the first up. Den mates weren't far behind them. Chase pulled Zadie into a dance while she was singing. Her lips switched from song to laughter as she let him put his arms around her. Hudson held a hand out to Nudara and then there was no singing, only drumbeats.

Two of the female performers sauntered up to the pureblooded brothers, soon pulling them up from the log and dragging them into the dance. Not that the males resisted. They looked pretty damn eager to grind against the females. Arms wrapped around the necks of the purebloods, the females rolled their hips and shoved their furry bikinis against the males' chests.

Justin stared at Taryn, who was seated on a log, arms folded, glowering into the crowd. When Wiley went to take another sip of moonshine, Justin snatched the mug, tipped it back, and gulped down the remainder of the brew.

"Hey!" Wiley said.

Justin shoved the empty mug back at him and stood, wiping his mouth with the back of his hand.

"I'm gonna ask Taryn to dance," he announced.

Wiley's eyes went wide, suddenly appearing very sober.

"Are you out of your mind?"

Justin merely grinned. "Maybe she'll want to make Chase jealous by dancing with me."

Without waiting for encouragement, Justin set forward. Wiley turned to Zackary. "No way she'll say yes."

"Nope."

Sure enough, Taryn scowled the moment Justin approached her. Her teeth looked as though they were biting the air when she spoke to him. Justin shrugged and turned away. Returning to their log, he smirked and said, "Maybe more moonshine, instead."

Wiley got to his feet, mug in hand.

"Good plan, but let's see if we can get two mugs this time. No offense, but I'd rather swap spit with a female."

"You and me both, buddy. You and me both." Justin slung his arm around Wiley and pulled him toward Jager and the bottles of brew he guarded on the edge of the glade.

Other couples got up to join the dance, including Sasha and Tabor. The wizard shifter placed his bandaged hand on his mate's hip.

Zackary scanned the glade, but Elsie still hadn't

arrived. He squeezed and relaxed his fists, taking another look around. One of the dance performers left the bonfire to join Lacy. The female who had been performing beside her walked over to where Jager sat, serving moonshine. The last female performer was the most petite. She'd stopped dancing and seemed to huddle behind the bonfire.

Zackary squinted. There was something familiar about her frame. His eyes popped wide open.

That wasn't Elsie, was it? It couldn't be.

He jerked his head to the side, staring at Tabor, but the wizard shifter's attention was wholly on his mate.

Returning his attention to the petite female, he noticed her backing slowly away from the fire toward the woods before slipping into the darkened forest.

Zackary got to his feet, skirting the glade and blundering packmates who kept getting in his way. He shoved a younger male named Carter, who bumped into him and grumbled, "Watch it, you lumbering giant." Zackary's snarl sent the mongrel fleeing into the crowd.

Upon reaching the last place he'd seen Elsie, Zackary raced into the woods. It didn't take long to catch up to her. Elsie moved quickly, but she wasn't running–not like Zack. He stopped abruptly to avoid running into her. He had no right to tackle her. All he really wanted to do was pull her into a hug and breathe her in.

Elsie spun around and yanked off the wolf mask. Her eyebrows were pinched together as she looked at the scrap of skin and fur in her hands.

"I feel ridiculous."

Head bent, it was as though she was too embarrassed to meet his gaze. Zackary had never seen her look vulnerable before. Was it because of what they'd done before he left, or was it the costume?

She pinched the hem of the deerskin skirt, frown deepening. It seemed to be the getup causing her distress.

"Elsie, you look beautiful."

She finally met his eyes, but there was no smile on her lips.

"I wanted to help out when they needed me for the dance, but I feel silly. Not fun silly."

The way she pursed her lips made Zackary laugh.

"You don't have to fit in with all of the hollow's customs," he said, daring to place a gentle hand on her shoulder.

"Dance duty is definitely not my thing. Welcome home, by the way." Her smile was like moonlight through the dense canopy overhead. "I was just headed to the communal cabin to change back into my dress."

"I'll come with you . . . and wait outside," Zackary quickly added.

Elsie giggled. Usually he found that kind of noise grating, but when Elsie did it, she sounded cute. She grasped the mask in one hand and wrapped her fingers around his with her other. Jolts of pleasure shot up Zackary's arm at the contact. All he could do was revel in her touch as he escorted Elsie to the cabin.

As they neared, they picked up on the sound of two shifters going at it within the log walls. Curtains shrouded the windows, but there was no glass to block the noise inside.

"You like that?" a male grunted.

"Oh, yeah. Take me harder. Make Mama Wolf happy."

Zackary and Elsie came to a halt. The witch shifter's eyes expanded as she turned to look at Zackary, her mouth gaping open in surprise. An instant later, Zackary saw her expression change and lips twitch. Laughter rose up his throat. He squeezed Elsie's hand and pulled her into the woods, running with her until they couldn't hold it in any longer. They doubled over, laughter bursting from their lips.

"Oh my gosh," Elsie gasped. "Who was that?"

"I think it was Ford and Polly," Zackary said, glancing in the direction of the communal cabin.

Damn den mates. They had their own enclosures to return home to. Why did they have to go hijacking the one communal structure for the single shifters?

"Uh, maybe wait a little longer to retrieve your dress," Zackary suggested.

Elsie laughed again, the mask dangling from her fingers. "Guess I'll have to keep the cavewoman look going a little longer."

"Want to go back to the party?" Zackary kept his tone light. After being away, he wanted to spend whatever time he could with Elsie. If they went back to the glade, that wouldn't be possible—not with Tabor around.

"The quiet is nice," Elsie said. "Maybe we could wait at Jager's hut. He has stools and a fire pit. Maybe there's even a fire already going. He'll still be at the party a while, won't he?"

Zackary scratched his jaw, recalling the eagerness with which Jager served moonshine to the pureblooded brothers—yet another reason he'd rather Elsie not return to the glade.

Grinning, he took Elsie's hand once more.

"Great idea," he said.

They cut through the woods, crossing the path that led to the den then stepped back into the underbrush. Zackary angled his body ahead of Elsie's, holding up errant branches before she could run into them.

The sound of muffled voices made Zackary's heart rate spike. He pulled Elsie down behind the base of an overturned tree. Roots shot out at the ends and the trunk was as wide as a giant boulder—enough circumference to hide them both when they crouched.

Packmates might get the wrong idea if they saw Zackary with Elsie alone in the woods. They hadn't even kissed . . . well, not tonight, anyway. Zackary frowned and glanced over at the pretty witch shifter pressed against his shoulder. Her head and eyes lifted like she was concentrating on the approaching footsteps. They kept hunched and quiet. The voices remained muffled even as they approached. One was deep, low, and male; the other soft and female. The couple stopped talking, but there had been no sound of them walking out of range. No footsteps or even the patter of paws if they'd shifted. No more conversation or . . .

The female's loud gasp carried all the way to where Zackary and Elsie huddled behind the fallen tree.

Oh, for the love of Moon. Not again.

Pleasured moans gusted out of the female.

Elsie's eyes expanded. She looked at Zackary, lips

parting in surprise. He grimaced.

A devious grin elevated Elsie's lips right before she turned and lifted her body inch by inch from where they hid. After looking over the uprooted tree, she dropped back down. She didn't even have to do it quietly, the female did nothing to muffle her eager pants.

Crouched beside him, Elsie mouthed two names, but Zackary couldn't decipher either. He shook his head. She placed a hand on his shoulder and leaned close until her lips were touching his ear. Zackary's dick jumped in his pants.

"Jordan and Raider." The names whispered down his neck.

The mating sounds faded the more Zackary thought of Elsie pressed against him in her furry bikini and scrap of deer hide plastered to her hips.

He turned his head, lips finding Elsie's. When she swiped her tongue over his mouth, he crushed his lips against hers, cupping the back of her neck to hold her against him. Elsie's fingers dug into his shoulder blades as though she meant to claw him with her nails. She didn't have to worry about roughing him up, but he needed to be mindful of the petite female in his arms.

"Don't stop. Don't stop. Don't stop!" Jordan bellowed.

It was as though she was encouraging them, along with her mate. A growl arose—one Zackary wasn't sure was his or Raider's. The sound of it seemed to vibrate in his throat.

He unfastened his pants and tore them off his legs then climbed over Elsie. A fierce glow entered her eyes when she stared up at him. Hesitating, Zackary pressed his lips together tight.

"Don't. Stop." Her words were a soft command. The playfulness had vanished from her expression, replaced by a silent demand. Her gaze flicked brazenly between his legs.

Heat flooded to Zackary's cheeks and sent blood rushing to his groin. He lifted the flap of deer skin above her thighs and found her wet and ready for him. He sank into her with an ecstatic sigh.

Zackary froze, listening for yelling or Tabor screaming a spell, but he could only hear Jordan's moaning.

When he rocked, the pleasure in his groin shot throughout his entire body. Zackary closed his eyes, momentarily overwhelmed by how good he felt inside her. He thrust, overcome with desire. Then did it again and again, moving to a rhythm that tugged at all the pleasure points inside his body. The ecstasy astounded him.

Elsie lifted her hips, and her eyes seemed to glow brighter. She made no sound, holding back to keep from being discovered by the passionate packmates. Jordan panted loud enough for all of them. Zackary wanted to pleasure Elsie the way Raider pleasured Jordan. He needed to make sure she felt satisfied. He couldn't let Raider outlast him. Zackary's dick had other ideas. This was his first time mating. Aroused beyond reasoning, he got the sense that things would soon be out of his control.

Rocking faster increased the pleasure. He pitched forward, nearly emptying inside her. Gritting his teeth, he groaned beside her ear.

"Protection spell? I can't hold on much longer."

"Nolosha para bos, nolosha para mangina."

Elsie whispered the spell. Once spoken, Zackary nearly lost it without resuming their mating. He rocked once and had to grind his teeth harder.

Elsie took up the rhythm. Her motion broke the dam inside him. When he tried to pull out, she wrapped her legs around his hips, squeezing him to her. That was it. No force on Earth could stop the flood of his release. His hips jerked forward, cock tunneling deeper into her blissful heat.

Jordan shrieked and Raider roared, as though they'd been in synch with Zackary and Elsie all along. Then the forest went silent.

Zackary and Elsie froze. Their eyes found one another's, locking on while they held their breath and listened.

"Was it good?" Raider asked.

"Like you have to ask," Jordan teased.

"I suppose we should return to the party and make sure our guests of honor are enjoying themselves," Raider said.

Jordan snorted. "Camilla and Rosalie are seeing to that. At least my sister's moving on."

"Maybe Hudson and Chase as well," Raider said.

Their conversation drifted away. Once no sound of the mated pair remained, Zackary eased out of Elsie. He hovered above her, searching her face for hints as to how she felt about their coupling.

"Are you okay?" he asked softly.

Elsie's lips spread into a grin. "I can't wait to do that again."

Chuckling happily, Zackary bent down and touched the side of Elsie's face. She was so sweet and lovely and beautiful. This must be a dream. He felt as though he'd claimed her, that she belonged to him. After this, there would be no staying away.

Mine, he thought.

This female is mine.

ELSIE FELL ASLEEP in Zackary's arms behind the fallen tree. Sometime later, she stirred and flipped around. Zackary immediately pulled her against his chest, spooning her body and wrapping his arms around her protectively. With a contented sigh, Elsie fell back asleep.

Dawn had not yet arrived when the soft crunch of leaves pulled Elsie awake. She grabbed her discarded mask and just managed to hold it in front of her face as Wolfrik rounded on them.

Zackary leapt to his feet, two large fists clenched at his sides.

There wasn't a stitch of clothing on either of the males.

Wolfrik wasn't looking at Zackary, his eyes were on Elsie—a smirk on his lips.

"I can still recognize you, Little Witch."

Zackary snarled.

Elsie lowered the mask and set it beside her with a shrug.

"You caught us," she said with nonchalance.

"He treating you good?" He nodded his head to the side in Zackary's direction without actually looking at him.

"Of course I am," Zackary snapped.

"Elsie?" Wolfrik raised his brows.

Zackary glowered at the pureblood. "What's it to you? You're not her brother."

Wolfrik turned slowly to face Zackary. "Be glad that I'm not." Ruthless eyes ran up and down the shifter's front. Wolfrik's teeth looked sharp when he grinned. "Then again, you have as much to fear from me as from the wizard wolf if you hurt Elsie—more actually." He took a large step toward Zackary.

"I'd never hurt Elsie," Zackary growled. His eyes squeezed together as though the mere thought brought him pain.

"Oh yeah? What about her brother? You beat him up for being part wizard."

"That wasn't me; that was Garrick." Zackary gritted his teeth.

Wolfrik lifted his nose. "I see. Just an innocent bystander."

"No," Zackary grit out.

"Wolfrik, stop," Elsie said. "Thanks for checking on me. I'm fine. You can go now."

Wolfrik gave a snort of amusement and folded his arms over his chest. "That's how it is then? Going to dismiss me the way you dismissed the boy?"

Zackary's forehead wrinkled when he looked at Elsie. "What boy?"

Elsie scowled at Wolfrik, who smirked before sauntering off.

"What boy?" Zackary asked again.

✦ chapter thirteen

Meat, moonshine, and erotic dancing . . .
Wolf Hollow certainly knew how to show migrant shifters
a good time.

Diego always found it fascinating to visit with other
wolf packs and observe their customs. Some were wary of
outsiders, while others jumped at the opportunity to play
host. Last night's entertainment had been a surprise, and
the moonshine was the best he'd tasted in a long while.

Would Glenn Meadows be as welcoming? Would
Hailey?

After a night of feasting, drinking, and dancing, he'd
nearly been too tired to shift. The hours before morning
were few, and soon enough the faint smell of smoke
tickled Diego's nostrils. He lifted his wolf head and scented
the air before shifting and rising on two legs. Grabbing
the borrowed jeans, he'd placed on the ground beside
him, Diego pulled the stiff material over his legs and hips,
leaving the top button unfastened. He stretched his arms
wide, bare chest lifting to greet the dawn.

Fully awake, Diego crept past sleeping shifters

sprawled over the ground still snoozing, some snoring, after the long night of partying.

He scratched his balls. Diego wasn't accustomed to wearing clothing, but their hosts were into the practice, so he'd go along with it until he and Raphael continued on their way.

Raphy was nowhere to be seen, not that Diego felt remotely worried. He knew exactly what his brother was up to when he'd taken off into the surrounding woods with one of the female performers. Good. Raphael needed to get laid. He'd been yapping Diego's ear off about his dry spell all up the coast of what had once been known as Oregon. They'd pissed on every city sign post they'd passed. Based on all the crumbling structures left behind, it was easy to deduce that humans had loved their coastal towns. That wasn't the case for wolf packs.

They'd come across a few stray shifters as they made their way up to the area of Washington, but those stragglers had taken off running before they could engage them in conversation. They hadn't had so much as a whiff of a female in many moons.

Diego didn't care about a romp in the woods. The moment he'd decided he was ready for a mate, he'd become committed to his female—even though he hadn't met her yet. He hoped it would be very soon.

Eager anticipation buzzed through him like bees over crocuses.

Several months ago, he'd decided he was ready to claim a female. Ready to spend the remainder of his days waking up beside his lovely mate. Ready to become a doting mate and father.

His brother was the best company. As soon as Diego shared his intentions with him, they'd agreed they must stick together and form their own little pack. Ideally, the female would be a pureblood who could keep up with their wanderings and birth pups who could do the same. Only the offspring of pureblooded mates came into the world in their animal form. They were unable to shift to humans until their twelfth year.

Once Raphael had gotten the teasing out of the way, he'd perked up at the idea of being Uncle Raphy—helping teach the pups to hunt and kill.

Maybe the search would end in Glenn Meadows . . . if Hailey was even single. Wolf Hollow's elder had insisted again and again that he would find out for them. He'd sent the pack's werewolf to make the trip over, while being elusive on the number of days it would take for him to travel round trip.

If Diego was in a rush, he would have gone himself, but such gracious hosts were rare in this world, and Raphael was getting what he needed.

Diego followed the scent of the smoke to the glade. Where it had been brimming with shifters hours before, it was now clear with the exception of the blonde female in a short floral sundress crouched beside a small fire above a cauldron.

The next beat of Diego's heart skidded against his chest.

Her name was Lacy. He knew because he'd asked another shifter that night. She wasn't a pureblood, but she'd looked so beautiful with her hair lifted into a ponytail, the same way it was now. There was a soft sweetness about her that immediately caught Diego's attention. While her packmates danced and drank, she had remained attentive, helping clear cups and offering warm smiles to any packmate she approached. No males had lingered around her, signaling to Diego that she was unattached. But the male who had told him her name also shared that she was grieving the loss of a friend.

Diego moved closer, sure Lacy would hear him, but she was on her knees in front of the fire feeding twigs in, looking fully focused on her task. Another look around confirmed that they were alone. Diego's heart sped up as he approached.

"Buenos dias, mi querido amigo."

Lacy blushed when she looked up. Getting up, she said a soft "hi," meeting his eyes dead on before looking quickly away. "Breakfast will be ready in a bit. I'm just getting it warmed up." She reached behind her head and tightened her ponytail.

"You are responsible for feeding your pack?" Diego stepped closer.

Lacy hurried around the cauldron, putting it between them. She grasped a long wooden spoon and began stirring. When she shook her head, her blonde hair swung from side to side.

"Just for this month. We change duties every new moon cycle. The single shifters, that is. The mated shifters take care of feeding their own families in the den, east of here."

Diego fixated on her lips as she spoke, keeping his gaze on them after she finished. More color crept into Lacy's cheeks. It was probably a good thing he had on pants, otherwise he might scare her off with the boner he'd gotten while watching her face flush.

Dios mio, she was bashful. If a flirty morning greeting got her this worked up, what would she look like beneath him as he took his time bringing pleasure to every inch of her body?

It was Diego's turn to feel overheated. His skin burned with desire to brand this female as his. What kind of sounds would she make once he was inside her? Would her entire body flush or only her face? What did she look like beneath her dress?

Futile thoughts, he admonished himself. She was not a pureblood. Not the type of female to run off with a couple of nomads. Her actions and words spoke of a dutiful and loyal packmate.

A dutiful and loyal mate for Diego, another voice taunted back at him.

Lacy's grip on the spoon tightened as he stared at her.

Diego tucked his silky shoulder-length hair behind his ears and flashed her a friendly smile.

"Can I help you, *mi amor*?"

"It just needs to warm up. Thanks. The Sakhir River is close. Just behind me," Lacy tilted her head back, "if you're thirsty."

Diego's eyes locked on her exposed neck. Oh, he was parched all right. He ran the tip of his tongue along the backs of his teeth, suddenly hungry for a taste of her cunt.

Diego didn't know what had come over him. She wasn't what he was looking for at all. He'd told Raphael he wanted a bold, feisty pureblooded female who could take down an elk with speed and skill.

That all had changed the moment he saw Lacy. He'd learned long ago to listen to his instincts. He was also the kind of wolf who got what he wanted. However long it took was irrelevant. Attracting a mate was like hunting a bison. As long as he stayed focused and kept after his prize, eventually she'd tire out and succumb to him.

Flexing his biceps, Diego rounded the cauldron and took the spoon gently from Lacy. "Allow me to stir this for you, *mi alma*."

"You don't have to," she said.

"I want to help you."

Her cheeks dimpled when she smiled. "Thank you. You are very sweet."

"Diego. My name is Diego."

"Thank you . . . Diego."

When she said his name, the flush crept down Lacy's neck, inching toward her bosom. Diego's hand froze over the cauldron. Steam warmed his fingers, becoming uncomfortably hot, but he didn't care. All he could do was stare at Lacy.

"Your smile could light up the entire world."

His words earned him a smile more blinding in its beauty than the first.

With a soft chuckle, Lacy spun around, busying herself at a wood table nearby where she carefully stacked bowls into a basket. After filling the basket, she carried it over to the cauldron where Diego diligently stirred the gruel to keep it from sticking to the bottom or sides of the large pot. A male of average height and reddish-brown hair jogged into the glade, rubbing his fists over his eyes.

"Just woke up, sorry," he said to Lacy.

"It's okay. Diego is helping."

The young male looked at Diego and blinked.

"*Hola*," Diego said.

"Huh?" *El tonto* squinted at him.

"Bring the rest of the bowls over," Lacy told him.

El tonto did as he was told just as shifters began entering the glade. The twerp had impeccable timing, making it appear as though he'd been helping all along rather than waiting until the last second to show up.

As Lacy walked past Diego, he frowned.

"Is this incompetent young male the only help you have?"

With a startled laugh, Lacy covered her mouth and leaned closer to Diego—so close he nearly dropped the spoon in the gruel.

"We change duties and patrol partners every moon cycle."

"Until you are claimed?" Diego asked gently.

Lacy lowered her lashes and nodded. He couldn't take his eyes off her. When shifters began grabbing bowls and lining up at the cauldron, Lacy looked him in the eyes.

"You can hand the spoon over to the first shifter in line. They can dish themselves up."

Rather than hand it over to the tall, skinny male at the front of the line, Diego kept it in his grasp.

"You should dish up first," he told Lacy.

"Oh," she said, smiling and blushing. "That's okay. I can wait my turn."

"You were up first preparing this food. You should eat first," Diego insisted.

Gazing at him closer, she must have recognized his resolve; Lacy grabbed a bowl and hurried up to the cauldron. When she reached for the spoon, Diego pulled it away, scooping up gruel that he dished into her bowl.

"More?"

Lacy shook her head. "This is plenty. Thank you."

She hurried away, taking a seat on a log. Diego handed the spoon to the male who had been waiting.

"Enjoying yourself?" a silky male voice asked as Diego was making his way to the back of the line.

He stopped and grinned at the hollow's pureblood, Wolfrik. He hadn't bothered committing many of the pack's names to memory, but Wolfrik stood out. Deep scars marred his body, and he had a manic gleam to his eyes, but apparently he was mated and expecting his first child in another eight months. Although he wasn't warm and fuzzy, he'd been welcoming, and even curious as to the territories Diego and Raphael had crossed.

"I am enjoying your pack's hospitality very much, *gracias*," Diego answered with a grin.

Wolfrik smirked. "But not as much as your brother."

"Have you seen him?"

"Seen him. Heard him—him and the two females he was pleasuring." Wolfrik's brows jumped.

Diego rolled his eyes. "Do you not have your own

female to spend the night with?"

"Better put Kallie out of your head, *esé*. Being mated doesn't mean turning a blind eye to what happens in my pack."

Diego squinted at Wolfrik's use of Spanish. Apparently he and Raphy weren't the only Latinos Wolfrik had run into. From the look of the pureblood's numerous scars, he'd been out in the world more than the rest of his pack. Diego offered Wolfrik a placating grin.

"I feel you, *hombre*. I wouldn't let my guard down with strangers around either."

"I'm glad we understand one another." Wolfish teeth gleamed from between Wolfrik's lips. "Enjoy the rest of your stay."

Shifters moved out of the way as Wolfrik sauntered across the glade. Diego was curious as to why he hadn't claimed the other pureblooded female from his pack, or Hailey from the neighboring. But looking around at all the attractive females in the glade, he had an inkling why.

As Wolfrik disappeared into the forest, Raphael strolled in with a satisfied smile jerking up his lips. Diego half-expected his brother to walk in with each of his arms slung around a female, but he was alone at the moment. He jutted his chin at Diego before planting his feet wide apart and placing his hands on his hips.

"*Mi hermano*," he said with gusto. "Thank you for sending your dance partner after me."

"Anything for you, brother."

They stepped into line, waiting their turn to get a taste of the unappetizing-looking mush inside the pot everyone waited to get a serving of. Switching to Spanish, Raphael proceeded to share news of the threesome he'd engaged in until the early hours.

"They couldn't get enough of me. You'd think they hadn't seen a male in months. So much appreciation, and up for anything." He winked. "You don't mind staying a little longer, do you?"

Looking across the glade at the cute blonde chewing a mouthful of mush, Diego grinned and answered, "Not at all."

THE CURTAINS WERE still drawn over the communal cabin's windows when Elsie tried a second time to retrieve her white dress before heading into the glade for breakfast.

Once she saw that the cabin was occupied, she spun on her heel and headed for the den. It shouldn't be too difficult to get her hands on a spare dress, especially since she'd donated the contents of the duffel bag William had brought to the hollow, everything except for the rifle, which Wolfrik had taken away for safekeeping.

Hopefully William had gone straight back home and stayed put. Elsie grimaced. She'd only told Zackary part of the truth. She couldn't tell him everything without revealing her reasons for rushing things along. It would only hurt his feelings and make him doubt hers—pure as they were.

Instead, she told him that William had come by with clothes for her and to see how she was doing. Assuring

Zackary that she had broken things off with the wizard years ago hadn't eased the troubled look in his eyes. He'd been upset that he had been away from the hollow when the "intruder" wandered in. It hadn't helped to tell him that William was harmless and that she hadn't even been alone with him since Wolfrik had appeared. That news had deepened Zackary's scowl.

She was eager to start patrol. They couldn't eat breakfast together with Tabor and Sasha hanging out with the pack. Elsie barely had time for breakfast, anyway. By the time she got a dress from the den and returned to the glade, patrolling partners were already heading out. Zackary and Chase had left. Hudson stood waiting with a bowl of porridge. Elsie grinned and jogged over, taking it from him.

"Thank you."

"Good morning, Elsie. Nice dress."

She looked down at the faded stripes and strappy sleeves.

"Thanks, mine got hijacked in the cabin while I was performing. Did you have fun last night?" Elsie asked between bites of porridge.

"Yup." Hudson grinned secretively. "Did you?"

"Uh-huh."

"Good. Ready to patrol?"

It was Elsie's turn to flash an elusive smile.

T HE BERRY BASKETS remained empty and discarded while Elsie and Zackary mated beneath a tree.

Curious to try a new position, Elsie had tossed off her dress and climbed over Zackary. She found a rhythm that caused his eyes to roll into the back of his head and groans of pleasure to bolt from his lips. Elsie panted with her exertions. At least she no longer had to be quiet.

Warm hands held her firmly by the hips. A couple times Zackary hissed, clearly fighting to hold on.

"You feel so good," he groaned.

She moved against him, loving the exquisite friction of his cock pulsing deep inside her.

His eyes focused on her shaking breasts. A predatory look flashed over Zackary's face right before he lifted her by the waist and flipped her onto all fours. The breath whooshed out of her as he positioned himself behind her.

Great bright moon above, he was going to take her doggy style.

She was panting and drenched as the head of his shaft dragged down her bottom until reaching her slick entrance. He pressed his thick, bulging tip there but didn't enter her. A whimper rose from Elsie's lips, an animalistic plea for him to penetrate her fully.

He spread her cheeks and entered her pussy slowly, taking his time filling her. Elsie's fingers stretched over the earth. Her nails dug into the rich soil with Zackary's first thrust. She gasped, feeling as though she would be the one who couldn't hold on when he was this deep inside her.

Zackary cussed and went still.

Elsie held her position. Her breaths rasped from deep in her throat, anticipation swelling inside her stomach.

"I wish I could stay inside you forever," Zackary said.

He pumped into her steadily, like he was concentrating on maintaining measured strokes. Bent under him, Elsie felt each plunge forward rub against her sweet spot. She could no longer think or breathe evenly. She could barely hold herself up. Every thrust brought stars floating across her vision and whimpers to her lips. She didn't hold back, didn't care that she sounded like a shifter in heat.

"Fuck! You feel so good." Zackary sounded emboldened by her unraveling.

Elsie clawed the soil, digging in her nails as Zackary thrust faster. His knuckles brushed her belly. Cupping her breasts in his palms, he tugged and held her securely against his chest. She seeped over his cock as he kept his hips in sway at her back.

The shade of the tree blanketed them from the morning sun. The cool air felt like heaven against her balmy skin. She was burning up, but there was nothing left to take off. Still, the pressure built and built. A carnal sob rose from her throat.

Cursing again, Zackary loosened his hold on her breasts and lowered her to the ground. Elsie pressed her arms into the earth, arching her back.

"Elsie . . ." Her name rasped down her spine. "Fuck. This is just . . . Just. Fuck."

Zackary grabbed her by her hips and moved like a wolf shooting out of the brush to take down a rabbit. His bulky weight slammed into her. Each time he jerked back he pulled her with him, rocking in rapid tandem.

Elsie gave up any further attempt to participate. Ecstasy burst through her body. It was like discovering a hidden power she'd never realized she possessed.

She cried out one last time before her body went slack.

Zackary pumped into her like his dick was on fire and only her wet heat could stop the burn. A guttural roar boomed over the clearing. Zackary's release felt like a tidal wave flooding toward her uterus. The spell would protect her ovaries. Elsie would continue using it until Zackary claimed her. After that, they'd talk.

Elsie rolled onto her side, catching the gentle wings of a butterfly fluttering past. She smiled happily when Zackary scooted against her back and wrapped an arm around her.

"I now understand the meaning of life." He'd never sounded so happy as he did when he spoke those words.

Elsie chuckled.

"Me?" she teased. "Am I the meaning of your life, Zackary?"

"You have no idea how much you mean to me," he whispered.

Zackary ran his tongue along the back of her earlobe. Elsie shivered against him, feeling like she might go liquid again. The way he took his time stroking her body, it was as though he needed to remind himself that she was really here, really his. And she was his. Elsie wondered if he had any idea about that.

"I wish we could stay like this forever," he murmured, brushing hair off Elsie's face.

Elsie flipped around to face him.

"Then claim me."

Zackary's eyes drifted to the ground, tugging his lips

into a frown. "Your brother would never allow it, and for good reason."

She sat up. "I won't let Tabor stand in the way of my happiness. Will you?"

Avoiding her gaze, Zackary chewed on the inside of his cheek. "Maybe after more time passes, he'll reconsider." The sag of his shoulders conveyed how little he expected such a miracle to take place at any period.

Elsie didn't have that kind of time. She'd achieved her first goal of hooking a wolf. Now she had to convince him to claim her within a week.

She tucked the hair Zackary had so tenderly swept aside behind her ear.

"I know that I'm young, and I know that I'm new here, but there is no other wolf for me. No other man. No other shifter. No other male in all the world I would rather make a forever life with." She met his eyes. "There is only you, Zackary. I don't want to wait. I don't want to hide our love."

Zackary rubbed his elbows and stared into the grassy blades around his toes.

"I don't either," he said. "I want to eat meals together. I want to be able to hug and kiss you in front of packmates." He looked up. "I want to do everything with you."

As though her chest had turned featherlight, Elsie felt her whole being lift with victory. She wanted all the things Zackary had said. She could already picture standing in line at the cauldron together, holding hands; spending her nights wrapped in his warmth; being assigned all future patrols as a mated pair; and raising a family with laughter and love.

"Good, now lie back," she said, pushing her palm against his chest.

Zackary's eyes flashed. "What are you doing?"

"I want to try something new."

Grinning wickedly, Elsie crawled between his tanned, muscled legs. He watched her intently as she wrapped her fingers around the base of his dick and guided the tip into her mouth.

Zackary's lips parted with a strangled rasp.

"Moon above, Elsie. You will be the end of me."

✦ chapter fourteen

ZACKARY FELT CERTAIN Chase and Hudson would see right through him when they walked over at the end of patrol. He'd spent the entire day mating and snoozing. Over and over he'd told himself he needed to stop. He couldn't spend every waking moment of the day having sex with Elsie. Tell that to his dick.

They had to hurry to fill their baskets when they realized how late it had gotten. Elsie kept crushing berries in her fingers and laughing. Zackary wasn't having much better luck with his picking. Rather than eat the ones he'd pulverized, he tossed them in smashed. The pack would just have to eat squishy blackberries that evening.

Elsie's laughter kept drawing his attention to her. She held up her stained fingers with berry bits all over them.

"You're cute," Zackary said, grinning.

"And you're sweet." Elsie leaned over and planted a quick kiss on his lips.

It was all he could do to stop himself from lifting her off her feet, carrying her to the shade of the tree, lifting her dress over her hips and planting himself inside her.

He forced himself to grab more berries and tossed them into the little crates.

"This is looking more like jam," Elsie said. "You're doing better than me."

"Hmm, what do I get if I fill up my basket first?" Zackary asked in a teasing tone.

A wicked gleam entered Elsie's blue eyes.

"Another kiss between the legs."

Zackary's nostrils flared as Elsie's eyes traveled down his chest, passing his hips before resting on his length. With no clothes covering him, his cock stood on end in plain sight and was growing bigger the more she stared.

He groaned. "If we don't get these berries picked, the pack will become suspicious."

"Then you better hurry and pick, especially if you want that kiss." Elsie lifted her brows and smirked.

As though he needed further encouragement. Zackary grabbed at berries, not caring as thorns caught on his fingers. He tossed them in carelessly, including stray leaves.

Elsie laughed and continued to pick berries steadily.

After Zackary finished filling his basket, he helped Elsie with hers. Once both baskets were finished, they set them in the shade of the tree over the flattened grass. Hudson and Chase would be arriving at any moment. The petite female tossed her hair back and grinned at Zackary.

"Guess you'll have to wait until tomorrow for your prize."

He grabbed his shorts off the ground, bending to get each foot in. After he pulled them up to his hips and fastened them as best he could, he folded his arms and pursed his lips, casting a considering look over Elsie.

"As the winner, shouldn't I be the one to decide the kiss?"

Elsie tilted her head to the side. "What did you have in mind?"

"Perhaps I would prefer to be the one to kiss you." His gaze lowered past her hips to the sweet spot covered by her striped dress.

"Oh." A blush entered her cheeks, something Zackary wasn't expecting but took great pleasure in. "Oh," Elsie said again.

His mind hummed with excitement, ready to taste her that second and devour his prize. The thought of her thighs pressed against his head as he lapped her up made his blood burn through his veins like lava. Even the sound of Hudson and Chase gabbing their way into the clearing wasn't enough to pull Zackary's eyes off Elsie. Not at first.

"Hi, guys," she said in a high-pitched voice. Her eyes darted away then returned right back to Zackary.

He wanted to tell the two clowns to get lost. He and Elsie were having a moment. If they were mated, he could have her all to himself rather than being forced to step aside and allow Hudson to escort her back to the glade.

Zackary clamped his mouth shut before he had a chance to bark at the mongrel to scram.

Lifting her fingers in quick farewell, Elsie joined Hudson's side. The pair headed into the neighboring woods, Zackary glowering at Hudson's back the whole while. Chase bent over Elsie's basket and frowned.

"These all look squished."

"Yeah, you didn't do a good job picking today," Zackary returned.

Chase huffed and rolled his eyes. "Getting ripe, are they?"

Zackary grunted in reply. He much preferred Elsie's company. She was right; the sooner he claimed her, the better. They couldn't let Tabor stand in the way of their happiness. So . . . what to do? Getting the half-shifter's blessings was out of the question. Nor could he kill him.

Zackary scratched his head before picking up his basket. His brain spun circles inside his thick head with each step to the glade.

How to go about making Elsie his mate?

Communication had never been one of his strengths. Words were just . . . frustrating.

"I know you've always hated me, but I want your sister," he pictured himself telling Tabor. *"I don't like you either. It's not like I went out of my way to fall for her. She's the only female I want to mate with. That's just the way it is."* In his mind, Tabor's face contorted right before he spoke foreign words and Zackary exploded into a million pieces of flesh and gore.

Elsie would protect him.

He huffed at that thought.

He wanted to be the one protecting her. It still gnawed at him that he had been away from the hollow when her ex-lover came skulking after her from the mountain.

Could Zackary even protect her from wizards?

A memory of Tabor flinging him onto his back with mere words pounded in his head. Zackary growled. Chase looked over and sighed without comment. They kept their heads forward, making no conversation. Zackary was busy having his own snarl fest with himself.

Yeah, words weren't going to help convince Tabor. Maybe Zackary should claim Elsie in secret then tell the wizard-shifter after the deed was done. He puffed out his chest and grinned. Tabor would never see him as anything other than a brute. In that case, why bother trying? Elsie wanted Zackary, and he wanted her back. It wasn't for anyone else to decide or interfere.

An entirely different conversation began running through his head in which he informed Tabor that Elsie was his mate. They'd claimed one another and expected him to respect their decision. Tabor really had no say in the matter. The wizard-shifter had his own mate to protect. Sasha would always come first for Tabor, the way Elsie came first for Zackary. The witch-shifter was his to protect now. The sooner Tabor accepted that, the better for all of them. Zackary would not back down, not when it came to the female he intended to claim as his mate.

T HE GLADE FILLED with chatter and laughter once more, now that the rest of their packmates had returned and there were new guests in the hollow. Elsie sat on a log with Tabor and Sasha at dinner, nibbling her stew.

"How long do you think they'll stick around?" Tabor asked Sasha.

"I don't know, but I imagine they won't linger," Sasha answered.

Tabor stroked his jaw. "Do you think Hailey would

really leave Glenn Meadows to join them?"

"I don't know. I've never met her."

Elsie only half-listened to the speculations involving the pureblooded brothers. She'd caught a glimpse of the males during the celebration, but hadn't stuck around long enough to be introduced. Raphael stood in the center of the glade, flanked by Rosalie and Camilla, who appeared to be having a contest to see who could touch him the most. From nearby, Diego mingled with the single males in the pack.

Elsie had her mind on a different male . . . him and his mouth . . . on her . . . tomorrow. Warm, wet heat seeped beneath the stripes on her dress. She replayed all the times they'd coupled that morning and afternoon. Her body heated as she anticipated doing it again tomorrow. Sneaking a glance at Zackary, she figured it was a good thing Justin currently held his attention. They might give everything away in one look if he met her eyes.

She needed to figure out a way to tell Tabor without inciting bloodshed. Elsie continued chewing, not swallowing until the bit of meat became part of the mush. She'd have to tell Tabor the truth, but only after the claim had been made. Knowing the fate she'd avoided, she hoped he'd make peace with her choice of mate. Most of all, she longed for him to let go of past grievances and recognize that Zackary wasn't a bad wolf. He was tender and sweet, and he made her happy. She wished Tabor could be happy for her.

After finishing the last bites of stew, Elsie got up and set her bowl in a basket with other dirtied plates. Lacy stood beside it and gave her a warm smile. There were so many nice shifters in Wolf Hollow, including the soft-spoken blonde who had lost one of her closest friends. Elsie smiled back.

"How are you doing, Lacy?"

The blonde blinked several times, her smile turning sad. "I'm okay. I still wake up forgetting she's gone. Then I look over at the spot where she used to curl up beside me and remember." She lifted her head and blinked again. "But I know she's in a better place. She's with her mom and dad. They were very close."

Elsie nodded. "We all end up in the After eventually."

What precisely that meant, she could only guess. There were wizards in her coven who believed in reincarnation, while others were convinced they went to heaven. Her father's theory remained consistent. He believed that after death, they became energy without consciousness or end. Tabor had told Elsie that the shifters of Wolf Hollow believed in the spirit world, and that they would turn into wolf souls running forever free in an ethereal dimension beyond this world.

Elsie knew it brought comfort in times of sorrow and fear, but she didn't give the question of life after death much thought. So many of life's mysteries would never be answered, and this mystery certainly not until death itself.

She hoped she wouldn't find out for a very long time.

STANDING WITH A small group of friendly male shifters, Diego recounted a winter bison hunt through heavy snowfall. He'd already told the story multiple times, but he didn't mind. Sharing the tale of a successful hunt never got old. With every detail he disclosed, he kept tabs on Lacy without openly looking.

When Lacy headed into the woods with a basket of bowls, Diego skipped over parts of his story, getting to the kill. Without appearing rushed, he lifted his chest and concluded the story before casually stepping away to wander across the glade before ducking into the woods.

Spotting a narrow trail, he followed it to the sound of flowing water. The basket had been set on the edge of the riverbank while Lacy waded in with a stack of bowls that she dipped into the current one by one.

Meandering closer, Diego lifted his chin. "Your patrol partner isn't very helpful, is he?"

Lacy smile sweetly. "I don't mind."

Well, maybe I do, Diego thought, keeping the comment to himself. This supposed helper of hers was a cur to stick Lacy with all the work and let her go off alone.

Snatching two bowls from the basket, Diego joined Lacy in the river. Her eyes expanded, looking down as the water soaked the lower legs of his jeans.

"You're getting your pants wet."

"Should I take them off?" Diego didn't mean for it to come out husky.

The blush that lit up Lacy's cheeks was blinding. Her lips twisted and she leaned back. The last thing he wanted to do was make her feel uncomfortable.

"I'll leave them on," Diego said, making himself sound casual. "It's still warm out and they'll dry."

Lacy rinsed the rest of the bowls she'd carried into the river before wading back, setting them on the rocky shore and grabbing several more to clean. Diego did the same, and soon all the bowls were rinsed clean.

He carried the full basket back to the glade, fuming to himself when he felt how heavy they were. That boy shouldn't be Lacy's partner–Diego should. Looking around the gathering, he couldn't imagine any of the single males doing a better job assisting her than him.

This wasn't his pack and it wasn't his place to step in as her partner, but that didn't stop him from hauling the next batch of bowls to the river and rinsing them with her.

"Are you not accustomed to seeing males naked?" he asked curiously after they'd waded into the water together.

"Oh, yes. I see them all the time," she answered cheerfully, as though he'd asked her if she'd ever clapped eyes on a full moon. Why then did she become bashful around him? Well, he was a stranger. Perhaps they didn't entertain many visitors in Wolf Hollow.

"You know you can trust me, *mi alma*?"

He forgot about the soaked jeans as water flowed past their ankles and their eyes locked. Lacy had bright blue eyes that considered him now with keen interest.

"You seem nice enough."

Nice enough? That was all?

He gaped at her. Before setting out to find a pureblooded mate, Diego had dallied with his fair share of she-wolves. Life on the go had made it easy to sow his wild oats without any kind of lingering obligations. The females before had fallen for his charms in swift succession.

Thoroughly intrigued, Diego vigorously rinsed the bowls he'd grabbed so he could set them out to dry while cleaning the rest until the next basket had been emptied of all its soiled vessels.

Lacy worked diligently. She might blush when he spoke, but his presence did nothing to deter her from her duties. Diego felt captivated by every little action the blonde performed.

When all the bowls were clean and stacked on the wood table in the glade, ready for the next morning's meal, Diego put his hands on his hips and grinned. "What next?"

"The cauldron could use a rinse." Lacy nodded at the large black bowl supported by three metal beams that were slanted like a tepee. It hung from a hooked chain.

Diego scratched the thick stubble covering his chin.

"Where did you find that thing?"

"Some of our elders came across it in a yard in the suburbs. They said it had logs in it, like it had been used as a fire pit, but we've always used it to cook up big batches of stew and porridge for all the unmated shifters."

"Hmm." Diego tapped the handle quickly, testing the heat. Although the fire beneath the pot had been smothered earlier, the solid steel structure looked like it could stay warm for hours afterward.

After testing that it was safe, he unhooked the cauldron and nearly dropped the damn thing as it plummeted to the ground. Diego's grip strained as he held tight.

"*Mierda*. Do you have to clean this thing after every meal?" It was like trying to lift a particularly large boulder.

198

When he looked at Lacy, he saw her cheeks dimpling and lips trembling as she fought back a laugh.

"Not after every meal."

Diego narrowed his eyes and grunted playfully. "Let me guess, you're honoring me with this difficult task because you noticed how strong I am."

Lacy shrugged and smiled. "You seem to be handling it okay. Shall we take it to the river, or would you like to hold on to it and talk a little longer?"

Oh, she was a cheeky one. A delighted smile entered Diego's face. Perhaps taking mercy on him, Lacy led the way to the river.

The dang pot seemed to want to pull Diego's arms from their sockets, but he didn't mind. After hauling the steel bowl to the river and thoroughly rinsing all food remnants from the bottom and sides, Diego hefted it back to the glade and hoisted it over the fire pit, attaching the handle to the iron hook. He stretched his arms to the ground afterward and groaned. "That thing should never be moved again."

Lacy laughed.

"Oh, you think that's funny, do you?"

"Yes," Lacy said, a shine in her eyes.

He took a step toward her then another. Lacy held her ground, laughing at him the whole while.

"I could still pick you up, you know?" Diego boasted.

"I'll take your word for it."

Diego hid his disappointment behind a chuckle when what he really wanted to do was lift her into his arms and hold her against his chest, then carry her off someplace private in the woods.

"Anything else I can help with?" he asked.

Lacy shook her head. "Some of the other shifters like to go for a run before sleep. Thanks for all your help." She turned on her heel and walked over to a female with light brown hair who Diego had seen playing a drum during the celebration night. The women linked arms and leaned their heads together before looking over their shoulders at Diego, turning back around and giggling.

His heart surged and chest puffed out. She was talking about him to her friend.

"*Mi hermano!*" Raphael belted out as he swaggered in from the woods, his pants unfastened at the top, tight enough to remain in place as he all but pranced forward. Raphy ran a hand through his hair, smiling smugly as he bumped his shoulder into his.

Diego chuckled. "You're in a good mood."

"You would be, too, if you were getting laid." Raphael tossed his head back and grinned.

Diego offered him a smug smile in return. "I'm not looking to get laid. I'm looking for love."

"Don't remind me." Raphael winced dramatically.

"Maybe one day you'll understand."

"Yeah? And maybe one day people will be driving around in automobiles again and flying in jet planes overhead. Oh, and watching pictures move on electronic screens."

"Dick," Diego said, rolling his eyes. The smile didn't leave his lips. Raphael wasn't the only one feeling pleased.

As much as he enjoyed their travels, it felt good to

be around other wolf shifters. Community was something Diego craved, almost as much as a mate.

Too bad Raphael would never agree to settle down in one place. The real question was, would Lacy be willing to leave her pack?

✦ chapter fifteen

THE SWIPE OF Zackary's tongue across her clit made Elsie's toes curl and sent waves of pleasure crashing through her core. They lay naked beneath their tree—their clothes tossed aside beside the baskets of berries, which they'd had the foresight to fill first so they wouldn't have to rush later.

Stretched on her back, Elsie alternated between closing her eyes and taking peeks of the cropped brown head between her legs.

When Zackary's tongue entered her, she squeezed her eyes closed and moaned. She felt his tongue retract and his hot breath tickled her thighs. Prying one eye open, she caught him staring at her in wonder, his lips parted slightly and eyes bright.

He looked as though he couldn't believe his mouth had the ability to give her so much gratification.

"More," Elsie said breathlessly.

Grinning, Zackary ducked down and lapped at her until she went over the edge.

After taking a moment to bask in the aftershocks of

pleasure, Elsie sat up and smiled. "I should let you win more often."

"Haven't I always won?" Zackary asked, chuckling huskily.

He drew her into his arms and kissed the back of her head as he wrapped his thick arms around her. Elsie leaned back against his toned chest and sighed happily.

"I never knew I could feel this way," she said.

"Me either." Zackary nuzzled his face against her bare shoulder.

They spent the remainder of the day naked. The burly shifter appeared to have gotten over his qualms about her nudity, especially when his body was pressed against hers.

For their part, Hudson and Chase remained oblivious to what happened each day after the trade. The following morning was the same as all the past ones. Hudson and Elsie walked straight over, Chase joined Hudson, Elsie flashed Zackary a smile, and the boys headed over to their territory without sparing them a second glance.

This morning, Zackary grinned so wide, Hudson did notice.

"What got you in such a good mood?" he asked, his eyebrows arched.

Zackary puffed out his chest. "I caught a nice juicy rabbit before breakfast. Got to eat meat rather than mush." He rubbed his belly for emphasis.

Hudson rolled his eyes. "Way to go, Zack," he said sarcastically. "The extra calories will come in handy for all the berry picking you have to do." He and Chase started away. They hadn't gone far enough for Hudson's next words to go unheard. "Me big male. Need meat."

Pressure detonated inside Elsie's head.

"Lavita sulumpa," she whispered harshly, without taking a second to consider the consequences.

Hudson's laughter broke off when he tripped and fell on his face.

"Nice going, dog," Chase said. "Looks like you're the one who could use the extra meat." He gave his friend a hand up, howling with laughter at his expense.

Hudson dusted himself off, growling something Elsie couldn't make out. She grinned with satisfaction as the males disappeared into the woods.

Zackary gaped at her wide-eyed.

She shrugged. "He was asking for it."

He stepped in front of her with a grave expression.

"Elsie, you can't use magic on packmates. If the council found out, they could banish you from Wolf Hollow."

"Okay," Elsie said with a shrug. It was a good rule to live by, and similar to the one at Balmar Heights. They didn't bandy around the threat of banishment, but casting spells on other coven members was against the rules. She lifted her chin. "I won't do magic on any of my packmates, even when they deserve it."

Zackary's stern frown wavered into a smile. He cleared his throat and attempted to look serious.

"I'm not one to lecture you, Elsie, especially after all the times I've lost my temper and acted without thinking first." He stepped away from her and hung his head. That action always made Elsie want to grasp his face and lift it back up.

All beings were flawed, and Zackary was particularly

hard on himself.

"No more magic," Elsie said. "Next time, I'll trip him with my foot." Zackary's head jerked. When his eyes met hers, Elsie laughed. "Or is that not allowed either?"

"If he ever insults you, I'll trip him myself . . . and by trip, I mean punch in the face."

Elsie's heart fluttered with excitement. She wasn't keen on violence among tribes, but Zackary's urge to protect her made a hum vibrate throughout her whole body.

"Hudson better not mess with me then."

"No, he better not."

They faced one another and locked eyes, smiles spreading high over their cheeks.

Elsie cleared her throat. "So, you caught a juicy rabbit this morning?"

Zackary grunted and shook his head. "No, just throwing those mutts off our scent."

"Good thing they aren't very observant." The entire pack underestimated Zackary. Elsie smiled, recalling the way Hudson had ate up Zackary's performance of playing the thickheaded male.

Zackary took Elsie's hand and walked with her to their tree. Beneath the canopy, he continued holding her hand and grinning wide. Elsie studied his face, but he was looking at the trunk . . . staring at it, actually. She followed his gaze to a heart carved into the bark. Elsie gasped. Inside the heart were the initials "E" and "Z." Releasing his hand, Elsie rushed up to the tree and stared at the carving up close. Her heart thumped happily inside her chest and, for some reason, tears welled inside her eyes.

She spun around.

"You're the sweetest male ever!" She sprinted the few steps back to him and launched herself into his arms.

Zackary caught her easily. When their lips met, they grasped at one another, tongues tangling while their faces tilted and mouths bore down on the others'.

Zackary pulled Elsie's dress over her head and slung it aside. His shorts were already unfastened, which made it even easier for her to yank down his legs. They lowered themselves to the ground, and Elsie climbed on top of her mountain of a male. She'd gotten in the habit of saying a protection spell on the way over, knowing how things were escalating between her and her soon-to-be mate. The barriers had crumbled to dust. Zackary offered no more protests when it came to mating. He groaned in pleasure as she rode him.

Elsie stole glances at the heart he'd carved for her, quickening her pace. Just when she thought Zackary would bellow and empty inside her, he lifted her off and switched their positions.

Elsie gasped when he slid back inside her and rubbed against her most sensitive spot.

Each pump of his hips brought stars rushing across Elsie's vision. Without meaning to, she let go. Zackary chased her release with his own.

After he'd emptied inside her, Zackary pulled her against him and covered her neck with fiery kisses.

"I can't believe this is really happening," he whispered.

Oh, it was happening all right and they were doing that again. But first, a nap snuggled against her male. This bold new side of Zackary was thrilling. She liked that he took what he wanted, and he wanted her.

They made time to fill their baskets and rinse off in the river before Hudson and Chase arrived. With the time they had left, they sat along the riverbank, holding hands as they watched the hypnotic flow of water over rocks.

"We need to tell the pack soon," Elsie said, watching a twig bob in the current.

"We should probably tell your brother first."

"You might want to claim me first. It might actually make it go easier." Elsie looked over and offered him a wry smile—one Zackary returned. He was behaving with a sturdy calm that set Elsie's heart at ease.

"I was thinking the same thing."

"You see? We were made for each other." Elsie grinned and pressed her shoulder against his.

When he turned to face her, Zackary's smile looked strained.

"Listen, Elsie. I want you to know that if you ever used your powers on a packmate and had to leave the hollow, I'd go with you. I'd do anything for you."

Elsie's stomach fluttered. "And I'd do anything for you, Zackary. But don't worry about having to leave Wolf Hollow. I'll try to behave myself, especially knowing I'll have my mate watching out for me."

"Tomorrow," he said, squeezing her hand. "I will claim you as my mate tomorrow."

Against all odds, she'd found her forever, and after tomorrow they'd be bound together for all time . . . with three days to spare.

ELSIE FELT HER whole face light up when she spotted Kallie in the glade. Her friend was already eating a bowl of stew on a log beside Wolfrik. Elsie skipped into line, bouncing in place as she waited her turn at the cauldron. Once dished up, she hurried over to Kallie and Wolfrik.

"I've missed you," Elsie cried out before she'd reached her friend.

Kallie made a face that was half grimace, half smile. "Sorry, I haven't been around much lately. I've had feathers to smooth."

"Feathers?" Elsie cocked her head to one side.

"Here, have my seat, Little Wolf." Wolfrik jumped to his feet and hurried away.

They watched Wolfrik down the remaining contents of his stew, shove his bowl into Carter's chest, and then barrel into the woods. He didn't take one of the trails connecting the glade to other areas of the hollow, but dove in between bushes, disappearing into the greenery.

Kallie snorted. "Integration is an ongoing process for my mate. Plus, he has trouble sitting still for long . . . kind of like you." Her eyebrows lifted as she smiled at Elsie.

"I can sit still, see." Elsie plopped onto the spot Wolfrik had vacated.

Kallie chuckled. "Oh, how I've missed you."

Elsie studied her friend. "What are these feathers you mentioned? Have you been stuck plucking feathered game?" Her stomach rumbled at the thought. The regular deer and rabbit meat was delicious, but Elsie loved the taste of fowl, too. Obviously, they weren't easily hunted in wolf form, but perhaps the den mates had devised a way of catching them in human form.

"Not those kinds of feathers," Kallie said with a sigh. "Even though Wolfrik is mated now, there are still shifters who want to keep him out of the den."

"What? That's ridiculous." Elsie's jaw hung open in outrage.

Kallie pursed her lips. "It's mostly Ford. I think he's still sore about Wolfrik taking his place on council. Palmer and Francine aren't helping matters, as can be expected. Even Heidi has suggested he wait until our pup is born."

"Heidi said that?" Elsie asked in disappointment. "I'll talk to her."

"It's okay; I'm working on it," Kallie said. "The situation is a bit complicated. Wolfrik prefers spending his time in the glade and its surrounding territories. Under different circumstances, I would have no problem settling somewhere near the glade, like Sasha and Tabor, but once our son is born, I want him to grow up around his young packmates."

Elsie grinned, perking up. "That's right. The soothsayer from Glenn Meadows predicted you would give birth to a son who would become a great leader. Have you thought of any names?" Elsie clapped her hands together in excitement. She couldn't wait to hold Kallie's baby in her arms and make him smile with games of peek-a-boo.

Kallie shrugged. "It's not original at all."

"You have to tell me."

"I was thinking Wolf."

"It's perfect!" Elsie squealed.

Kallie grinned. "You think so?"

"Definitely. It's part of his father's name and it's strong, just like our species." Elsie rocked over the log in her excitement.

Kallie laughed. "Well, I'm glad you like it."

"I love it. Wolfrik must too."

"He said it was fine by him, but he did smile pretty big."

Elsie bumped her shoulder against Kallie. "He loves it. He just doesn't know how to express himself. Not all males are good at verbal communication."

She had believed Zackary was one of those males when she first met him, but Elsie had underestimated her big wolf, just like everyone else. The more time they spent together, the more he opened up and shared his feelings with her. She recalled his comment about putting Hudson and Chase off their scent earlier that morning and nearly laughed. Her heart felt as though it were glowing inside her chest. This was a side of Zackary she felt sure no one had seen besides herself.

Kallie leaned closer and lowered her voice. "Speaking of communication. I actually came over tonight to find you and talk to you about Wolfrik's progress with the council. They were open to allowing Aden to claim a mate should he ever wish to, but Sasha said that lifting Zackary's punishment wasn't for the council to decide. She said that was up to Tabor." Kallie pressed her hands to her chest. "You know Tabor will never lift the ban."

Elsie sagged over the log. She hadn't taken one bite of stew. She doubted she'd get anything in her belly that night. All the elation she'd felt moments before faded like the sun.

"I love Zackary, and he loves me. That's not something I can walk away from."

Her friend frowned and studied her face for several beats. "What are you going to do?"

"Claim one another and then tell Tabor. If he banishes Zackary for loving me and saving me from the curse, then I'll leave with him. I'll stick by my mate."

Elsie felt certain Tabor wouldn't send Zackary away if it meant losing her, but she did worry that her brother would attempt to hurt him for going behind his back. Maybe she should talk to Tabor first, prepare him. Tell him all about the curse and Brutus. Perhaps she should wait until the day before her birthday when it would be too late for him to try and do anything about it other than give her and Zackary his blessings. Yes, that was the best approach. She and Zackary would claim one another in secret then wait a couple of days to announce their status as the pack's newest mated pair.

Warmth filled her cheeks when she smiled. Every time she thought of them being an official couple, joy radiated through her body. She loved the feeling of belonging with someone—of being two halves making up a whole. Or maybe they were two wholes becoming something bigger.

The bowl in Elsie's hands still felt warm. Lifting it to her lips, she tilted the ceramic vessel until a small amount of stew slid into her mouth and found she had an appetite after all.

Switching back to the subject of the den, Elsie asked, "Have you decided what kind of enclosure you want for your den?"

"Something small and sturdy," Kallie answered, "and not a treehouse." She stretched her injured foot.

Elsie rarely paid attention to the deep scars gouging Kallie from ankle to toes. Her mind lit up at the idea of residing above ground.

"I want to live in a treehouse!"

Kallie chuckled. "Why am I not surprised?"

Elsie tapped her lower lip, taking a closer look at Kallie's injured foot. "But I want you to be able to come over and visit whenever you want." She stopped tapping and looked up, grinning wide. "I know what I'll do. I'll just have to float you up to see me, and back down when you're ready to leave." Yep, Elsie had it all figured out. Hopefully the den mates would be welcoming of Zackary. He was strong, respectful, and helpful—well mannered, unlike Wolfrik, not that Elsie wanted the wild wolf to ever change. She liked Wolfrik the way he was, and so did his mate, which is what really mattered.

"What do you mean by float?" Kallie asked. Her eyebrows lifted. Despite asking, there was a knowing look on her face, most telling in the curve of her smile.

"I'd show you, but I think it might scare other packmates."

"Maybe wait then, until you've secured a mate and a treehouse."

Elsie grinned extra wide. Kallie was going to love floating—so were the pups in the den.

After finishing their supper, Kallie gave Elsie a warm pat on the shoulder then stood.

"I can take your bowl over," Elsie said.

"Thanks. I'm going to find that mate of mine." Hands free, Kallie limped to the edge of the glade, pulling her dress off when she reached the woods. Wise woman, shifting to track her mate down in wolf form. In another couple months, Kallie would be too far along in her pregnancy to shift to wolf form. Once that happened, Wolfrik better settle down and stick by her more often otherwise Elsie would be the one having words with him.

She smiled to herself before depositing their bowls in the dirty basket. Looking around the glade, her eyes landed on Zackary standing with his friends. He met her gaze instantly. Warmth flooded her chest. She smiled, her grin growing when Zackary smiled back. Wiley looked over and waved, so Elsie returned the greeting before spinning around and heading into the woods.

Even if she hadn't been cursed and running out of time, she still would have been ready to hurry up and make this claim. They didn't live in a world of waiting. Elsie wanted to start spending the remainder of her nights with Zackary as soon as possible. Even waiting for morning patrol felt too far away. She wouldn't be able to kiss him for nearly half a day. Granted, she would be asleep for most of that time, but still . . . torture.

Maybe Zackary could sneak away, follow her into the forest to give her one last kiss good night—one on the mouth and one lower. Elsie's cheeks flushed. She looked over her shoulder hoping to see her male stalking down the trail after her, but all was clear . . . that is until a crow landed on a nearby branch and cawed at her insistently.

Elsie had a visitor from her coven.

She lifted her head to the crow.

"Okay, then. Show me."

Black wings lifted the bird from the branch. The crow flew several trees away, waiting for Elsie's pursuit.

Lazarus had come, she felt certain. She was glad for it. He would be relieved by her news.

The crow took off toward the Sakhir River. When the current came into view, Elsie frowned. Her heart sank as William appeared on the other side of the river.

Before she could take another step, William floated a foot off the ground and drifted over the water, landing a couple feet in front of Elsie on solid ground.

"We need to talk about your father," he said grimly.

✦ chapter sixteen

"HAS SOMETHING HAPPENED to him?"

Elsie's legs nearly buckled in fear that something bad had befallen her father. Perhaps Brutus had come looking for her at Balmar Heights and hunted down Lazarus after discovering she was no longer on the mountain. Hugging her arms around her middle, Elsie's vision blurred so that she didn't notice William's scowl until she blinked several times.

"Lazarus is fine," he said in a clipped tone. "You never have to worry about the almighty wizard. He's untouchable."

"What does that mean?" Elsie demanded, dropping her arms roughly to her sides.

William lifted his nose high. "It means it's time for you to learn the truth about your father. Your mother was never in love with Lazarus. Wolf shifters have never wanted anything to do with wizards. But Lazarus had to have her so he placed an enchantment spell over her before raping her repeatedly."

His mouth moved, but what he said made no sense.

Elsie's mouth hung slack. William's hateful words felt like freezing rain pouring down on her out of nowhere. He'd stooped to an all-time low.

Nostrils flared, she glared at William for telling lies. His desperation had turned him deranged. Whatever ploy he was attempting to get her on his side wasn't going to work.

"Why are you saying this?" she demanded.

"I refuse to keep his secret any longer, not when it's affecting your judgment. The only reason I kept my mouth shut is because I didn't want to see you hurt, Elsie. But your father doesn't deserve your loyalty. You are sacrificing your freedom for him and his coven even though your very existence is a result of his treachery. My parents kept their mouths shut because they were afraid of Lazarus. He's a monster, Elsie. That's why you need to stick to my plan. Allow Brutus to claim you, then let me take care of the rest. We'll run far away where Lazarus can't find us. I'll protect you from him. I won't let him or anyone else come between us."

Fingers trembling, Elsie felt her stomach turn to stone. Even Brutus hadn't made her feel this sick sense of dread.

William took her silence as encouragement to continue.

"He did the same thing to your brother's mother. The enchantment he used on her was too strong. It made her obsessed with him. Once Lazarus succeeded in getting a child in her, he didn't want anything more to do with the crazy she-wolf. The next time around, he diluted the spell and succeeded quite nicely with your mother. She thought she loved him, without going insane in the process. She even moved in with him at Balmar Heights after becoming pregnant with you. Unfortunately, both versions of Lazarus's spells ended up making the she-wolves sick and killing them before their times." William's eyebrows slashed over his forehead in angry strikes.

Elsie shook her head. "My father wouldn't do that."

And yet he'd suggested she enchant a wolf shifter to claim her as a mate and save her from Brutus. Mind manipulation was considered taboo for good reason, not to be toyed with . . . ever. She'd taken her father's words as just that . . . words. Something to say for the sake of comfort.

She remembered getting acquainted with Tabor when she first joined his pack. Elsie had wanted to know everything about his life among the wolf shifters. She could still recall the sadness in his voice when he spoke of his mother's illness and death.

She dragged her nails down her cheeks.

"No." She shook her head. "He loved my mother. He wouldn't force himself on her."

"He didn't have to." William huffed as though Elsie was trying his patience with her stupidity. She glared at him.

Did he think he could show up uninvited, unannounced, unwanted, drop this steaming pile of shit on her then whisk her off to live happily ever after in a secluded community of their own? Oh, and murder Brutus while they were at it? No big deal.

"I need to talk to my father."

William folded his arms. "Why? So he can force you to love him too?"

"No one can force me to love them," Elsie gritted out,

hoping he'd take the point.

"Maybe not, but he can wipe your memory of this knowledge. You need to stay away from Lazarus. Claim Brutus, let me kill him, and then we'll get out of these godforsaken woods." William loosened his arms and started toward Elsie.

"Stay away from me," she cried, jumping back.

William's eyebrows slanted. "I'm not the enemy."

"I've found a mate in Wolf Hollow, William. Brutus can't have me, and neither can you. If you continue pursuing me, how are you any better than my father?"

William scowled. "This is different. I'm protecting you."

"I don't need your protection. I can protect myself, and so can my mate. After tomorrow, I will be a claimed woman. End of story. Go back to Balmar Heights, William. Or leave if you truly hate it there. But don't come back to the hollow, and don't come looking for me again."

Elsie took off running, tears streaming down her cheeks the moment her back was turned to William. She sprinted for the glade even though the communal area was the last place she felt like going. If William had the bad idea to chase after her, he'd find himself surrounded by a group of angry wolf shifters.

Sprinting over tree roots and rocks, Elsie didn't slow down until she had nearly reached the glade. She stopped and looked over her shoulder, getting her breathing under control so she could listen for movement in the trees. There were no signs or sounds indicating that William had come after her.

Sinking to the forest floor, Elsie squatted and cupped

her face in her hands. William's words blackened her mind like smoke.

"Raped repeatedly."

Bile rose up her throat. She vomited into the dirt. Tears joined her dinner, flowing down her cheeks.

William was only trying to manipulate her, she tried to reason. That thought was interrupted by a cruel inner voice reprimanding her for being so blind and naïve. What kind of wolf shifter would willingly leave her pack to live inside a villa on the mountain with a wizard?

Why hadn't he enchanted another she-wolf after her mother died? Perhaps because he'd had a doting daughter to keep him company. An innocent witch wolf who'd believed he could do no wrong.

Elsie pitched forward, catching her weight with her wrists before she could fall into her own sick. She heaved again.

Love had not brought her into this world. It had been sorcery. Deception. Rape.

More tears came flooding out.

There was a darkness inside her, and now she knew where it had come from. Recalling the spell she'd cast on Hudson to bring him to the ground earlier, a strangled sob burst from her lips. She was awful. Terrible. And she had everyone fooled. They thought she was kind. If only they realized. Elsie was more dangerous than Wolfrik could ever be. If the pack knew even a fraction of what she could do with her powers, they'd send her away.

Zackary thought he didn't deserve her, but she was the one who didn't deserve him. She'd pursued him relentlessly, practically given him no other option but to yield to her.

Her father would be proud, she thought bitterly.

Worst of all, there was no altering the course she'd set out on. She would still keep her secret and claim Zackary. But she swore to the moon and the stars above that she would spend the rest of her days loving her mate with her whole heart. His happiness was hers. She just needed to keep this one secret. Well, two secrets. She didn't want Zackary to know how she'd been conceived. And she never wanted Tabor to find out about his mother. Why cause him needless pain and rage?

The next time she was alone with her father, she'd ask him why he'd done it. She'd give him a chance to explain himself before she shut him out. If he didn't have an acceptable defense, she didn't know that she could ever look into his face again.

CURLED UP IN the fetal position in a patch of moss, Elsie didn't sleep much that night. Instead, she replayed past conversations with her father and how he'd responded when she asked about her mother. There had been nothing malevolent in his tone or gaze, only sadness for the forever mate he'd loved and lost. How could he do something so vile to a female he obviously cared for? She couldn't picture it. She didn't want to. Not ever.

Her mind switched to more recent conversations—encounters with Brutus when she'd run across him in the forest.

"What kind of brute would want to take a female who hated him?" she'd demanded.

"You should ask your father that question," Brutus had returned gruffly.

She had always blown off his responses, only half-listened before moving on to her next attack.

"What kind of animals would steal young children and use them as bargaining chips?"

Brutus had growled in outrage, loathing seeping into his eyes.

"The kind who had no other way to protect themselves against your father's dark sorcery. He'd already taken our home, our place of gathering. Your father snuck up the mountain after our clan had changed skin to hunt. My father was the first one back. He tried to defend our territory, but Lazarus struck him down with a bolt of lightning he conjured from the sky. Your father took our home. It's a good thing our females weren't around or he might have taken them too."

Elsie hugged her knees to her chest. Anger built inside her body, splintering in her chest. Seething thoughts turned toward William for telling her this awful secret. It was easier to hate the messenger than the man who had done these horrid deeds.

Anguish and revulsion warred inside her, but she couldn't hate her father. She owed him an opportunity to explain himself first.

But what could he possibly say to make it better?

Elsie had the feeling that, like death, there was no coming back from this revelation.

Blurry eyed, and so exhausted she could barely stand up straight, Elsie stumbled into the glade for breakfast the next morning. She sat on a stump and slouched, not sure she had enough energy to wait in line. She really didn't want to draw attention to herself either.

"Elsie, what's wrong?" Zackary asked in a low voice.

She looked up and met his eyes. His brown irises shone with concern. Before she could answer, Tabor stormed over with clenched fists.

"Leave my sister alone, Zack." Tabor's voice carried across the glade, causing heads to pop up and look over. Elsie winced, frustration sweeping through her belly that her brother had brought more attention to her.

"He was just asking if I was okay," she said moodily.

Tabor frowned. "Why? Is something the matter?"

"No. I couldn't sleep, and now I'm tired . . . and cranky. So leave me be." Elsie stared pointedly at her brother.

Tabor's frown deepened. He cleared his throat and turned his head to Zackary, narrowing his eyes. She could practically read his mind yelling at the other male to *"Go away!"*

With stiff movements, Zackary left her side, making his way to the line at the cauldron.

Elsie folded her arms and narrowed her gaze on her brother. "Why do you have to be such an ass to him?"

Mirroring her, Tabor folded his arms. "Because I've known that mongrel my entire life. Everyone knows he can't be trusted. Maybe he thinks he can fool you since you're new here and don't know any better. The only reason he's still around is because I allow it." Tabor narrowed his eyes. "I've seen how he looks at you. I'm not blind, Elsie."

Tears formed in her eyes. She squeezed her arms tighter to hold herself together, and keep her heart from falling out of her chest.

Relaxing his stance, Tabor sighed. "I know it may feel flattering to have the attention of a packmate. This is all still new to you, and I'm sure you have a romantic notion of claiming after seeing me happily mated, followed by Jordan and Raider, then Kallie and Wolfrik. And I know you just want to fit in and be friends with everyone, including befriending that mongrel who doesn't deserve your kindness."

She wished he'd stop talking.

The resentment Tabor harbored for Zackary might never go away. They would have to leave the hollow. She would never see her family or friends again.

"I'm asking you to stay away from him, Elsie. That's my only request."

Her head snapped up. "Request or demand?"

Tabor rubbed his lips together, studying her face.

"Maybe I'm going about this all wrong," he said slowly. Tabor pulled his arm free and opened his palm, face up, staring coolly at his fingertips. "Perhaps Zackary is the one I should be warning to stay away."

Elsie understood what Tabor meant. Her brother wouldn't be warning Zackary away from her so much as threatening him.

"I think you've made your wishes clear enough," she

said bitterly.

"I'm only looking out for you, Elsie. Our father would do the same."

She scowled. Their father was the reason for her dark mood this morning. Tabor had managed to draw the clouds in thicker.

If Tabor knew what she'd learned, he wouldn't speak to her so coldly. He should meet Brutus and William, maybe then he'd open up his damn eyes and see how well Zackary treated her. But, oh no, that didn't matter, not when Tabor had a grudge he was unwilling to let go of. Stubborn fool. He was ruining everything. What did her happiness matter?

She kicked a clump of loose soil and pinched her lips together.

Tabor straightened his back. "If you're tired, maybe you should sit out patrol. I'm sure Hudson would understand. I can speak to him."

"No," Elsie grit out. "I can handle patrol."

"Want me to get you something to eat?"

"No."

Tabor frowned and studied her face. Concerned he'd start speaking again, Elsie got off the stump and headed to the cauldron saying, "I can get it myself."

AFTER TRADING PLACES with Chase in the clearing, Elsie apologized for her brother's behavior at breakfast.

"He can be so thickheaded," she complained. Tabor

needed to stop treating her like a child and recognize her as his equal. He'd managed with Sasha. Why couldn't he see his little sister as a grown woman?

She paced beside their tree with the heart carved into the trunk.

"He's trying to look out for you." Zackary shrugged, keeping his distance from her.

Elsie stopped her pacing and narrowed her eyes. "I can look out for myself. Always have. Always will."

Zackary scrubbed his jaw, frowning the whole while. If Elsie weren't so annoyed at her brother, she'd probably be blinking away more tears. Things had been going so well between her and Zackary. They were supposed to claim one another today, but she no longer felt in the mood, all thanks to William's revelation. She got the feeling the boy wizard was out to sabotage her if she didn't succumb to his wishes. He was despicable. Again, she seethed at her brother's impaired perceptions. He said he wasn't blind, but he was wrong; he saw nothing. Knew nothing. Her world was caving in and all he did was order her around, same as Brutus and William.

No. That wasn't fair. How could her brother know? Zackary was right. In his own misconstrued way, Tabor was trying to protect her even if his actions meant her doom.

Zackary cleared his throat. His hand moved from his chin to the back of his neck.

"You said you didn't sleep well."

This time, the tears flowed freely. Zackary took three wide steps toward her before sweeping her into his arms and hugging her to his chest. He didn't ask her what was wrong. He simply held her to him, running a gentle hand through her hair.

Elsie pressed her face against his bare chest, inhaling his woodsy scent. They stood like that a long time, saying nothing. Time stretched on. The sun edged its way across the sky higher. Elsie's sniffles faded. Still, Zackary said nothing, providing comfort while respecting her privacy.

God, how she loved this shifter. He was there for her the way no one else had ever been. He knew what she needed without having to ask or be told. He was pleasure, comfort, and companionship all rolled into one big attractive man.

Inhaling him a final time before stepping out of his arms, Elsie looked over at their initials etched in the tree. She returned her attention to Zackary and blinked.

"I think my father may have done terrible things." She looked down and pulled at the hem of her dress.

Leaving a stretch of silence, Zackary lowered his voice when he asked, "Why do you say that?"

"How did he end up mating two different she-wolves? Did your parents ever tell you what happened with Tabor's mother?"

When Zackary didn't answer, Elsie looked up and found him frowning. She could see the questions swirling behind his eyes. He rubbed his neck.

"Everyone said she'd been bewitched, but that's only because she mated with a wizard, so they just sorta passed it off as that."

"Why else would a wolf shifter mate with a wizard?" Elsie asked, hoping Zackary could come up with an answer to let Lazarus off the hook.

"I was still in my mother's belly when it happened, so I'm just guessing here, but they must have been attracted to one another so they . . . you know?" Zackary attempted a smile. "Jager knows more, but I do remember hearing that Lucinda was crazy about your father."

Elsie's jaw locked. *Crazy* was the apt word. What had her father done to the poor she-wolf to make her lose her mind?

"What if he really did bewitch her?" Elsie found herself asking aloud.

Zackary furrowed his brows. "Why would he do that?"

"So he could breed with her," Elsie jabbed her toe against the earth.

Zackary shook his head. "Lucinda loved your father. That much I know."

"Maybe she didn't have a choice."

"You can't force someone to love you . . . can you?"

"We're not supposed to," Elsie said defensively. The etched heart in the tree blurred along the sides of her vision. "But maybe my father did," she whispered.

Zackary stood his ground rather than rush over to comfort her again. Perhaps his eyes had finally been opened to the danger she posed.

"What made you think of this now?" he asked.

She looked at the ground, searching for an explanation that didn't involve William or Brutus. When no answer appeared in the soil, she looked into Zackary's eyes as though he might help her.

"I was thinking about our claiming," she began slowly.

"And it got me to thinking about my mother. I never knew her so I only had my father's stories to go on. He said he'd been a guest of my mother's pack long ago after setting out on a quest to find shelter for his coven. My mother's pack lived along a lake and welcomed my father and his travel companions with food, drink, and shelter. He wondered if the wolf pack was still there on the lake, so one day he set out to see for himself. Not only was the pack still there, but he was introduced to my mother and it was love at first sight."

"That's a nice story," Zackary offered.

Elsie used to think it sounded so romantic—her father searching out the first wolf pack he'd ever known and finding his new forever mate in the process. Now she didn't know if any of it was true. Perhaps he'd gone back and hidden in the woods, waiting for the first female to wander off alone before casting his spell. She'd seen him creep through the forest before—admired his stillness and patience when they'd first traveled to Wolf Hollow to find Tabor. Without being a shifter, Lazarus still possessed the survival skills of a cunning predator. To think she'd been proud of his abilities. It churned her gut.

Elsie stared glassy eyed across the clearing, straight to the flowing river bordering the hollow.

"It's just strange that none of my mother's packmates ever tried to visit. I asked around and our elders all said the same thing. Abigail was the only wolf to ever come to Balmar Heights."

Zackary squeezed his bottom lip between his fingers then let go. "When a shifter joins another pack, they become their family. I'm not surprised your mother's old packmates didn't seek her out, especially on a mountain full of wizards."

Elsie shook her head. "That's the other thing. He took that mountain from bear shifters—forced them from their home. If he's capable of stealing a community for his coven, what else would he be willing to take? He lost his forever mate at a young age. They were never able to have children. Lazarus always said that kids were the best way to continue his legacy—to pass on his powers. He boasted about creating a superior species to thrive in this new world." She doubled over, feeling sick again. "I think he forced himself on Tabor's mother and on mine."

There was no sugarcoating the truth. Her mother never had the chance to fight back. He'd treated her worse than a dog forced to submit to her master.

Sobs wracked Elsie's body. She pitched forward, thinking she'd fall, but Zackary was there to catch her. When her legs gave out, he scooped her up and carried her across the clearing until reaching the riverbank where he set her gently down, taking a seat beside her. His fingers caressed the top of her hand in soothing strokes.

"Maybe it's not what you think. Either way, I'm sorry to see you hurting."

Elsie sniffed and laid her head against Zackary's shoulder. "Thank you for being so sweet."

Zackary grunted. "I know a thing or two about bad fathers."

"You're right. I'm sorry. I'm being all weepy, when you actually lost your father to madness. I can't imagine what it would feel like seeing your father that way—still alive, but no longer himself."

Zackary pulled his hand off hers, resting it on his knee. He stared at the river.

"He used to hit me."

Elsie's head jerked up. "What?"

"He smacked me around a lot, so seeing him rabid isn't so different . . ." Zackary shrugged. "He was mad all the time even before he went crazy."

Heat flashed through Elsie's body and her heart pounded.

"Your father hit you? That monster," she growled.

Zackary shrugged again. "He was bigger and stronger, though that had changed before the rabid wolf got him. I could have taken him if I really wanted to."

"No child should have to fight off their parent," Elsie cried, her heart breaking. She wanted to throw her arms around Zackary, but he might think she was coddling him. What he'd shared with her was big. Huge. She knew it had to be hard. Most males didn't want to admit any kind of weakness. She could imagine the only reason Zackary had shared was to make her feel better about her own monstrous father.

This male of hers was amazing. He would always put her well-being first, even at his own expense.

Zackary swallowed. "I only saw Lazarus once—the time he appeared in the glade to tell Tabor he was his father. But it was clear he cared deeply for you, both of you. When Tabor refused his invitation to Balmar Heights, he insisted the pack welcome you into the hollow. He asked

Tabor to teach you how to be a wolf. No matter what he has done in the past, I believe your father truly loves you."

Tears ran down Elsie's cheeks.

Even if that was true, was her father's love enough? If he'd bewitched her mother, could she ever forgive him?

Elsie crawled over to Zackary, settling between his legs. She leaned her back against him. His arms wrapped protectively around her and together they spent the remainder of the morning watching the river flow by.

"Zackary?"

"Yes?"

"Can you claim me tomorrow?"

Zackary cradled her in his arms. "I will claim you the moment you want, Elsie."

As risky as it was to wait another hour, let alone day, she had to hold off.

Tomorrow. They'd start fresh tomorrow. They'd bury the past and create a brighter future together.

She still had three days left. Elsie would save herself from every troublesome male in her life: Brutus, William, and her father. And if Tabor didn't want her to be happy, then maybe he didn't belong in her life either.

✦ chapter seventeen

HAVING MEMORIZED LACY'S routine, Diego entered the glade several hours before dinner when he knew she would be filling the cauldron with ingredients for the pack's stew. She stood with her back to him at the table, hacking meat into chunks with a large knife. Not wanting to startle her while she chopped, Diego waited until she'd set the knife down to call out a greeting.

"*Hola, mi amor.*"

Lacy turned and grinned. "*Buenas tardes,*" she returned.

Hearing her use the Spanish he'd taught her gave him a thrill even if it was only two words.

As Diego sauntered closer, the scrappy male on duty with Lacy emerged from the woods with a bucket of water. Diego stopped and frowned at him.

"I will assist Lacy with dinner," Diego informed him, lifting his chest. "Go do whatever it is you do when you're not helping." The male set the bucket down and gaped at him. "You understand English, *si*?" Diego lifted a brow.

"Um." The scrapper looked at Lacy, but she held her

tongue and stared at Diego as though he was in charge. His chest expanded even more.

"*Andale, andale,*" Diego said, shooing the male with his hands. "You are no longer needed."

The male frowned at Diego, standing his ground.

"It's okay, Carter. Diego wants to feel useful. You can go," Lacy said patiently.

Still glowering, the male took his sweet time walking away. Diego didn't care if he moved at a crawl so long as he left the glade. Once reaching the clearing's perimeter, the male stomped into the woods.

Lacy placed the hand that had been chopping meat onto her hip.

"Carter was in charge of fetching water for the stew. I assume you're going to take over that task now that you've sent him away."

"No problem," Diego answered. "Or I could cut up the meat."

"While I fetch the water? Nice try." Lacy laughed at him. Diego shrugged and smirked before striding over to the bucket of water and lifting it easily. The scrapper named Carter had barely filled it halfway. Weakling.

"This goes in the cauldron?" Diego asked.

Lacy nodded. "And we need about five more of those. Think you can handle it?"

"Easy." Diego lifted the bucket above his head as he walked to the cauldron. Reaching the steel bowl, he lowered the water and dumped it inside. "I'll be back," he said cheerfully as he headed in the direction of the river.

"I'll be here," Lacy returned.

On his return trip with the first full bucket of water, he dipped his fingers inside as he passed Lacy and flicked water at her.

"Diego," she chided, unable to hide a smile.

"*Si*, that's my name."

Lacy huffed. "You're unbearable."

Diego smiled wide as he filled the cauldron, then hurried back to the river so he could return to the blonde beauty in the glade.

Once the cauldron had enough water in it, Diego set to work lighting the kindling beneath the pot by rubbing two sticks together.

Looking over, Lacy laughed. "We have a bow drill you can use."

Diego batted the suggestion away with his arm. "Nah, I do this all the time. My brother and I don't carry supplies. We mastered the skill of fire-starting years ago—among other talents." He winked. "We've never needed any tools to get by," he boasted.

Lacy returned to the table, cutting onions next.

The gusto with which Diego had been rubbing the sticks lost its satisfaction once Lacy's back was turned. He did admire her backside, though. Light blonde hair hung from her ponytail over her slender back. He felt an urge to spin Lacy around and dance with her while serenading her with a love song his mother had sung to them when they were little.

As fire sparked from the stick Diego rubbed back and forth, he snuck looks at the blonde shifter to see if she was watching him at all. She wasn't. Disappointment engulfed his chest, but he successfully lit the prepared kindling. He could practically light a fire in his sleep. Not that Lacy seemed impressed.

Diego blew on the flames, feeding more twigs in until the logs burned with gusto. Swiping his hands back and forth, he got to his feet and strode over, running his eyes along Lacy's lovely backside.

"What can I do next?"

"All this needs to go into the cauldron." Lacy nodded at the chopped meat and vegetables on the table.

They worked together filling a pan, which Diego then took and emptied into the cauldron. It splashed into the water. He went back and forth until every last scrap of meat and vegetable had made it into the mixture warming above the fire.

Diego fetched another bucket of water and dumped it over the table, giving it a thorough rinse.

"Now what?" he asked, setting the bucket beneath the table.

"Now we wait for the stew to heat."

Diego grinned. "That's it?"

"Every now and then I give it a stir." Lacy walked up to the cauldron and turned the long wooden spoon several times before letting go.

Diego joined her, lifting onto his toes as he looked into the soupy mixture.

"How long before it needs to be stirred again?"

"Not for a while. The fire just got started, the water's still cold, and there's a lot in there to heat through."

"Okay," Diego said. "So now what?"

Lacy glanced around the empty glade. "I usually hang out and wait until it's time to give the stew another turn with the spoon."

"Hmm, I wonder how we can pass the time?" Diego tapped his lower lip three times with his pointer finger.

"You can tell me about your travels," Lacy said with a grin. "Heath and Alec made them sound quite exciting."

Diego pursed his lips. Usually he enjoyed recounting his adventures, but what he had in mind didn't involve talking. It did, however involve his lips and Lacy's—maybe a little tongue if she allowed it.

Gaze turning hooded, he stepped closer to Lacy. She didn't look away as he devoured her in his gaze, leaning forward, caressing her cheek before he kissed her. Soft lips pressed against his hungry mouth, igniting a fire that trailed from his tongue to his groin.

Diego deepened the kiss, tilting his head to get in closer. He gave up breathing as the delicious blonde went after his kisses like she wanted this as much as he did. Lacy wrapped her arms around his neck and pressed against him. If Diego could give up clothes and wear her for the rest of his days, he'd be one happy wolf shifter. He rubbed against her, showing her how hard she'd made him. Lacy squeezed him tighter as she sucked his mouth.

Dios mío.

He stroked her tongue while grinding against her. Lacy's fingers dug into his shoulders, causing blood to rush his pelvis. He slid his hands down her back slowly, caressing her through the thin cotton of her dress as he went. When he reached her ass, he cupped both her cheeks in his palms and pulled her against his groin. Lacy's feverish kisses continued. Diego warred with the urge to take it slow and the need to bury his cock inside her.

When his hands gripped the hem of her dress, Lacy grabbed his wrists in a surprisingly tight grip and broke off their kiss.

Taking in deep, gasping breaths, she shook her head.

"That's as far as I go. I'm holding out for my forever mate."

Diego's mouth gaped open. He had the biggest boner straining against his jeans, swollen lips, and the taste of Lacy lingering on his tongue.

"You've never mated another male before?" he asked in shock.

"I know it's uncommon," Lacy said.

"But–" Diego didn't know what else to say. He rubbed the back of his neck, staring at Lacy perplexed. "Not once? Not ever?"

Lacy shook her head, the end of her ponytail sweeping from side to side. She chewed on her lower lip, staring at him with flushed cheeks and puffy pink lips. Damn, she was cute and sensual–kinda a tease, too, but that only made her more desirable. Diego wanted to be the first male to bring her to climax and empty his seed inside her . . . the only male. His chest puffed up at the thought.

A crazy thought occurred to him. He zeroed in on her lips, sure it wasn't possible, but still curious to know.

"Had you ever kissed a male before?"

Lacy grinned and gave a slight shake of her head.

"You're kidding!" Diego exclaimed.

"No, I'm not. You are the first male I kissed. I . . . liked it." The pink flush in her cheeks turned deep red.

Diego ran a hand through his hair. She was an unexpected delicacy meant only for him. He had to have her, all of her. No one else could. They could keep their grubby paws off his beautiful blonde virgin tease. Realizing he'd begun pacing in front of Lacy, he stopped and chuckled to himself.

"Very well, *mi amor*. I was waiting to tell you this, but I might as well share. I've intended to claim you since the moment I saw you."

Lacy adjusted her ponytail, which had been knocked askew when they'd kissed, then looked at him head on. "If you want me, you will have to claim me *and* reside in Wolf Hollow."

One moment he was soaring, the next, plummeting from the edge of a cliff.

Diego's smile slipped off his face, avalanching to the ground below, along with all the plans he'd imagined for his future.

✦ chapter eighteen

ELSIE SLEPT EASIER after being comforted by Zackary all day.

She was ready to put the past behind her and begin a happy future with her wonderful forever mate in Wolf Hollow.

She was ready to break the curse.

Too excited to eat breakfast, Elsie sat on a log with Tabor and Sasha, tapping her foot relentlessly over the earth.

Tabor looked over and squinted. "What's up with you?"

Elsie stopped shaking her foot. "What do you mean?"

"You've been acting funny lately."

"Funny how?"

Sighing, Tabor looked to Sasha for help, but the pureblooded she-wolf continued eating her porridge without comment. When Tabor cleared his throat and raised his brows, Sasha set her bowl in her lap. "If Elsie has something she wants to share, she'll do so when she's ready."

Elsie flashed Tabor a triumphant smile. "You have such

a wise mate, Brother."

Tabor grunted. "Fine, but you know you can tell me anything."

"Uh-huh."

"I mean it."

"I know."

Tabor rubbed his jaw. "So, anything you want to discuss?"

"Not particularly."

When Tabor next turned to Sasha, she stood.

"I think I'll have a little more," she said, rubbing her flat belly. The motion caught Tabor's attention. He jumped to his feet, accompanying Sasha to the cauldron.

Elsie smirked. Sasha certainly knew how to make her mate heel.

Feeling guilty about tripping Hudson, Elsie offered him a bright smile when they met up at the edge of the glade.

"Good morning, Hudson. It looks like it's going to be another beautiful day."

Hudson nodded. "Hard to believe we're heading into fall next month."

"How do shifters keep warm in the winter?" Elsie asked curiously.

At Balmar Heights they were able to power the electric fireplaces with magic. The villas had fireplaces on both levels, in multiple rooms. Some were the old-fashioned wood-burning stoves. Elsie had always found it cozy. As far as Wolf Hollow went, she doubted cook fires provided enough warmth to shifters in skin.

"We single shifters spend the coldest months mostly in fur," Hudson said. "For families with kids too young to shift, they bundle up and spend lots of time inside their dwellings."

Elsie shuddered. "I'd go stir crazy."

Hudson chuckled. "Yeah. Mates take turns shifting and going for runs. The kids get pretty fed up, too, and end up coming out for playtime and exercise. They're pretty hardy to the climate, even in skin."

"Hmm," Elsie said, thinking. "It would be really nice to have a communal enclosure that was heated for the children in the winter. You know, a place where they could play games and stuff–get out of their huts and treehouses."

Hudson scratched his head. "Uh, yeah. That sounds great, but how would we heat it?"

"With a stove," Elsie suggested.

"Good point." Hudson laughed.

"Do you plan on ever claiming a mate?"

Hudson's laugh turned into a choking sound. "After Vallen took Rebecca from me, I didn't think I'd ever love again. I ended up asking Jordan, but I wasn't really in love with her; I just wanted to stop her from making a mistake."

"You don't think she should be with Raider?"

"They seem to be into one another so whatever," Hudson grumbled. "I mean, if she wants to give her former friends the cold shoulder, that's her decision."

"Love sorta sidetracks people. I'm sure she'll come back around in time," Elsie offered.

"Doubtful," Hudson answered moodily.

Elsie smiled. "Or you can make new friends, like Zadie

and Nudara."

Hudson perked up, his eyes glowing a little brighter. "Yeah, they're pretty cool." He elbowed Elsie playfully. "You are too. Can we be friends?"

Elsie placed her hands on her hips. "I thought that we already were."

Hudson chuckled. "I suppose so."

They walked side by side while the trail was wide enough then switched to single file where it narrowed. Elsie went first, picking her way through the brush toward the clearing.

"As your friend, I need to apologize for letting you get stuck with Zack," Hudson said to her back.

She whipped around and narrowed her eyes. "Hey! Zackary is my friend. There's more to him than meets the eye."

Hudson lifted his arms in a calming gesture. "Don't bite my head off. I'm glad he's being nice. If he wasn't, I'd have to set him straight."

Chase lay on his back, eyes closed, in the clearing. Walking closer, Elsie couldn't tell whether he was asleep or resting his eyes.

"What a lazy ass," Hudson joked.

Chase stuck his tongue out, eyes still shut.

Zackary stood in front of the bushes, filling a basket with berries. Eager to get his duties out of the way, Elsie thought with a wry smile.

Chase rolled over, stretched his arms above his head and yawned. When he'd finished, he smacked his lips. "Well, not much more of this before the new pairings. I like this new practice of trading. Great idea, Elsie."

"She's full of ideas," Hudson said with a teasing smile.

"Well, see you later," Chase said.

Elsie waved. As the males headed to the woods, Hudson paused beside the tree with the heart. Elsie's heart rate picked up, worrying he had noticed the initials and would turn back around asking questions. But when Chase gave Hudson a playful shove, the boys laughed and disappeared into the forest.

Arms swinging, Elsie joined Zackary in front of the bushes.

"Hey," he said, smiling at her.

"Hey," she said back.

"I thought we could get the berries picked first."

"Good idea."

Elsie took up the second basket and began filling it, her heart pattering. By the end of the day she would be a claimed female. She imagined herself holding hands with Zackary in the glade, sitting together to eat their morning and evening meals on a log with Justin and Wiley. Every night, they'd find someplace private to make love before drifting off into sweet slumber wrapped in one another's' arms. Her vision of partnered bliss fizzled when she thought of her brother. This could only happen if Tabor chose to forgive and forget past grievances once and for all.

If not, Elsie would start a new life with Zackary someplace else. Perhaps Raphael and Diego would allow them to join in their nomadic cross-continent run. They could become a wandering wolf pack. She wondered how the brothers felt about a half-witch, half-wolf shifter.

Elsie's fingers moved fast even as her mind drifted. She filled her basket soon after Zackary who waited to walk with her to their tree where they set down the berries.

Taking both her hands in his, Zackary stared into her eyes. "We don't have to do this today."

Elsie lifted her chin. "I'm ready. Are you?"

"Are you sure you want me as your mate? Once we break skin with the intention of claiming, we will be bound to one another."

Elsie rose on her tiptoes and planted a soft kiss on his lips before lowering herself back to the ground. "You're the only one for me."

Eyes brimming with love, Zackary bent down and grazed her neck with his teeth. A shiver of pleasure skidded across Elsie's skin. Her heart rate picked up as Zackary's hot breath caressed her lower neck. His bite started out gentle. As the pressure increased over her skin, a dull ache burned up her neck. Zackary bit down, breaking through her skin.

The sharp pain made Elsie whimper. She clamped her mouth shut while Zackary finished the mate claim. A sense of completion and belonging rushed through her. It was as though a well inside her chest had been filled and would never run dry.

Once releasing her neck, Zackary licked the wound on her neck clean of blood.

Elsie bit him next, sealing their claim with the blood on her tongue. It was done. She was safe. She was mated to her forever.

"You are mine now, Elsie," Zackary said, guiding her

to the ground.

She touched the tender skin where he'd bitten her while Zackary removed his shorts then straddled her beneath their tree. He pushed her dress up to her belly and entered her, joining with her in their first time as claimed mates.

"And you are mine, Zackary," Elsie said as her mate groaned his pleasure with each thrust of his hips.

He was thick and long, stretching her apart, filling her completely. Her big beautiful mate. She'd been claimed. She felt like stars should shoot across the sky. Maybe tonight when she could actually see them.

Desire built inside her. When she first woke up in the morning, she'd whispered her protection spell. She preferred not interrupting moments like these. Now that they were mated, perhaps she wouldn't be using the spell for long. She'd wait until Zackary was ready. He'd already taken a huge leap in claiming her.

Pulsing, in the throes of pleasure, Zackary ground his hips against hers and groaned, gritting his teeth, holding on. The next time he thrust, a male shouted, "Get the hell off her, you mongrel!"

Hudson and Chase appeared over Zackary's shoulders; their faces mottled red and the whites of their eyes blazing.

"No," Elsie cried as they yanked her mate back and threw him to the ground.

As though she had ceased to exist, Hudson and Chase came at Zackary from either side with their fists raised.

Zackary got to his feet with a snarl. His muscles corded.

Even though it was two against one, he could take Hudson and Chase on with his brute size and strength.

Yanking her dress down, Elsie sat up. "Guys, stop. It's not what you think. Zackary is my mate."

Ever so slowly, Hudson and Chase turned to face her with gaping mouths.

"Mate?" Chase asked in disbelief.

Hudson's eyes rounded as he zeroed in on the fresh bite wound on her neck. Elsie touched the tender spot tentatively with the tips of her fingers. Nodding, she pushed herself off the ground and dusted off her dress.

"We were going to tell everyone at supper tonight."

Hudson's neck corded. "Elsie, you can't go claiming someone you hardly know. And you," he said, pointing a shaky finger at Zackary, "you know damn well you're not allowed to claim a mate after what you did to Tabor. Is that what this is? Payback? Thought you could force yourself on his little sis?"

With a loud groan, Elsie stepped between Hudson and Zackary.

"That's not what happened," she snapped. "We fell in love. Why do you think we hid it? Because we knew packmates would react this way."

Hudson shook his head. "This can't be."

Zackary growled and Elsie put her hands on her hips. Chase rubbed absently at his arms, looking from one face to the next. He cleared his throat. "So, you're telling us you want to be Zack's mate?"

"I *am* Zackary's mate, and yes, I want him as my forever." Elsie lifted her chin.

"Tabor needs to know about this," Hudson said, still shaking his head. "He needs to know now." He gritted his teeth and took off in big sweeping steps for the woods.

Chase grimaced then jogged after his friend.

Jaw tight, Zackary glared in the direction the guys had gone.

Elsie forced a smile. "Well, Tabor had to find out today, anyway. Hudson really should have let me be the one to tell him, though. No matter. We can talk about it when he finds me."

Zackary put his head between his hands. "This won't end well."

"It has to. We're all family now," Elsie insisted.

She wondered how long it would take for Hudson to track Tabor down. She faced the forest, ready, waiting. With her focus so intent on the woods, she didn't see the figure creeping in behind her from the river.

A growl rose up Zackary's throat. He rushed past her. Elsie spun around, gasping when she saw William glaring at Zackary.

"Is this the animal you chose to claim?" he demanded.

It was as though a storm had rushed over the sky as her vision clouded.

"William, I told you never to come back here!"

Zackary's head jerked. "This is the boy?"

Nostrils flaring, William sneered at Zackary. "I'm no boy. I'm her *first*; her *forever*. And you're just the animal Elsie was forced to claim in order to avoid mating a much worse beast."

A frown dragged down each side of Zackary's chin.

"Elsie? What is he talking about?"

Words stuck in her throat, like she was choking on a large chunk of meat.

William looked Zackary up and down with a scathing jeer. "I take it you are oblivious to the curse placed over Elsie by her father. She's turning twenty in three days. If she didn't claim a shifter mate by then, she would have been forced to become a bear's mate. Lazarus owed the bear shifters for stealing their home. He promised them his firstborn daughter. At least she doesn't have to worry about Brutus any longer. You took care of that by claiming her in time."

Rather than snarl, Zackary turned to Elsie with a grim twist of his mouth. His eyes were unfocused and dark, unable to hold her gaze for long.

"Elsie, is this true?"

She opened her mouth to deny it, explain. William had it all wrong. But that phantom chunk of meat was still blocking her airways.

The one voice she was sick of hearing filled the clearing, as William explained how her father's first forever was barren and he never expected to have children. Then he explained about Lazarus seducing female wolf shifters and forcing them to mate with him. He offered no sensitivity on the subject, circling back around to the curse and how at least the "bastard wizard" had the foresight to word his binding promise carefully. He'd promised Elsie to a shifter. "Shifter," William repeated slowly, as though Zackary were daft. "Not a bear shifter specifically. So you served quite nicely as a replacement. Now that you know the truth, I'm sure you won't bind Elsie to you indefinitely. You did a good thing, sparing her from a terrible fate. For that, you have our gratitude."

Zackary's spine bowed like a bent over tree when he looked at her.

"This is why you wanted me," he said flatly. "To break some curse."

"No," Elsie said, her voice cracking on that one short word. Tears swarmed her vision.

"It makes sense." Zackary's head bobbed slowly. "How could anyone truly love a mongrel like me?"

With heavy footsteps, Zackary headed for the woods, not bothering to pick up his shorts as he passed them blindly.

"That's not true," Elsie cried after him.

William made a sound between a sigh and a huff. "We should get going, Elsie."

"You!" she snarled, fangs protruding from her gums. "You ruined everything. I hate you!"

William frowned. "You don't mean that."

Claws poked out from her fingertips. William's eyes widened.

"You better get out of here before my wolf breaks out and rips you apart." A growl erupted from Elsie's throat, causing William to take a step back.

"Elsie?" he asked uncertainly.

"Go!" she bellowed.

William turned and ran for the river. The angry wolf inside her wanted to chase after the meddlesome weakling, rip open his chest, and pull out his intestines.

But going after her mate was more important. First, Elsie made sure William cleared out of the hollow's territory. In his hurry to get away, he ran across the river, getting his pants soaked. Once he reached the other side, he kept running, fleeing into the woods on the other side.

Elsie's fangs and claws retracted. She sprinted after Zackary, afraid he'd already shifted and taken off on four legs. Dense trunks and foliage blocked out the sunlight when she entered the forest. She found Zackary hunched over beside a thick tree beyond the edge of the clearing. His back was turned to her, his shoulders shaking. At the sound of her footsteps, he went still.

"Zackary," she said softly, her heart twisting inside her chest.

"You needed a male wolf shifter to break your curse," he said in a hollow voice. "Someone dumb enough to be fooled into a quick claiming."

"No," Elsie cried.

"Was I even your first choice? Or was I just the most convenient?"

Elsie rushed over, but Zackary kept turning away from her. She grabbed his arm and opened her mouth to tell him she loved him. The words shriveled inside her throat when she saw the tears streaming down his cheeks.

Elsie's heart split open, torn violently apart. Seeing her mate in such anguish shredded her soul. She had caused this. She'd hurt the male she loved most in the world.

Elsie released his arm and sobbed. "No. That's not what happened."

Zackary turned his head away, unable to look at her.

"I can't . . ." His teary voice was cut off by a soul shattering sob. He took off, arms swiping aside brush in his hurry to get away from her.

Elsie didn't pursue him this time. She could barely breathe or stand. She collapsed on the ground, a sob-scream rising from her lips. The forlorn sound made her cry harder. She wrapped her arms around her middle, rocking and crying her heart out.

That's how her brother found her. He and Sasha ran up to her the moment they caught sight of her on the ground. Sasha dropped down and put an arm around her. Tabor's neck corded and lightning-like flashes streaked through his eyes. The rage awakened his powers.

"I am going to kill Zackary," he said in a chillingly calm voice.

Before Elsie could scream at him to stop, he was gone, just gone. Had he figured out teleportation on his own?

Sasha froze and blinked several times while tears flooded down Elsie's cheeks.

A firm arm squeezed against her.

"Did Zackary hurt you?" Sasha demanded.

Shaking her head, Elsie erupted into a fresh rush of tears.

"No! I hurt him," she sobbed.

 chapter nineteen

THE WORLD HAD ended. Not the world before. Not the old one Zackary's father used to rant about.

"Asshole politicians" and "stupid fucking people" who had "destroyed the planet and brought disease upon the whole of humanity."

"Morons deserved to die out," Vallen used to say.

Despite the turbulent relationship he had with his father, Zackary figured he was better off in this new world. At least Vallen had brought him into a strong community of wolf shifters. Their pack was the only family Zackary had ever known. Wolf Hollow was the place where he had grown up and made friends . . . the place where he thought he'd met his mate.

He was a fool. He should have trusted his instincts from the start. Only the most desperate female would allow him to claim her. And Elsie . . . His mind clouded on her name. Elsie had been in a race against time to claim a wolf shifter—any wolf shifter—before a bear claimed her.

He remembered her singling him out, calling to him to join her swimming in the pond, trying to get a kiss out of him after she'd first arrived. The moment she'd returned from Balmar Heights, she'd sought him out straightaway—because she had a curse to stop.

What had she truly seen when she looked at Zack? A dupe? A mindless mongrel easily manipulated?

He yanked a branch off a tree and snapped the wood in half, throwing the pieces roughly onto the ground.

Had she recognized the hopeless romantic in him—the one who had opened his heart to her and made himself vulnerable as he'd never done before?

Zackary doubled over, tears spilling from his eyes. Damn it!

He was pathetic. All weepy over a woman. What a sissy he'd turned out to be. He didn't need Vallen around to tell him how stupid he was for letting himself get duped into believing a female as beautiful and clever as Elsie had really chosen him above all others to be her mate—that she loved him so much she couldn't wait to be claimed.

She'd broken his heart permanently. It was all too much for his wrecked emotions to handle.

Zackary fell to his knees in the dirt. He wanted to keep falling—for the ground to swallow him up and bury him without a trace. Let the rest of his pack search for him and trample him in the process. He wouldn't be missed. Only Justin and Wiley would care, but they'd move on. No one mentioned Rebecca or David any longer. How soon until they stopped talking about Jolene and Patrick? Jolene's two closest friends were no longer sniffling in the glade at every meal. Hell, they were smiling again. That was just the nature of life. Live or die, everyone moved on.

Would Elsie miss him . . . even a little? She'd seemed so genuine in her affections. How did someone fake that? Had she faked everything?

Zackary breathed in the earthy loam below him. He dug his fingers into the soil. If the ground would swallow him up, maybe he could bury his broken heart.

As his fingers closed around loose soil the ground seemed to shake beneath him, as though the weight of his emotions might cause an earthquake. Leaves rustled from branches overhead. An unnatural breeze swirled through the forest.

"Zackary!" Tabor bellowed, murder in his voice. A cold wind blew over Zackary's hunched back.

"Let him come," he thought bitterly before shifting into wolf form.

His body contracted, becoming more agile and lean. Sight and scent heightened. Energy filled his limbs. He could hear Tabor's two-legged approach.

Zackary streaked through the woods. It wasn't fear that drove him, but heartache. If he moved fast enough, perhaps he could outrun his emotions. All he knew was he couldn't stand still.

Large paws landed on the earth, pushing away to lift him over the forest floor. He made his way to one of the hollow's trails, which was easier to speed along. Front paws. Back paws. Lifting and landing. The path was clear. Packmates used it to travel to and from patrol, which kept them dispersed throughout the woods, fields, bluff, knoll, falls, and pond.

Zackary wasn't headed in any particular direction—just

running as hard as he could.

A rumbling growl behind him announced the raging pursuit of Tabor's wolf. He'd caught up fast.

Zackary shot forward. Tabor was lighter, leaner, and faster. He sprang into the air, landing on Zackary's lower back. His hind legs bowed from the abrupt weight. Zackary spun around and snarled. Saliva dripped from Tabor's fangs. They circled one another growling. Tabor lunged at him, but only snapped air with his teeth when Zackary sprang away.

When Tabor next charged, he managed to knock Zackary over and wasted no time biting at his underbelly. Zackary kicked at Tabor with all four upended legs, nails clawing at the other wolf's neck. Teeth sunk into Zackary's hind flank. He snarled and snapped viciously, rolling over onto his side and dislodging Tabor in the process. The moment Zackary was on all fours, he lunged at his attacker.

At least in wolf form, Tabor couldn't use sorcery on him. They were evenly matched. Zackary didn't want to harm a packmate, but he wouldn't allow him to injure his wolf.

They leapt at one another, quickly becoming a manic flurry of biting fangs and vicious snarls that rang out across the forest. Tabor sank his teeth into Zackary's neck and bit clean through fur and flesh. Zackary reared back, Tabor coming at him. He grabbed hold of the wolf's leg and bit down hard. Tabor howled and yanked free then jumped at him, swiping his claws at Zackary's snout. It was hard to hear anything over their thunderous snarling. Zackary thought he caught the sound of screaming, but it spurred the two wolves on rather than inspiring them to cease fighting.

"Tabor. Zackary. Stop!" His wolf's ears heard the sound of Elsie's screams, but he couldn't stop. She tried to get to them, arms jerking at her sides as though she thought she could pull them physically apart.

Tabor snapped down on Zackary's neck below his jaw and shook. A jolt of piercing pain went through Zackary. He cried out.

"Tabor, no!" Elsie screamed.

Zackary clawed at Tabor until he released him but as soon as they were separated, they lunged at one another again. Tabor's intent was clear—this was a battle to the death.

Elsie backed away and raised her hands to her cheeks. Sasha arrived, jogging up to Elsie. The scent of human fear was strong in the air.

"Tabor, stop it!" Sasha yelled.

The wizard wolf listened to his mate as much as his sister—which was not at all. He lunged at Zackary with his razor-sharp fangs already coated in blood.

In the next instant there was a third wolf—female—jumping into the fray, snarling up a storm. Sasha had shifted and joined them. Tabor immediately pulled back before he could accidently harm his mate in the brawl.

Sasha growled low in her throat, a warning not to resume their fight.

"You both need to shift right now," she communicated.

Tabor snarled in Zackary's direction. *"Not a chance,"* his bared fangs said.

Zackary wasn't going to shift before Tabor, leaving himself exposed. No chance in hell.

"Go lick your balls, half-breed," Zackary returned.

Tabor's lips lifted over his gums right before he lunged. Zackary pounced, ready to cleanse his mouth of Elsie's blood from the mate bond and replace it with Tabor's after he got the mutt on his back. He wasn't about to be made a fool twice in one day. Losing to the half-breed was out of the question, especially since Elsie had shifted and was now barking at them. He'd show her what a strong, capable male he was. No wolf would take him down.

Sasha yipped, but this time it was a bone-chilling snarl that caught everyone's attention. It erupted from the bushes. Zackary and Tabor stopped and lifted their heads, a momentary pause, before Vallen leapt onto the trail, the fur along the ridge of his back sticking up razor sharp. His growls were ceaseless.

Horror crashed through Zackary. His female was here in wolf form, as was a pregnant packmate.

All four of them snarled back at the rabid wolf. They held their places, lips drawn up, growling. Zackary's attention was now fully focused on Vallen. He was an intruder, a danger to his pack. Vallen needed to be killed, but Zackary had to watch out for the mad wolf's lethal bite.

When Vallen lunged at Tabor, Zackary dove around and went for the crazed wolf's hind leg, only to end up biting the brute's tail. Forgetting Tabor, Vallen roared and turned around, glaring at Zackary. He opened his jaws, going for Zackary's neck, only missing by a couple inches.

Zackary's heart raced. His ears drew back flat against his head.

He came at Vallen, turning sideways at the last second and throwing his weight into the other wolf. The rabid beast was knocked aside but kept his footing. Zackary moved to face him, standing tall and alert while Vallen crouched low near the ground, snarling. The old wolf's tongue lolled from his mouth as foam dripped from his jaw. All of his wiry hairs stood on end like prickly pine needles.

Vallen charged Zackary head on, his jaw open wide as he came at him.

Angry, vicious teeth sank into his neck. Time stuttered to a stop as he was sucked away to another time.

Drumbeats and firelight danced through the trees as a young Zackary snuck in from the den to spy on the adults' full moon ceremony. Justin and Wiley were supposed to accompany him, but they'd chickened out at the last minute.

The music and merriment drew Zackary in closer. He wondered what he'd see. He had half a mind not to share any information with his friends for tucking tail. Then again, he imagined the fun he could have taunting them with everything they'd missed.

He could hear laughter and loud, slurred speech. He was almost near enough to peek in through the bushes when a large figure stepped out of the shadows blocking him.

Zackary's breath stalled. Why was it that the last person he wanted to run into was the one who had to discover him sneaking in? Did Sky Mother hate him that much? She wasn't around to ask. Darkness cloaked the forest but not the sneer on his father's face.

"What are you doing here, boy?"

Vallen didn't bother making a fist. The back of his hand across Zackary's face was enough to upend him. He hurtled backward, landing roughly on the ground. Vallen lifted him by the neck and pushed him down again.

"Stop it," Zackary said.

"What are you going to do about it?" Vallen slurred in a mocking tone.

When Zackary tried to get to his feet, Vallen tackled him. Angry tears sprang from Zackary's eyes.

"I think you should crawl back to the den like the baby you are." Vallen's cruel words were spoken an inch from his ear.

Zackary kicked his dad, but the brute didn't even flinch, just picked him up by the neck again and squeezed. Pinched.

Broke skin.

Pain lanced through his neck where Vallen had bitten him.

Throughout his childhood, Zackary's father had taken away his sense of self-worth, now the bastard had stolen his soul in one final bite.

Fuck that!

Before he succumbed to madness, or was put down by the pack, Zackary would make sure Vallen never hurt another wolf again.

With nothing left to lose, Zackary flipped around and lashed out at the rabid, beastly animal, slashing at Vallen with his claws. Blood filled Zackary's nails as he raked them down Vallen's hind flanks. The rabid wolf snarled his fury. He snapped his jaws near Zackary's face, but Zack dashed to Vallen's other side and bit the side of his neck. Vallen shook him off and tried to get the upper hand, but Zackary darted around him, snapping at the mongrel's hind legs. He charged Vallen from the side, knocking the other wolf over. Vallen's legs flailed, attempting to find purchase, but Zackary was there locking onto his neck, shaking side to side. The blood filling his mouth fueled his frenzy. Jaw clamped as tight as a metal trap, Zackary shook his head, yanking Vallen's throat viciously until it ripped open and blood flowed freely, leaking from his jaw to the ground.

With one final triumphant jerk, Zackary released Vallen.

There were no cries from the rabid brute, not even a final snarl of goodbye.

✴ chapter twenty

MAYBE ELSIE SHOULD have remained in wolf form. She was the first to shift, prepared to knock everyone out to save them all from the rabid wolf.

But she was too late. Still crouched naked on the ground, her heart gave out as she watched Vallen bite Zackary.

"No," a soft voice croaked inside her head.

It was as though her mind had gone hoarse along with her throat from all of the earlier screaming.

"No," she thought again and again. *"No. No. No. No. No."*

"Elsie? Are you okay?" Sasha's voice made her body jerk.

She turned to find Sasha and Tabor staring at her. Zackary was the only one who hadn't shifted. He would never shift again.

"No. He's okay. He killed Vallen. He hasn't run off."

The madness had yet to claim him.

"Was he bitten?" Tabor demanded.

"No." The lie caught in Elsie's throat before she could utter a sound.

"He must have been, but I'm not certain," Sasha said, frowning at Elsie.

Zackary remained in wolf form, blinking at the wolf he'd just killed. He behaved as though he wasn't aware of his packmates' presence. His wolf stood still, panting and staring at the ground in a daze.

"They were fighting too close. Vallen had to have gotten his teeth in him at some point. Everyone stand back." Tabor stretched his arms from side to side as though to create a human barrier.

"No!" Elsie yelped, finding her voice. She darted in front of Tabor, serving as the new barrier between wolf and humans. "He'll be okay. We can fix him," she pleaded.

Tabor grimaced. "Elsie—" he started.

"No! Don't hurt my mate. I can reverse this. I'll find a way."

"Elsie, I'm sorry. He's as good as gone." Tabor sounded firm this time. Resolute. "You might not want to watch."

She went still—not with fear, but with determination. Magic sizzled along Elsie's veins and flared inside her chest. It had a heart of its own that pumped with mystical electricity.

Things would not end this way. She wouldn't stand by while her brother killed her mate. It wasn't fair. It wasn't right.

She'd find a way to save him. What better use for her powers than for the sake of true love?

"Hold on, Zackary," she thought as her voice rose above the forest.

"Ferus matangi. Ferus vonku. Na veigacagaca alle.

Khob formella cov lus no."

She shouted the spell so that no one could interrupt. She swept her arms above her head then ran to catch Sasha before the pregnant female fell unconscious to the ground. Tabor fell over like dead weight. She only had time to help one of them, and Sasha took precedence.

The forest, which had been filled with such grizzly sounds moments before, went silent in the wake of Elsie's incantation. There wasn't so much as a peep from the birds' overhead. At least none fell out of the tree. Maybe the snarls had already scared them off.

After gently easing Sasha to the ground, Elsie surveyed the scene. Everyone had been knocked unconscious, including Zackary's wolf, who had fallen onto his belly, front legs flanking his muzzle on the ground as though he was snoozing.

A sob broke through Elsie's lips as she rushed over and dropped down beside him. She covered his body with hers, hugging him, reassuring herself that he was still warm and breathing, his soft fur against her naked body. She eased up, stroking the beautiful wolf's head. Her fingers trailed along his furry back.

"I love you, Zackary. I love you so much. Don't leave me, my love. Not like this. Not ever."

The side of her neck where he'd bitten her throbbed from their recent claiming. Elsie held two fingers to the love bite, her other hand resting on her beloved wolf mate.

Tears burst out of her. She cried harder and harder until a torrent of agony soaked her face in anguished sorrow.

Howls echoed from too close.

"Go away. I want to be alone," Elsie thought. Her jaw tightened.

Four wolves ran in and circled the fallen group. Elsie was not able to place who they were. As the fur on their ears began to recede, Elsie said her spell again, knocking them out before they had a chance to shift.

She needed more time.

"There has to be a way," she whispered. "There must. I'll do anything. Make any bargain . . . any sacrifice. Just give me back my mate."

Was this the kind of desperation Lazarus had experienced when he made that long-ago bargain with her future?

If given the option, would she be willing to promise her firstborn child in exchange for her mate's life?

"Yes," she thought.

Without her mate there would be no child. Without him, there was no life worth living. These thoughts were pointless, anyway. It was an entirely different situation. But William was right about one thing . . . Lazarus was a powerful wizard. More importantly, he wasn't afraid to cross lines.

Her father owed her. If he ever wanted her forgiveness, then he would cure her mate.

Zackary had saved her from Brutus then he'd sacrificed himself to protect them all. He could have run away. Instead, he'd killed his father ensuring the mad wolf didn't destroy any more lives.

Vallen did not get to take Zackary away from her.

But what if it was truly too late? What if her mate's mind was lost forever?

"No," Elsie said. That two-letter word played on endless repeat inside her head.

If Lazarus could make a shifter lose her mind, then he should be able to do the opposite and make a mad wolf shifter sane again. Right?

She fell over Zackary, her shoulders shaking as she sobbed.

"That stupid curse makes no difference. If I could be with anyone in the world, it's you. You had my heart from the very beginning."

Her tears rained down on Zackary, wetting his fur.

"Elsie, what has happened?"

At first, she thought she'd imagined her father's voice.

Wet faced and sagging, Elsie turned her head until she spotted Lazarus standing beside Tabor's fallen form. Their father's gaze locked on hers and his frown deepened.

"What are you doing here?" Elsie asked.

"William took off. I assumed he was headed your way to cause trouble. The neighbors saw him sneak into my villa while I was with Shannon then leave soon after. I figured he'd taken an article of your clothing for a location spell and beaten me to the hollow." Lazarus rubbed his chin, taking in the scene. "What is going on here?"

Elsie's fingers curled in Zackary's hair one last time before she stood up. She covered her breasts with her long brown hair and locked eyes with Lazarus.

"Did you enchant my mother? Did you make her love you and breed with you?" Her voice came out cold and calm, the opposite of how she felt.

Lazarus scowled. "How could you ask such a thing? Has Jager been feeding you this nonsense?"

"William told me."

Lazarus made a snarling sound as though he too was part wolf shifter.

"That blockhead speaks without knowledge. When he returns to Balmar Heights, I'll place a tracking spell over him so that he won't be able to go anywhere without me knowing. William will never bother you again."

I narrowed my eyes.

"Answer the question, Lazarus. Answer it honestly."

"I am your father." He sighed and shook his head. "I loved your mother with my whole being. Abigail and I had an instant connection, but our love was considered taboo. Shifters have a misplaced sense of exclusivity within their species—especially wolves. Years of programming confused Abigail into thinking on behalf of her pack rather than her feelings and what she wanted. I just helped her choose what she really wanted—me."

Elsie narrowed her eyes. He could tell her anything and she'd have no way of knowing if it was the truth. What she needed was a truth spell, but that required candles—something the hollow didn't have.

Do you really want to know the truth?

It would be so much easier to believe what he'd told her.

"What about Tabor's mother?"

"I came across her in the woods during a solo trek I made shortly after losing my first forever mate, Lillian. I gave poor Lucinda quite the fright. I may have used a spell to keep her from shifting, but only so I could explain I meant her no harm."

Elsie's stomach soured. She pursed her lips.

"You're saying she went from being afraid of you to madly in love?"

Lazarus's head turned and lowered. He looked at Tabor, who had landed face first on the ground.

"Lucinda and I loved one another very much. Unfortunately, she became too unstable to bring back to Balmar Heights."

"What did you do to her? Why didn't you fix her?" Cold, dark trenches dug their way through Elsie's stomach. If Lazarus hadn't been able to help Lucinda, how would he help Zackary?

"I cannot alter another being's personality," Lazarus answered sharply. "Lucinda wasn't altogether sane from the start. She'd stepped away from her home territory. I found out she was prone to wandering alone. I didn't realize how deep her personal issues ran when we met."

"So you thought, hey, here's a convenient female all by herself—what a great opportunity to breed?"

Lazarus scowled. "That's not how it happened. We talked. It was nice. We agreed to meet up again. We got to know one another first."

"You just said you were unaware of her mental instability. Now you're telling me you met up multiple times for a friendly rendezvous in the forest."

Streaks of light crackled inside Lazarus's irises.

"I don't appreciate this line of questioning, Elsie. Everything I've done has been for our coven's safety and continued survival. I loved Lucinda and Abigail. That's what's important. That's what you need to remember. And I love you. The moment you entered this world, you were the pride and joy of my life."

"You loved me so much you promised me to a bear shifter." Elsie scoffed.

"That was before I ever dreamed I'd have a son and daughter of my own—as you well know."

"Do I? Maybe that story about the captured children was just that—a story."

Bolts of yellow light crossed over her father's pupils. "I would never make up something so horrible," he thundered. "Those missing kids were my responsibility. It didn't matter who the parents were—I am this coven's leader. The safety of our people is my responsibility, a responsibility I take more seriously than my own life. We all feared for Noah and Layla. Your questioning my commitment to our community hurts me more than you realize. I was willing to do anything to save them. I agreed to the bear shifters' terrible terms even knowing what it might cost me in the future. Your mother, may she run forever free, knew the risk, but she also knew that if we should be lucky enough to have a daughter that you would be able to choose a mate from your wolf side and avoid the curse. My last promise to her before she died was to ensure you didn't end up with Brutus or any other bear or shifter you did not want to be with. Now why don't you tell me what's really going on here? Why are your brother and his mate unconscious? And—is that a dead wolf? What happened?"

Elsie felt the tears running down her cheeks in twin streams. The finality of her father's words brought her back to the present and the tragedy she didn't have the strength to face.

"The dead wolf was rabid. He bit my mate. I think Tabor was going to kill Zackary. I had to stop him."

Lazarus looked past Elsie to the motionless wolf. "You were successful then? He claimed you? The curse is broken?"

"What does it matter?" Elsie asked angrily. Her vision blurred. Couldn't her father see that she was dying inside?

"You saw the rabid wolf bite your mate?" Lazarus asked slowly.

"Yes. Tell me there's a way to stop the madness."

Lazarus frowned. "You know I would if I could."

He might as well have shoved her off the highest mountain to jagged rocks below or thrown her down the deepest, darkest well.

"No. There has to be a way," Elsie insisted, stiffening. She lifted her head to the sky ready to call upon any deities that might reside in the heavens.

"You love him?" Lazarus studied her with intense green eyes.

"More than life itself," Elsie answered.

Her father lifted his chin considering her for many labored heartbeats. His fingers twitched at his sides. Elsie recognized that look of possibility. Right now, it captured her breath in her lungs. If he had a way to save Zackary she would breathe again, but not until he reassured her.

"There might be a way to recover your mate."

"Anything," Elsie exclaimed, gripping her hands.

Lazarus sighed. "You should listen to what it entails before you get too eager."

"As long as I get my mate back with his full mental capabilities, then I don't care how you do it."

Lazarus smiled sardonically. "Are you certain? A moment ago you didn't sound keen on me using spells on wolf shifters."

Elsie growled. "This is different."

Lazarus raised his eyebrows and shot Elsie a pointed stare before revealing his idea for rescuing Zackary from madness.

"We can force a shift," he stated. When Elsie gaped at him, he continued. "His human form wasn't bitten and will be safe from rabies."

Elsie's eyes expanded. Why hadn't she thought of that? It was brilliant! It felt unnatural to smile when she had felt minutes before that she would never do so again. Hope lifted her chest.

"Yes," she said, happy to move away from all her previous no's. "Of course, yes." She'd done something similar for Emerson when the shifter had become violently ill and begun to waste away in human form. Emerson had been too weak to change into her wolf form, which would cure her from her malady and allow her to fully recover before switching back.

Lazarus held up a hand. "It's not as simple as it sounds."

"Sure it is. I can make him shift right now." Elsie turned to face Zackary. She'd get him back in human form and convince him of her love . . . with words, not spells.

"Elsie, wait." She glared over her shoulder. She was done waiting. She wanted her mate back.

Lazarus clasped his hands together. "Once he's switched, he can never change back into wolf form."

That statement hit her like a thunderclap.

"What?" Elsie rasped.

Nodding solemnly, Lazarus cast a pitying look at the unconscious wolf on the ground.

"Once bitten, he's infected. In the olden days there were vaccines for this kind of thing. Now . . ." Lazarus heaved a sigh. "His wolf is infected, so if he were to shift back into animal form he'd become what he was before: rabid."

"But he wasn't rabid when I knocked him out." Elsie waved a slender arm feebly in Zackary's direction.

"Not yet," Lazarus said. "But the virus is in his wolf's blood. It's only a matter of time"

Lying so still and quiet, Zackary's wolf looked harmless. He could have been taking a snooze before getting to all fours to stretch and wag his tail at her.

She understood what her father was saying, but it still didn't compute. Once they forced Zackary to shift into human form, there was no going back to four legs.

Her head fuzzed over. Never able to change back. What kind of shifter would that make him? Without his wolf, he would simply be human.

What kind of life would he live, unable to shift, to run, to hunt, to howl?

But if she didn't force the shift, he would be lost forever.

"This is my only option," she said absently.

"I'll do it." Lazarus took a step forward. "You can blame it on me."

Their eyes met. Her father had always been her ally. He'd never once uttered a harsh word to her. Love was all she'd ever known from Lazarus. Love and support. He'd never held her back. Age had not diminished his powers or stature. He stood tall and unapologetic. Patient green eyes set above a proud, lean nose watched her, waiting for her decision. Was this really the face of a monster?

"He's my mate; I will take care of him," Elsie said.

She stood over Zackary and pressed her palms over her heart.

"Please forgive me," Elsie thought before voicing the spell.

"Du lupus a du mansklig magnus. Ra le lanna formella."

Zackary's wolf quivered at her toes. A faint whine seeped through his lips. This was followed by a sharp snarl. It was as though he was fighting the shift. With Emerson, Elsie only had to say the spell once, and it had worked instantly.

She repeated her words firmly, pulling her hands off her chest and opening her palms, inviting the natural world to use her body as a conductor to intensify the magic.

The wolf below her jerked, and Elsie was about to say the spell a third time when she noticed the fur finally receding into his body and his shape reverting to human. Zackary hovered over the earth on his hands and knees, belly to the ground in the same position his wolf had last laid.

Relief, guilt, and sorrow slammed Elsie back a step. Stumbling, she nearly collapsed to the ground. She took a quick look over her shoulder only to find that sometime during the spell, her father had disappeared.

She'd wanted to be alone with her mate. Now that he crouched over the ground, heaving in raspy breaths, her throat tightened and her heart bled. What could she possibly say to make him feel better? He would hate her for what she'd done.

✦ chapter twenty-one

THE SMALL FIRE in front of Jager's hut gave off little heat. Zackary avoided its light, sticking to the shadows. He stood among the trees, as still and solid as oak.

The council sat on stumps in a circle that included Tabor. The wizard shifter rubbed his elbow, all his earlier anger drained from his face. Now he looked into the fire with dull eyes. Elsie sat on a stump outside the circle, head bent, and hands folded in her lap. She wore her long white dress, the one she'd first appeared in, but instead of the sweet angel Zackary had first seen, he knew her for what she really was—a scheming temptress looking out for her own interests.

He was less than a mutt now. He could only ever be human—that or completely mad. Maybe the council would vote to banish him from Wolf Hollow before the night was out. What place did he have among shapeshifters?

Jager smacked his hands together, calling attention for the meeting to begin. "The good news is: Vallen is dead and burned. Jolene's and Patrick's lives have been avenged, as have Toby's, Roger's, and Rebecca's—may they run forever free. Vallen will never take another pack member from us again."

Zackary held back a bitter huff. His father already had. He'd given him that final, fateful bite. Vallen was the one he despised, but the old bastard wasn't around to direct his anger at. However unfair, Elsie was more convenient. That, and she'd betrayed his trust, his heart, his soul. She'd destroyed all of him. A shadow had fallen over him that no amount of daylight could ever chase away. If Zackary wasn't so broken, he might have felt vulnerable, stuck on two legs. Right now, he didn't care what happened to him. The pack could allow him to remain or send him away. It didn't matter. He had no place there. No place anywhere else. No more purpose.

Being unable to shift meant he couldn't be put on duty—right when he was beginning to be accepted back into the fold.

Life could be a real bitch.

Jager cleared his throat. "Now onto a more serious matter." The old man took a long pause to look at each face in the circle. Beyond that, Zackary and Elsie might as well be absent. This was a trial of sorts, one they weren't to interrupt.

Recently, it had been announced that Sasha was head of council, but she'd turned tonight's proceedings over to the pack's elder.

"I feel it is only fair that I step down as head given my relationship with Elsie," she'd explained.

"Today magic was used against seven pack members." Creases formed around Jager's mouth when he frowned.

The council members shifted uncomfortably on their stumps.

In addition to knocking out Zackary, Tabor, and Sasha, Elsie had gone and done the same thing to Hudson, Chase, Emerson, and Alec when they'd run over to see what was going on.

He avoided looking at the female in question. It was hard to feel sympathy for her, even seeing her under scrutiny. She still had her powers, her ability to shift, and she'd succeeded in breaking her curse.

"Tabor was going to kill you; I had to stop him," she'd told him. *"I couldn't lose you to madness."* Her tears had fallen on deaf ears.

Zackary was stuck in this big, blundering, dimwitted human form for the remainder of his life. The only time he'd ever felt at peace with himself had been in fur and . . . with her. He clenched his jaw, turning his anger inward at his own weakness—still wanting her despite her betrayal. If he wasn't worthy of her before, he definitely wasn't now. That, and how could he trust her ever again?

"Elsie used her powers without permission or regard to pack rules. She struck down seven of our packmates, and she forced a shift." Jager's voice turned stern. A cold, determined gaze entered his eyes—one that even his proximity to the fire could not thaw. "I recommend immediate banishment."

Zackary forced his expression to remain firm and to hold still, even though it felt like someone had punched him in the chest. Moisture stirred behind his absent gaze, but his eyes remained dry.

"She didn't mean to," Tabor said. "Zackary had been bitten, and I was about to take care of him before he had a chance to turn on us. Elsie wanted to stop me. She never meant to use her powers on anyone else."

"That's not what I heard from the other wolves," Jager said stiffly.

Tabor's eyes darted from the elder to his sister. He was the only shifter who had spoken up on Elsie's behalf. Even now, Zackary was incapable of protecting his mate.

Mate. Bitter laughter filled his head. Her neck bore the marks of his teeth from their claiming earlier. The happiest day of his life had turned into the most wretched.

"I have tried to be open and understanding," Jager announced. "When Tabor used his powers against the vulhena, it was to protect his pack. Elsie used her unnatural gift against the shifters of Wolf Hollow. We also know now that she tricked one of our packmates into claiming her to avoid her commitment to a bear shifter."

Tabor sprang off his stump. "That was our father's doing, not hers," he blasted.

"It matters not who made the arrangement," Jager said impatiently. "A bargain was struck between the two clans decades ago. Lazarus cheated the bears yet again, and his daughter was his accomplice."

Elsie made a choking sound.

"Tabor, I know you feel responsible for your half-sister, but you have your own young to think about. Community is built on trust. We sent Sidney away when she acted out against the pack—Sidney, who was born and raised among us—who was one of us." Palmer's head bobbed in agreement. He was the only other elder left, and he'd allowed the council to send his youngest daughter away. Elsie didn't stand a chance. Confirming this, Jager continued, "Elsie is new to our pack, and already she has betrayed our trust on a colossal scale."

Scowling at Jager, Tabor turned to his mate.

"Sasha, say something," he demanded desperately.

The pureblooded female sat up straight and offered Tabor a sad smile. "It is for the council to decide."

"You are the council."

"Part of it. Yes."

"And what is your opinion on the matter?" Tabor asked impatiently.

"I don't think it is wise for me to speak until everyone else has had a chance. My relationship with Elsie and the affection I feel for her shouldn't affect the outcome."

"Screw that!" Tabor bellowed. "This is my sister we're talking about. It doesn't matter that she used magic. She would never hurt a member of this pack. She *didn't* hurt anyone. If she hadn't stepped in, at least one more life would have been lost today." Tabor's piercing green eyes found Zackary in the shadows. The wizard's lips curled. "Well, aren't you going to speak up on behalf of your *mate*?" he asked bitterly.

Zackary clamped his mouth shut and folded his arms over his chest.

"Once a coward, always a coward," Tabor huffed. For once, the slur had no impact on Zackary. He was too numb to care.

"Tabor!" Sasha admonished.

278

"What?" he demanded, whirling on her. "He had no problem biting her, claiming her, mating her," he made a hissing noise, "but now that her future in the pack is up for debate, he stands there like a useless stump while Jager tries to throw my little sister out on her ass."

"We are still discussing the matter," Jager spoke up.

Tabor sneered at him. "You've already made your verdict, old man. The rest of the council will follow your lead unless someone speaks up."

"I know Elsie meant no harm," Heidi from the den said. "Give us time to talk it over, Tay."

"Maybe she should be stripped of her powers, so to speak," Wolfrik suggested, looking Elsie over with consideration. "Give Elsie the chance to choose whether she wants to be a witch or a wolf."

Tabor scoffed. "That's not something we can choose."

Wolfrik kept his eyes locked on Elsie. "You screwed up, Little Wolf."

Elsie gave a slight nod. Her lips remained pressed together. Zackary kept expecting her to justify her actions, explain herself to the council as she'd tried with him. But it was as though she didn't care what the council decided. Like she'd given up. They both had.

Emerson sucked in a breath and lifted her chest. "Elsie, I know I owe my life to you," Palmer's head jerked up. Zackary's eyebrows drew together, wondering what Emerson was talking about. The blonde shifter swallowed. "But I don't appreciate being knocked unconscious. I'm not saying that I'm voting you out; I'm just speaking my truth. Whatever you did took away my ability to defend

279

myself or even retreat. I didn't like it one bit." For such a beautiful female, Emerson's frown was fierce.

"That's it; I've heard enough," Palmer said, getting to his feet. "The witch shifter is out. She's a danger to our pack."

"We haven't voted yet," Sasha said.

"Sit your ass down, Palmer," Wolfrik said gruffly.

Palmer glowered at the pureblooded male.

"You don't run this council, son."

"Son? I don't think so." Wolfrik chuckled darkly then ran a finger along his bottom teeth like he was considering biting into the elder den member.

Brows lifted, Palmer turned to Jager. "She knocked out seven shifters at once. Seven! She tricked Zackary and forced him to shift. It might have saved him, but she still used her unnatural abilities to take control. Who knows what else she's done?" He cast a questioning stare at Emerson before jerking his attention back to Jager. "And who knows when she'll use her power next?"

"This is outrageous!" Tabor cried. "As though Zackary needed tricking." Tabor huffed in disgust. "He took advantage of the situation. He didn't even bother waiting to get the council's permission to claim a mate, which he clearly knew he wasn't allowed to do. Stop making him the victim." Tabor whipped around and took two shaky steps toward him. "Moon above you're pathetic letting my sister take all the blame."

Zackary narrowed his eyes. His fingers twitched with the old urge to punch Tabor's lights out. Past feelings of disdain prickled over his skin like thorny branches being dragged against his bare arms.

Elsie stood up slowly. "I will go back to Balmar Heights," she said softly to the council in their circle around the fire.

The anger drained right out of Zackary at the sound of her sad voice. It drove another fissure through his heart.

Tabor's mouth hung open as he whirled around. "Elsie, no. You don't have to. You didn't do anything wrong. You were just trying to protect us. No one got hurt."

Elsie's eyes shone when she looked at Tabor. It was the same teary gaze that had bore into Zackary's after she'd forced his shift.

"I betrayed the pack's trust," she said with soft, sad resolution.

Zackary's stomach threatened to bottom out. *No*, he told himself. *Don't be an idiot. Didn't you learn your lesson the first time? Don't you dare pity her. She used you. Never forget that.*

How could he? The only female he'd ever truly loved had ripped out his heart. It felt worse than all the beatings his father had ever given him.

"You are justified in voting me out of Wolf Hollow," Elsie said. "I am not sorry for what I did, and I would do it again." He wasn't ready to look at her, but the tragic pull of her emotions drew him in. "I could not live in a world without you. Even if we aren't together, you will always be in my heart. I will always love you." Elsie took in a shuddering breath and looked away, addressing the council. "I never wanted to hurt anyone. I waited so many years to finally meet my brother. At least I got that much." Her voice broke. Elsie quickly cleared it. "I am so sorry for the hurt I've caused." Her gaze went to Zackary then shifted down to her feet. "You welcomed me into your community. I wish I had been worthy of a place here."

"Elsie . . ." Tabor's voice cracked, and tears glistened in his eyes. He turned away from the group, giving them his back while he tried to collect himself.

When Zackary's eyes misted, he clenched his jaw. He'd already cried today, he wouldn't do it in front of a damn audience.

An awkward silence followed in which the council members took sudden interest in the soil around their toes. Heidi wiped at the skin beneath her eyes. Sasha looked at her mate with a trembling lip. Zackary had never seen the pureblooded female this close to crying. This day was getting shittier by the second. It was all too much. He wanted to get away from them all and be left the fuck alone for a while.

The pained silence was broken by Emerson.

"Um, guys, where did Elsie go?"

Heads shot up and mouths fell open as they stared at the spot where Elsie had once stood. She had simply vanished. Seeing her gone turned the hurt in Zackary's heart to panic.

Everything that had happened to him that day still felt too fresh, too raw. He'd lost too much, and now he'd lost the one person who mattered more to him than life itself.

Where had his voice gone?

Elsie wasn't his enemy. Words were. Expressions. Emotions. Zackary had struggled his entire life to communicate. He'd all but given up. Who cared about articulation in a post-apocalyptic world?

Elsie had sacrificed her place in the hollow to save him. She'd said she couldn't live in a world without him. But that wasn't enough for Zackary. He couldn't live without her period.

✦✦ chapter twenty-two

THE RUSH OF the Sakhir River at her back flowed with the force of her tears. Elsie was leaving Wolf Hollow for good. Her home. Her family. Her beloved. A sob burst through her lips. She bit her tongue.

Stop it!

She couldn't fall apart so close to the hollow. She'd only just crossed the river. Her teleporting skills only extended about fifteen paces. After that, she'd masked her scent with magic—no sense holding back now—and picked her way carefully through the woods between Jager's hut and the Sakhir.

At least she had a home to go back to. Bitterness soured her tongue and coated the back of her throat. She couldn't imagine sharing a villa with her father again. Maybe Charlotte's family would take her in.

Elsie pitched forward, tears erupting from her eyes.

She didn't want to live with Charlotte's family or in Balmar Heights—she wanted to be in Wolf Hollow with her mate.

Her anguish carried through the trees as she made

her way north on foot. Shifting to wolf form would be too easy. She deserved to walk the whole way back and wallow in despair. She welcomed the pain with open arms. How could she ever forget Zackary's face at the council meeting? He could barely look at her. Even Wolfrik and Emerson despised her powers. She was a witch. If they didn't like magic, they didn't like her. She'd never had a place in Wolf Hollow—shifters and wizards were simply not meant to mix.

A freak of nature, that's what she was. Her father's sick little experiment.

A fresh stream of tears gushed down her cheeks. They dripped over the top of her dress, wetting the white silky fabric.

She was in no hurry to reach the mountain. Once again, she'd be a lone wolf. Solo moonlit runs would resume. There would be no answering call when she howled.

She was selfish to think such thoughts when her mate could never shift again, but that didn't stop her aching heart from mourning the loss of her entire pack. She hadn't even gotten to say goodbye to Kallie. She hated that her friend, or anyone else in the pack, would think ill of her. She'd truly wanted to fit in. To belong.

Keeping her ears open for the sound of her name on Zackary's lips, Elsie peered over her shoulder frequently, hoping her mate would come after her. Why she insisted on this delusion was beyond her. The hurt she'd seen in his eyes would haunt her for the rest of her days.

She wanted to remember the good moments they'd

had together, however fleeting, but all she could think about was this cursed day from the moment William showed up to Zackary shaking with tears then the horrifying sounds of him fighting his father.

The forest animals offered no comfort. A squirrel raced across her path and skittered up a tree chattering and tugging her inner wolf who tried to convince her she needed a snack.

Elsie placed one foot in front of the other, somehow making her way through the woods without collapsing into a blubbering heap.

No one came after her. She was entirely alone and it was terrible.

With dusk came gut-stabbing hunger. Elsie gave in to her stomach, pulling off her dress to shift and hunt down dinner. After feasting on rabbit, she remained in fur the rest of the night, her senses alert to potential dangers. No matter how much her heart ached, her survival instincts refused to be ignored.

It was the longest and loneliness night of her life.

When morning light filtered through the trees, Elsie pounced on an unfortunate squirrel looking for a place to bury his acorn. After eating the rodent—and the acorn—she shifted and pulled her dress over her head, resuming her trek across streams, through meadows and dense woods, each step taking her closer to Balmar Heights.

It was a good thing she'd run around Balmar Heights barefoot all her life and toughened the bottom of her soles. She'd been called an odd child growing up, but her coven had still accepted and loved her. Lazarus had said she refused to wear shoes the moment he tried to put her first small pair on. He'd chuckled with delight at the memory, claiming it must have been her animal side rebelling against footwear.

Elsie walked over the rough, rocky terrain without any trouble. If only she could harden her heart as easily.

Did Zackary miss her as much as she missed him? Did he miss her at all?

She understood that he felt betrayed, but she had told him she loved him again and again. Had he lost all faith in her? Would he ever search her out? Should she bother holding out hope?

He'd looked so closed off at the council meeting. Remembering the vacant look in his eyes brought the tears back.

"Ugh, I hate being sad," Elsie groaned aloud.

She altered her course midday to avoid the caves where Brutus dwelled. The bear shifter had made his den uncomfortably close to the mountain on which sat Balmar Heights. His brothers had chosen to venture farther off. They certainly weren't pack animals.

Elsie picked her way over a rocky path that followed a trickling stream before leveling out into a plateau. The open space felt freeing, even if it left her temporarily exposed. There was no fear in her, only a deep unsettling emptiness and too many jumbled thoughts.

The path Elsie walked was one of her own making. She chose areas she could navigate easiest on foot. It was silly to continue on foot, but she still wasn't ready for that final climb up to Balmar Heights.

Passing blackberry bushes brought another onslaught of tears to her eyes. Would Zackary resume berry picking without her? How could he let her walk away? Well, okay, maybe she hadn't given anyone the chance to stop her after her disappearing act. Should she have been the one to dig her heels in and try harder to remain in Wolf Hollow with her mate?

The proceedings hadn't exactly felt like they were going in her favor. Better to make things easier on everyone and leave on her own.

A single tear slipped down Elsie's cheek. She rubbed it with her fist, smearing her cheek in dampness.

Stepping closer to the bushes laden with dark purple fruit, Elsie pulled a berry free and closed her eyes. When she opened her mouth, she imagined it was Zackary setting the blackberry on her tongue. It could have been the sweetest berry in the forest, but without him it had no flavor.

She swallowed the pulpy juice and seeds past the lump in her throat.

The bushes seemed to make up a natural wall that went on and on, curving then straightening for long stretches before curving again. Rabbits that had been out sunning themselves scrambled beneath the brambles when they heard her coming. They continued to dart out of sight around every bend. When she rounded the corner, the fur ball twenty paces off was bigger than bunnies . . . massive. Huge. Brutus.

Of all the rotten luck. She really was cursed. Her annoyance at running across the bear shifter supplanted any fear. Why today of all days? Why now?

She held still, watching him munch berries straight off the bushes. He was too busy stuffing his face to notice her. She took a tentative step backward, followed by another and another until she had cleared the bend and gotten out of sight.

Elsie scarcely breathed as she listened for the sound of a large animal charging for her. When none came, she grinned to herself.

Phew! That was a close one.

She turned slowly, as though the big, bad bear was still in sight, before taking tentative steps over the trampled wild grass. Backtracking her way toward the plateau, Elsie hadn't quite cleared the blackberry bushes when she rounded a bend and came upon Brutus again—only this time he was in his human form . . . naked.

Elsie gave a squeak of surprise.

His hands were on his hips, chin jutted up as though he'd been waiting impatiently for her arrival.

"What are you doing here? There are still two more days left." Brutus turned up his nose.

Elsie gave a sardonic laugh. "How romantic."

God, what a caveman. No, he was worse. A caveman would have worn a loincloth—the wild dark brown thatch of hair above his cock didn't count, nor did his hairy chest and legs work as a substitute for clothes. Elsie wrinkled her nose. Brutus looked like Sasquatch in human form. If he had a more pleasant personality, she would have given him credit for the muscles sculpted beneath all the hair, but the brute repulsed her with his barbaric behavior.

"Guess you figured there was no sense waiting any longer," Brutus said, ignoring her sarcasm. He scratched his beard. "As long as you're here, you might as well make yourself useful by cleaning the bones out of my cave. I like to eat in." Brutus flashed her a cruel smile through the bristle lining his lips.

Elsie's upper lip curled. "I don't think so. Clean your own damn cave. Or sleep in your own filth for all I care."

"That's no way to speak to your mate." Brutus glowered at her.

A smile lifted Elsie's cheeks. "Actually, I already have a mate, so I'm gonna go ahead and pass on the whole cavewoman lifestyle, as charming as it sounds." She probably shouldn't have smirked at a mammoth-sized bear shifter, but she couldn't seem to help herself. After the shit-ass day she'd had, it felt too good to toss out some sass.

Brutus stormed over and grabbed Elsie's arm in one meaty palm while shoving her hair off her shoulder with the other. His jaw tightened as he took in the bite mark on her neck.

"What's this? You've been claimed?" he roared.

"By one of my own kind—a wolf shifter," Elsie informed him as she tried to yank free of his grasp.

Brutus's grip tightened. "That's not allowed."

"My father made a promise for me to mate a shifter— not a bear shifter specifically—and that's what I've done."

Brutus's next roar rang in Elsie's ears. Her eyes squeezed closed as she winced.

"That son of a whore! That backstabbing weasel of

a wizard!" Brutus raged, shaking Elsie in his anger. "He took my home, and now he took away the mate I was promised."

"He didn't take me away . . . I chose someone else," Elsie corrected him.

It didn't matter what she said. Brutus had gone into a blind rage. He jerked his head in fury, wild-eyed, breathing hard, and digging his fingers into her skin. There would be bruises on her arm the next day, if not sooner.

"You're hurting me!" Elsie yelled. This she followed with a spell in case breaking the cursed match with Brutus had also freed her ability to use magic against him. *"Formella lavita!"* It should have sent Brutus flying off her, but he remained where he was with his crushing hands. Using her powers on him had been a long shot when he still had the symbols carved into his arm, but it had been worth a try.

A vicious chuckle rumbled past Brutus's thick lips. "You can cheat me, Little Wolf, but you can't hurt me."

Elsie was air born in seconds, tossed roughly over Brutus's broad shoulder. Blood rushed to her head as she dangled precariously close to Brutus's toned butt cheeks.

"What are you doing?" she screamed.

Brutus started walking toward the plateau. "You were promised to me. I don't care if you suckered some wolf shifter into claiming you. You are mine, Elsie, and you will obey me."

Elsie burst into laughter—laughter that was cut short when Brutus spanked her across the ass.

"Did you just fucking spank me?" she bellowed. She

wasn't looking for an answer. Elsie kicked out with her legs and scratched at Brutus's lower back with her nails.

"Stop squirming unless you want me to spank you again . . . or maybe you like it." Brutus chuckled.

"You bastard bear!" That did it. Elsie stopped struggling and calmed her breath, but only so she could shift. The blunt nails that had been scratching at Brutus turned into claws that punctured his skin, drawing blood.

"Oh fuck," Brutus muttered when he realized what she was doing. He threw her to the ground with such force Elsie smacked her head against a thick tree root. She wasn't sure if she was wolf or witch when she began to lose consciousness . . . or some monstrous combination of both.

SHE REOPENED HER eyes to darkness—darkness and firelight flickering around cave walls. Elsie coughed and blinked through the smoke. A campfire in a cave wasn't the smartest placement, but Brutus wasn't very bright. At least she could see the cave's opening from here.

Looking around the sandy floor, Elsie saw that Brutus hadn't been joking about the bones. The place was littered with cartilage and skeletons of small animals.

She screwed up her face in disgust.

Her arm ached where Brutus had manhandled her, and the back of her head throbbed. When she tried to rub it, both hands moved.

What now?

Eyes adjusting to the dim light, Elsie found that her wrists were bound tightly in rope. Not only that, her dress had been removed and replaced with a fur bikini top and skin loincloth. Elsie's nostrils flared in outrage.

"What the hell is this?"

"These are the clothes I will allow you to wear, woman."

Elsie's head jerked in the direction of Brutus's voice. He sat against the cave's wall, nearly blending in with the rocks, looking her over with smug satisfaction.

"You put your hands on me after knocking me unconscious?" Elsie demanded. She glared at him through the smoky darkness.

"I only changed your clothes, and you knocked yourself out after attempting to attack me." Brutus sneered. "I have no desire to touch you, Little Witch. At least now you are tolerable to look at."

Elsie growled as she scrambled to stand, careful that she didn't hit her head again on the rocky ceiling. She needn't have bothered. Brutus's cave was large, like the beast that inhabited it. Her lip curled as she looked down at the crude scraps of animal hide and fur. Ugh. First William, now Brutus trying to dress her up as he pleased. How long had he been holding on to this getup waiting to humiliate her?

"You may stand, but you cannot leave." Brutus issued the command with cool patience.

"You can't keep me here," Elsie snarled.

He bristled. "I can and I will. Your father made a promise long ago."

"Yeah, yeah, yeah. His firstborn daughter must claim

a shifter. I claimed a shifter."

"Then where is your mate?" Brutus taunted.

Elsie looked at the cave's entrance as though Zackary would magically appear in the opening. Seeing only more darkness and hearing silence that stretched on for miles, Elsie's lower lip trembled. She attempted a halfhearted shrug. Brutus's lips puffed out through his beard.

Smug fucking bastard.

"Did he kick you out of his den, or did you run away, Little Wolf?"

"Stop calling me little."

Brutus scratched his beard, looking her over.

"Or maybe you performed one of your little magic spells on him. Dumb mutt didn't even know what hit him until it was too late. You got what you wanted and now you're running home to daddy."

"You don't know what you're talking about, asshole!" Elsie's scream echoed through the cave. It entered her brain and magnified the pounding at the base of her skull.

"I know plenty," Brutus answered calmly. "I know exactly what you and your father are capable of. You're worse than the wretched humans pillaging what's left of the world. You'd screw over your own mother if she were still alive."

"Shut up, Brutus! You are the foulest being I've ever had the misery of knowing." Hot, angry tears slid down Elsie's cheeks. His rotten words festered inside her mind.

"What kind of weakling wolf did you trick into mating you? I bet he was a scrawny, pathetic little thing. Little wolves humping in the woods."

"My mate is not little. He could kick your sorry ass," Elsie said between clenched teeth.

"You wish so," Brutus said with a smile.

"I know so."

Brutus lumbered over, his broad shoulders towering above the flames and blocking the entrance. "It doesn't matter," he said with finality. "You are mine now."

"You think you can keep an eye on me day and night," Elsie snorted. She might as well sit back down and wait for Brutus to go to sleep or leave the cave in search of food. The moment he left, slept, or let down his guard, she'd shift into full fur—not the stupid scraps covering her breasts—and be on her way.

Brutus grinned. Elsie didn't like it. She narrowed her eyes.

"What's so amusing?" she demanded.

Brutus shuffled back to the wall of his cave and reached behind some large rocks. He kept his body turned sideways, one eye on Elsie, one on what he grabbed. The sound of metal clinking together sent cold fury coiling around Elsie's stomach. The rage and dread magnified when Brutus pulled out a metal chain. He lifted an old frayed collar next, smiling triumphantly.

Elsie scowled. "There's no way you're putting that on me."

Brutus grinned. "Not everything from the human world is a waste. I'll give you a choice. You can put the collar on yourself, or I can do it for you."

He tossed the horrid woven circlet at her feet. It made a soft jingle with the metal heart-shaped name tag still attached. Elsie's stomach roiled. She kicked it into the fire. Brutus shot over in an instant and fished the filthy thing out of the flames with a stick. After dragging it across the sandy floor, he picked it up and sighed.

"I guess I'm going to have to touch you."

"Don't you dare."

She darted to one side of the fire, attempting to misdirect him when she jerked back and went for the other side. Brutus had the advantage on being in his home turf. Size didn't slow him down inside his cave. He moved shockingly fast, surging toward her, his big, beefy arms locking her in their grip.

"Let go!" Elsie screeched. She slammed her heels over his feet and twisted from side to side in his arms. Rubbing torsos with the brute was seriously disturbing, but getting away trumped all.

Brutus had to let go to get the collar around Elsie's neck. When he loosened his hold on her, she pushed away from his chest. Brutus's arms shot forward with the blasted choking device. In his rush, he slammed into her throat, choking her. The brute didn't bother easing up to allow her to breathe. He finished, wrapping the tightly woven material around the back of her neck and securing it tightly.

Her violent coughing brought tears to the corners of her eyes. Elsie was still hacking when Brutus hooked the chain to the metal loop by the collar.

"Finished. You can sit and relax now," he said calmly.

Elsie dropped to the ground, still hacking. With the collar so tight, she felt like she might never find her breath again. Tears continued to spill out. All the while, her hatred of the bear shifter grew. She'd been willing to walk away, but now she had half a mind to kill the beast before she left.

"You are the worst of the worst," she seethed as soon as she could speak without coughing her way through every other word.

"You're mistaking me for your father."

Brutus backed away, dragging one end of the chain with him to the wall of the cave where Elsie noticed a round metal hoop hammered into the rock. The bastard had planned this all along! He clipped the metal leash in place and folded his arms, raising his eyebrows as though expecting Elsie to yell at him.

Oh, she wanted to do more than scream. Disembowelment had a satisfying ring to it.

"You never wanted a mate," she accused. "You wanted a slave. A prisoner. A pet."

Brutus growled, matching her hatred with his own. "I did want a mate, but not you. Someone in my family had to see to it that Lazarus and his offspring suffered. My brothers bitched about it, so I stepped up and offered to make the sacrifice."

"How noble of you," Elsie said bitterly.

"At least my father died knowing that vengeance would be served." Brutus wrapped his fingers around the chain and gave it a slight tug, not enough to pull her over, but to show her he could. Elsie glared at him. Brutus nodded. "I have metal hoops secured all around my territory so that I can keep you with me at all times."

"You planned to collar me all along," Elsie said again,

her heart sinking.

"I knew you had no honor," Brutus fired back. "I knew once I claimed you, you'd take off. You've already proven my point. You let a wolf shifter claim you and then you left him. You're not leaving me, Elsie. If I have to keep you on a chain for the rest of your life, that's your own damn fault."

Angry tears splashed over Elsie's cheeks. She was so sick of crying.

"I hate you," she said between clenched teeth.

"The feeling's mutual." Brutus settled in beside the chain, laying an arm over it and his head on top.

When he closed his eyes, Elsie lifted her bound wrists to her neck. The name tag and links of chain clinked before she had a chance to try and twist the collar around to reach the fastening. Brutus's eyes opened. He watched her, looking way too relaxed about the situation.

Huffing moodily, Elsie turned her back to him and lay on her side, facing the fire. As eager as she was to leave, she needed to dredge up some patience and wait until Brutus was well and truly asleep. After that, she just needed to slip the collar off without making a sound. Hopefully the bear shifter was a loud snorer.

Waiting meant thinking and replaying all the terrible things Brutus had said about her. What hurt the most was they weren't entirely untrue.

No one wanted her, not even the hairy brute. He only desired her punishment. Maybe this was exactly what she deserved.

chapter twenty-three

ZACKARY CRASHED THROUGH brush, racing the sky. Dusk had come, but he would continue to run until he could no longer see his legs below him. A full moon would have been helpful tonight, but he couldn't seem to catch a damn break.

Ignoring the darkness that fell over the forest like an all-encompassing avalanche, it wasn't until Zackary stubbed his toe and ran into a tree that he gave a great groan. Better to wait out the rest of the night unless he wanted to end up with a twisted ankle and no wolf to carry him through.

Grumbling, Zackary got to the ground, not caring that roots and pebbles dug into his back. He didn't want to waste time sleeping while his mate was somewhere in the wilderness all alone, but dusk had fallen, and he couldn't see in the dark. That ability was lost to him forever. It still hadn't sunk in. Maybe it never would.

It wasn't as though the night gave him the benefit of rest either. Mosquitoes swarmed him, making a merry meal out of his arms and neck. Their incessant buzz was the worst part. Zackary slapped at the ones that came near his face.

"Fuck off!" Zackary growled. As though the mosquitoes would listen. He sat up and blindly clapped the air around him. The forest momentarily quieted. He placed his hands in his lap, replaying the last moments of the council meeting right after Elsie disappeared.

"Well done, everyone. Now my sister's out there all alone," Tabor had said bitterly.

Emerson had rolled her eyes and flipped her long blonde hair over her shoulder. "She's hardly defenseless. And I didn't vote to kick her out. I just told her how I felt about being on the receiving end of her spell."

Jager had nodded. "Council members must feel safe to openly discuss pack concerns."

"I didn't vote her out either," Wolfrik had chimed in. "Elsie is a grown woman. She doesn't need to be coddled."

Tabor's scowl had said otherwise.

Zackary, having heard enough, stepped away from the circle. When asked where he was going, he'd answered, "To find my mate."

It didn't matter that he no longer had the ability to sniff her out or catch up. He wouldn't stop until he got to Balmar Heights.

Zackary rubbed his jaw.

The trouble was, he'd never been to Balmar Heights. Knowing which direction the mountain lay probably wouldn't get him there anytime soon. Thinking ahead had never been one of Zackary's strengths. It was his heart that had led him into the woods. He'd climb every damn mountain in the forest if that's what it took.

Zackary lifted his knees and rested his face against them.

Bzzzzzz.

"Fuck!" he bellowed, slapping his cheek. Too late; the little fucker had bitten him.

A male grunted in the dark. "You kiss my sister with that mouth?"

Zackary leapt to his feet, his fingers curling into fists. Turning in a circle, he searched the shadows for the wizard.

"Did you follow me here to kill me?" Zackary demanded.

Flames burst from a rotted out log a couple paces away. Zackary jumped back, crouching, preparing himself for an attack. But the next voice was Sasha's. She walked past the flames naked.

"We're coming with you," she announced, chin raised high.

Zackary quickly turned around to give her privacy. "You mean to start a new pack?" he asked in confusion.

For a moment, he forgot he was no longer a wolf shifter. Even on four legs, it would have been awkward as hell. What an odd mix they'd make: a pureblood, a wizard, a witch, and a shifter who couldn't shift.

"No, we're getting Elsie back, then we're all returning home to Wolf Hollow. A female has a right to protect her mate, and you risked yours to save the hollow. The council has decided that you and Elsie will live in the den. They are in desperate need of extra hands for structural repairs and projects. How does that sound?"

Facing the dark trees, Zackary went still. "If the den needs my help, I am willing to give it. What would Elsie do?"

"She could help tend the garden and watch over the children until the two of you have your own."

The subsequent growl was unmistakably Tabor's. Whispers, followed by low arguing hit Zackary's back before Tabor stopped bickering long enough to huff.

"We'll sleep here for the night," Sasha announced. "Tabor, is there anything you can do about the bugs?"

"Build a bigger fire?" he suggested.

"Let's get to it," Sasha said.

Zackary helped gather twigs and feed them into the flames Tabor had conjured up. He was careful to avoid looking at Sasha's naked form, keeping focused on the task. When they'd built the fire up enough to last the night, they curled around it. Zackary wondered why Sasha and Tabor didn't shift into wolf form for the night. He wondered why they didn't press on without him. Yet he was glad they didn't. He wanted to be the first to reach Elsie, even if that meant arriving with a group. At least this way he could find her faster and not waste time fumbling through the forest. It gave him enough peace of mind to drift off to sleep . . . that and the break from the infernal mosquitoes.

In the morning, Tabor and Sasha hunted down a couple of rabbits. It was another reminder of Zackary's new shortcoming. He wouldn't be able to feed himself let alone his mate. Without a knife to skin the animal, Zackary couldn't even share in the small feast. At least he'd have the tools he needed in the den. Children weren't capable of shifting until their twelfth year, which meant butchering wild game into hunks of meat suitable for roasting over an open flame. Zackary would be like a big child who never reached the age of shifting.

Could be worse, he reminded himself. He could be mad. Or dead.

"You have a mate who loves you," Sasha said softly. "That's what's important." Yet again, she'd shifted without him noticing, and she had an uncanny ability of reading his mind.

"Let's go find Elsie."

Tabor took the lead in wolf form since he knew his sister's scent best. Zackary kept his focus on where he walked and on the direction the wolf led them, doing his best to not accidently look at Sasha.

It felt strange traveling together again. This journey led them deeper into the wilderness—north rather than south. Their query was different.

"I am sorry your father wasn't a better man," Sasha offered somberly.

"I'm glad he's dead," Zackary gritted out.

"You're nothing like him, you know." Zackary kept his mouth clamped tight. "You will make Elsie a good mate," Sasha continued.

"What good am I to her now?" Zackary ground out. He'd never known how to take a compliment, nor pretend like everything was going to be okay.

Staying quiet for several heartbeats, Sasha looked over, offering a gentle smile. "Only you can determine your own self-worth."

Her words didn't bring the intended comfort. He knew she was trying to be nice, and he appreciated it—not many packmates bothered. But Zackary wasn't strong-willed like Sasha. Elsie's love was the only thing that had ever made him feel like a better man—one capable of being more than what his father had seen. She brought out the best in him and made him want to be even better. Living without her didn't feel like any kind of life. He could learn to go without shifting into his wolf so long as he got to be with his mate.

Zackary was encouraged by Tabor's intent nose sniffing over the ground, but they still had to stop when another night cast its shadow over the forest.

"We're getting close," Tabor said as they built up a fire. "For some reason she's traveling in human form."

"Why would she do that?" Stunned, Zackary gaped at Tabor over the low flames rising from the twigs and brush they'd gathered. Tabor shrugged.

Zackary didn't like the thought of Elsie leaving herself exposed to lurking predators, the vulhena among them. The vicious creatures had kept away from the hollow for the past couple months, but that didn't mean they weren't slinking around the outskirts.

Zackary's hands began to sweat. He tightened them into fists then loosened them, repeating the motion.

Sasha cleared her throat. "I think she's walking because she never wanted to leave Wolf Hollow and is hoping Zackary will catch up and bring her back home."

Zackary blinked before the tears had a chance to form. He should have spoken up sooner, returned Elsie's love at the council meeting, admitted that her reason for hastening their claiming didn't change his feelings for her.

"I love her," Zackary said. "I feel like I can't eat or sleep without her." He gripped the back of his neck with one hand and stared into the fire.

Tabor huffed. "You don't deserve her."

"I know."

"Everyone deserves love," Sasha said.

When he looked up, Sasha smiled at him warmly. Tabor's arms were tightly folded and his green eyes seemed to flicker with the flames.

"My sister's happiness better become your number one priority. In the future, you stick by her side no matter what—are we clear?"

Zackary kept his lips pressed tight as he glared at the wizard shifter.

Sasha clapped her hands together. "Excellent. Now that that's settled, let's try and get some rest so we can catch up to Elsie tomorrow."

THEY ROSE AT first light. Tabor and Sasha skipped their morning snack, as eager as Zackary to get going. Tabor said Elsie's scent was getting stronger and, with the early start, they might catch up to her before midday. Zackary's heart pounded with anticipation.

Several paces ahead, Tabor stopped to sniff at a rough trail up a slope with streams trickling down. The wolf picked up his pace, head down, sniffing intently. When Tabor started up the slope in a jog, Zackary and Sasha ran after him, catching up at the top.

Tabor looked from one direction to another before taking a path that leveled out along blackberry bushes. Seeing the berries made Zackary's stomach clench. He nearly tripped over the wolf when Tabor jerked around without warning and headed back the way they'd come. This time, the wolf took off at a sprint and it was all Zackary and Sasha could do to keep him in sight.

The thought of Elsie being close by sent adrenaline spiking straight down Zackary's legs. He ran for all he was worth. A life of labor had strengthened his human body. He pounded over the firm ground leading away from the bushes and back into the forest. Sasha's labored breaths faded as he left her behind. The pureblood could always shift if she needed help catching up.

The sound of Tabor's enraged snarl jolted Zackary into triple speed. He thundered past trees and hoisted himself over a fallen log, swinging his legs over the thick wood before hitting the ground running on the other side.

Through the thicket, he could make out a small clearing with sunlight pouring down, lighting the space in front of the opening to a large cave set into a hill.

What Zackary saw when he reached the clearing nearly brought his wolf out before he clamped it back and the madness that came with it.

Elsie stood with her wrists bound in front of her, wearing a fur bikini top and loincloth, similar to the costumes the females wore during the full moon celebration dance . . . only there was no mask covering the angry red blotches on Elsie's face. And this was no celebration.

The worst offense was the collar wrapped around his mate's neck and the chain binding her to the beast of a man holding the other end. The bastard was naked and ungroomed. He towered over half a head taller than Zackary and showed no alarm at their appearance.

The pounding in Zackary's ears brought out a guttural roar. Before he could make a move for the mongrel, Tabor shifted, pushed out his arms, and yelled, *"Formella lavita!"*

"Tabor, no!" Elsie yelped. "Magic doesn't work on him."

The hairy mass holding Elsie's chain rumbled with laughter.

"And who is this fool? Your half-breed brother?" He laughed again.

Tabor lowered his arms slowly, glowering. "You must be Brutus. Since you're obviously not very bright, let me explain things to you. My sister already has a shifter mate, so you have no right to her."

"Elsie!" Sasha gasped in horror, having just run in.

Neck corded and arms shaking, Zackary came at the man. Brutus's eyes lit up at Zackary's approach. He yanked Elsie to him and she fell to her knees. Zackary stopped and growled, his vision clouding over in fury.

"You weren't lying about your mate not being small," Brutus said, sounding delighted. "This *is* your mate, isn't it?"

Elsie pressed her lips together and glared furiously at Brutus.

"Did he touch you?" Zackary demanded. "Did this filthy beast force himself on you?"

He was going to rip Brutus limb from limb. He'd knock him out with a rock and chain him to a tree first so he could go back to the hollow and borrow an ax. The end of Brutus the bear would not be merciful.

"No," Elsie said. "He's not interested in me that way. He's only trying to humiliate me."

The relief was like the first wisp of breeze on a blistering day. His mate had not been violated. Thank the moon.

Zackary still wanted to kill the beast.

"I'm sure the rest of you have as much honor as the little witch, which is to say none," Brutus said. "Her father made an agreement with mine over two decades ago. She was promised to me as recompense for the sins committed against my family by Lazarus and his coven."

"How does forcing an innocent to become your mate make past grievances any better?" Sasha folded her arms over her breasts.

Brutus smiled at her slowly.

"That is no innocent you welcomed into your wolf pack. But you're right. Taking the little witch-wolf doesn't begin to make up for stolen territory. My brothers and I have been too lenient while waiting for Lazarus to fulfill his end of the bargain and hand over his daughter. Perhaps she was a decoy all along." Brutus turned to Elsie and sneered. There wasn't the faintest glimmer of interest in his gaze, not even lust. For that, Zackary was grateful, but the brute could still harm his mate.

Noticing the rage brewing on Zackary's face, Brutus gave a nod of understanding.

"I can see you want to fight me, and I am game for that. How do you want to do this, tough guy? Bear to wolf or man to man?"

"Man to man," Zackary ground out, eyes locked on Brutus.

The bear shifter dropped the chain and cracked his knuckles. "Fine by me." He jutted his chin and smiled smugly. Zackary's fist tightened.

"Just walk away, Brutus. You're outnumbered," Elsie said.

The brute's smile turned into a sneer. Skin wrinkled around his eyes and he growled through his beard.

"Shut your mouth, woman."

Snarling, Zackary threw the first punch, smacking Brutus square in the jaw. Brutus's big head snapped back. He jerked forward with a roar, rubbing his chin through his bristling beard. Zackary lifted his fists, ready for the bear shifter to come at him.

Brutus tugged at his beard, shoulders relaxing. He gave a rumbling laugh. Zackary narrowed his eyes.

Puffing up his hairy muscled torso, Brutus beat his fists against his chest then started forward, eyes intent on Zackary. The next time Zackary swung at the brute, Brutus ducked and shoved him. Stumbling backward a couple feet, outrage burned through Zackary, made worse by Brutus's laughter. He heard his father's cruelty in that taunt.

Zackary charged, only to be flung to the ground.

Elsie gasped.

Zackary refused to look at her, not until he'd beaten the bear shifter. He wanted Brutus on the ground bleeding.

Jumping back to his feet as though he'd never fallen, Zackary made as though he would storm Brutus again only to stop at the last second. As predicted, the bear shifted leaned forward to grab him, only to stumble when his hands hit air. Brutus scowled. Zackary might have smirked if it weren't for the fact that he was still seething at the sight of his mate nearly naked and chained like a sex slave. Zackary spread his arms wide, making himself appear bigger. He'd always felt abnormally large, but in front of Brutus it was as though he'd shrunk down to average size.

They circled one another, their chests jutting forward and their arms spread high. It felt like a savage dance in which one wrong move could lead to injury and pain. After Zackary made another false attempt at attacking, Brutus copied him, barreling forward. Zackary shuffled aside on quick feet. Normally, his mass made him feel slow, but today he was matched with a male on the bulky side. Brutus wasn't particularly fast or stealthy. The more they circled and tested one another, the more Zackary learned of the bear shifter's fight tactics. Brutus was a lumbering beast who breathed heavier as their scuffle dragged on.

Zackary lowered his arms and took a step back. When Brutus came toward him, he walked backward with a smile, leading Brutus into another circle around the small clearing.

Brutus no longer chuckled. His expression turned pinched and angry, and he emitted low huffs whenever he appeared to think he'd catch up, only to end up chasing air.

"Wise choice fighting in human form," Brutus said. "My bear would have had your entrails strewn across the clearing by now."

"My wolf would have ripped open your throat before that ever happened," Zackary bluffed since he couldn't use his animal's help. The rabid beast might have no interest in a bear and go after his packmates instead or flee. Even a mad wolf kept a sense of self-preservation.

"Is she worth it?" Brutus asked.

"I love her." Saying it aloud made it easier to express over and over—even to a thickheaded bear shifter who wouldn't know what love was if it bit him on his hairy ass.

Brutus snorted. Yep. Zackary had been right about the moron.

"Her breasts are too small." Brutus braced himself, clearly expecting Zackary to charge. He bounced on the balls of his toes, keeping his spot, building his energy for the right moment.

"My mate's body is none of your concern," Zackary said in a calm, even tone.

Brutus narrowed his eyes. "You don't care that she was using you."

Zackary shrugged. "I got a mate out of it, which is more than I can say for you."

With a roar, Brutus charged. Zackary sidestepped the enraged shifter and used the force of Brutus's own weight to shove him from behind. He pushed with all his might, his clammy palms slapping the male's hairy muscled back. Brutus stumbled forward, nearly catching himself until losing his footing and landing on his hands and knees. Wasting no time, Zackary lunged at the fallen brute, swinging his fists, pummeling him on his exposed back and sides. He held nothing back.

Brutus scurried forward over the ground, getting up before Zackary could stop him. He whirled around, bringing his fist with him. The impact against the side of Zackary's skull sent him reeling. The ground rushed up at him, which is how he noticed the thick fallen branch near his feet.

Spots of light danced in front of his vision. He hunched over, blinking rapidly. It was shocking that Brutus didn't attack him after stunning him with his blow. The bear shifter was either slow in the head or extremely confident he'd win this fight. Zackary kept his sights on the heavy branch just in case.

"I've got my eyes on him, Zackary. I'll warn you if he decides to shift," Tabor called out.

Brutus growled. "I will do no such thing. We agreed to fight man to man, and man to man we shall fight until one of us wins. I keep my word."

While the bear shifter bellowed over his integrity, Zackary made a split-second decision. Once his arms were in motion, there was no turning back. He lunged to the ground and grabbed the fallen branch, comforted by its dense weight. Jumping up, he spun around and ran at Brutus, swinging the branch back. He aimed for the male's face, taking in Brutus's shocked expression. The bear shifter only had time to open his eyes wider before the branch struck him. They heard a sickening snap that sounded more like bone than branch.

Brutus bellowed in pain, hands cupping his face. When he pulled his fingers away, blood gushed from his nose.

Maybe it had been a cheap shot, but honor wasn't something Zackary prided himself on.

Once a mongrel, always a mongrel. He'd do anything to protect his mate.

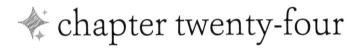 chapter twenty-four

"TIME TO GET out of here," Sasha hollered.

Zackary kept hold of the branch, focus on the hairy male. Brutus wasn't on the ground yet. As blood continued to run over the male's thick lips, horror entered his eyes. Brutus turned, running for the cave.

"Zackary, let's go!" Tabor yelled.

Blinking rapidly, Zackary took notice of his packmates headed in the opposite direction of the cave as though they intended to sprint for the woods as soon as he joined them. During the fight, someone must have helped Elsie out of the collar and ropes binding her wrists.

Worried, beseeching blue eyes found his. "Please, Zackary. Let's go," she said.

He nodded and jogged toward his group. They ran the way they'd come and continued running until they'd reached the bottom of the hill.

"I'll shift so all my senses remain alert in case he tries to follow us," Tabor announced, glancing over his shoulder.

"I will too," Sasha said.

The mated pair changed into fur within several blinks

of the eyes. The wolves took up the rear while Zackary and Elsie set a brisk pace back to the hollow.

"Am I allowed to go back?" Elsie asked softly, eyes on the ground.

Zackary repeated what Sasha had told him, leaving out the part about starting their own family.

"Do you still want me?" Elsie's voice was no more than a whisper.

Zackary tugged on his ear. Their claiming had been followed by a shit storm of revelations, violence, and life altering consequences. He was ready to put it all in the past.

Zackary stopped in his tracks and turned to her, taking her delicate fingers in his hands. "I will always want you, Elsie. I love you."

Tears glossed over her eyes. She sucked in a shaky breath.

"You'll forgive me?" He didn't like how small her voice sounded, as though the joy had been crushed out of her.

"You saved me," Zackary said.

"I . . . tricked you." Elsie wrinkled her nose.

"You could have told me the truth from the start, you know."

Elsie shook her head. "No. I couldn't. You would have thought that was the only reason I wanted to be with you, then you would have never known the truth." Fresh tears filled her eyes. "I love you so much it hurts, Zackary. I didn't want this damn curse to get in the way of you believing my feelings for you were genuine. No one has ever meant as much to me as you."

Zackary felt himself falling for Elsie all over again, wanting to win her over, mate her, and make her his. Leaning forward, his eyes hooded, Zackary's kiss was cut off by a low growl.

Elsie's eyebrows lifted. She and Zackary turned to find Tabor's wolf glaring at them with his lips lifted over his teeth.

"Uh, I guess he wants us to keep moving. Lots of ground to cover," Elsie said.

"Yeah, I'm sure that's it."

When Elsie smiled at him, Zackary chuckled. Soon they were both laughing. He held on to her hand, walking forward, because the wolf wizard was right to urge them on. The farther they got away from the bear shifter's cave, the better. Brutus didn't know that Zackary could no longer shift, and he wanted to keep it that way.

"So, my brother's really okay with us?" Elsie asked, sneaking a peek over her shoulder.

"Yeah, couldn't you tell by how happy he sounded a moment ago?"

Elsie put her free hand to her mouth, stifling a giggle. She lowered her fingers, grinning up at Zackary. "Was that a joke?"

Zackary grinned and shrugged. He didn't care when his hand turned clammy or that he could have used it for balance, he kept hold of Elsie's hand until they found a place to stop for the night. A steep, earthen shelf jutted along a mossy patch of ground. There was enough overhang to act as a ceiling, not that there were any clouds in the sky.

"No fire tonight," Tabor said after shifting. "We don't want to alert Brutus to our whereabouts in case he pursues us."

"He probably thinks we're long gone in wolf form," Sasha reasoned.

"Still," Tabor said with a frown.

Sasha nodded. "We'll shift back to wolves and hide in the bushes farther up in case he happens to amble this way."

Zackary and Elsie were still smiling at one another when Tabor faced them and scowled.

"You two, keep quiet. No funny business."

Zackary had a few choice words for Tabor's commands, but given the circumstances, he held his tongue. They weren't home safe yet.

"I mean it," Tabor said as he got onto the ground to shift.

Zackary turned his back to him and rolled his eyes.

Sasha joined her mate on the ground. Once they were in fur, they trotted off silently into the woods.

Elsie's chin dropped as she looked down and frowned, picking at her fur bikini.

"Ugh, I wish I'd gotten my dress back before fleeing. I never saw what he did with it—probably shredded the thing."

Like that, rage billowed straight back up to Zackary's head. "He undressed you?"

Elsie looked up and scowled. "Don't worry. Brutus said he didn't cop a feel, and I believe him. He seemed truly disgusted by me."

Zackary growled. "If I wasn't so relieved, I'd knock him over his thick head for insulting my mate."

Chuckling, Elsie lifted onto her tiptoes and kissed Zackary on the cheek. He craved more than kisses, but it was a nice start.

"So, no fire," Elsie drawled, glancing around. "I guess you'll have to keep me warm tonight. No funny business, though." She wagged her finger at Zackary and laughed.

Tabor could keep his rules. Zackary had his mate back and he got to hold her in his arms all night long.

Elsie WOKE TO strong arms hugging her middle and her mate spooning her from beneath the earthen shelf where they'd lain down to rest. At first, she feared she was dreaming, but Zackary's steady breath at the back of her neck reassured her that not all was lost. She would have liked to snuggle longer, but all too soon Tabor walked over and frowned at them.

"Time to go."

They continued their brisk pace, keeping conversation to a minimum. It gave Elsie lots of time to think and for the guilt to seep back in. As the sky darkened on the last night before they reached the hollow, Elsie felt a cloud settle over her heart.

As with the previous evening, Tabor and Sasha took to wolf form and hid a short distance off in the brush. Zackary had found a soft patch of moss behind a boulder where they would cuddle up and get some sleep before the final trek home.

Elsie held back as Zackary made himself comfortable, lying on his side. He patted the area in front of him. Uncrossing the arms she'd wrapped around her middle, Elsie took a seat beside her mate.

"I'm so sorry, Zackary," she whispered, not meeting his eyes. "For everything, and especially for the loss of your wolf."

Zackary sat up and placed his hands lightly on her shoulders, leaning forward. He didn't speak until she looked into his beautiful brown eyes.

"I would have lost myself completely if it hadn't been for you."

She nodded sadly. "I still feel horrible."

"Well, stop." Zackary's firm tone made her sit up and pay attention. She blinked. A smile curved up Zackary's luscious lips. "Claiming me was supposed to be the key to your happiness, remember?"

He lowered his hands off her shoulders and nudged her arm with his. Elsie pursed her lips, not convinced she was ready to stop wallowing.

When Zackary's finger trailed down her collarbone to the valley between her breasts, her breath hitched. A satisfied smile lifted his lips.

"What would you say to some funny business?" he asked huskily.

Like that, Zackary turned her frown into a smile. Her mate knew exactly how to cheer her up.

APPROACHING THE HOLLOW the following

afternoon, Elsie reached for Zackary's hand. He gave her a reassuring squeeze.

How would the pack react to her return? Had she lost the few close friends she'd made? Would packmates merely tolerate her? Ignore her? Despise her?

After crossing the Sakhir River, Elsie's steps slowed. Zackary turned to her and offered a warm smile.

"It's going to be okay."

She nearly laughed. Her mate was the one who had lost his wolf, and yet he was comforting her.

Tabor and Sasha shifted to human form after crossing the river.

"Home," Sasha said happily, her smile brightening as she lifted her head to take in the familiar trees.

They headed down a trail to the glade. From the position of the sun, it was just after midday. Most shifters would be on duty so at least Elsie didn't have to parade in front of a large gathering. She wasn't expecting a warm welcome, but even more than that, she really wasn't expecting to find Brutus in his brown fur pacing the glade. He knocked over a table with clean bowls, sending them crashing to the ground.

"Hey!" Elsie yelled.

Lacy and Diego ran in from the woods, eyes widening when they saw the bear and broken bowls.

Brutus stood on two legs and roared.

Tabor and Sasha took one look at each other then dropped to the ground to shift. Brutus came down onto all fours with a thump that shook the ground. When he started for Tabor and Sasha, Elsie ran along the edge of the glade, waving her arms.

"Hey, Brutus. Over here!"

The bear growled and went after Elsie.

"No!" Zackary shouted.

Elsie scrambled up the nearest sturdy tree, adrenaline sending her up with the speed of a squirrel. She grabbed at branches and pulled herself up higher as Brutus appeared below bellowing in outrage. A rock flew at his back and bounced off. Brutus's jaw opened wide as he roared.

Four wolves snarled back.

While Brutus had chased Elsie, Lacy and Diego had undressed and shifted. The four wolves stalked toward the bear, their ears flattened against their backs and their lips lifted over glistening fangs. Their growls chorused around the glade, soon echoed by howls from around the hollow.

Brutus charged the wolves who circled around him easily. He spun around, batting the air with his great big paw. The wolves sprinted behind him, making him turn and turn and turn, bellowing the whole while.

Six more wolves ran into the glade. Now ten wolves snarled and snapped at the bear, putting him on the defense. Brutus circled frantically in place, raking a paw through the air to keep the wolves from closing in on him.

When four more ran in, he charged through the group and took off running across the glade in the direction of the Sakhir River. All but two of the wolves gave chase, howling in pursuit. When their cries began to fade off, one of the wolves who had remained behind lifted her head and issued a piercing howl.

Elsie wasn't surprised to see the female wolf shift into

Sasha afterward.

Zackary rushed over to the tree, helping Elsie as she climbed down.

As Tabor shifted, Jager limp-hopped into the glade, worry lines wrinkling his forehead.

"What in tarnation is going on?"

The first wolves back from the chase were Lacy and Diego. The blonde shifter changed form beside her discarded dress, pulling it back on before jogging over to the broken bowls. Her hand covered her mouth and she said, "Oh no. So many broken."

Elsie lowered her head. She'd brought this havoc to the hollow. Zackary put his arm around her and pulled her against his side. It was tempting to bury her face into his chest and hide.

Wolves entered the glade from all angles—some returning from the chase, others arriving from patrol areas farther out. One by one, they shifted into human form, filling the grassy expanse as though the gong had summoned them for dinner stew. Elsie winced with each new arrival. They'd all hate her for sure.

"Elsie! Zackary!" Wiley hollered, lifting his arm from across the glade before jogging toward them.

Well, maybe not everyone.

Justin sauntered over, scratching his chin. "Welcome back, lovebirds. Glad you worked everything out."

Before Zackary or Elsie could respond, a shrieking female caught everyone's attention.

Francine screamed from the middle of the glade. "What happened here?" she demanded.

"Everyone, calm down," Sasha said, stepping in front of Francine. "The matter is dealt with. A bear shifter charged into the glade. He's gone now and I doubt he'll come back, but we'll keep a patrol on the lookout."

"What was a bear shifter doing in the hollow?" Francine asked in her shrill voice.

Elsie wrapped her arms around Zackary's middle, wishing she could disappear from sight.

Sasha's eyes found Zackary. She lifted her chin and smiled.

"Zackary fought the bear shifter after the brute captured his mate. He fought him and won. The bear shifter obviously wasn't happy about the outcome."

Stunned faces turned to stare at Zackary with open mouths. Justin was the first to break the silence.

"Way to go, Zack!" He gave a cheer and jumped up, fist pumping the air. "You the man—taking down a bear."

Wiley nodded eagerly, lips grinning.

Francine's head jerked to Sasha. "How is that possible? We were told Zackary can no longer shift."

"They fought in human form," Sasha said.

"I bet the bear shifter is a big man," Wiley mused.

Elsie loosened her arms from around Zackary's waist to stand straight. "Bigger than anyone here," she couldn't help saying.

"Bigger than Aden?" Wiley asked.

"Oh yeah," Elsie said.

"Wow." Wiley's eyes widened, bringing a smile to her lips.

Francine folded her arms, but Elsie lost sight of

the cantankerous den mate as shifters came forward, surrounding her and Zackary, asking for details of the fight since Sasha wasn't one to embellish. Besides, it was Zackary's tale to tell.

He was the victor.

The hero.

The champion of Elsie's heart.

⚚ chapter twenty-five

WHILE THE SHIFTERS in the glade spoke in boisterous groups, Lacy crouched beside the overturned table, picking up shards of porcelain and placing them inside an empty basket.

Diego knelt beside her and helped. Lacy paused, turning to smile at him. That gorgeous grin was all the motivation he needed to pick up every last sliver of broken materials.

"All right, everyone," the pack's elder said, clapping his hands together. "Back to patrol. You can talk more tonight during supper."

"Where's your brother?" Lacy paused just long enough to look around the gathering.

Diego chuckled, unworried. "Probably exploring beyond the hollow's boundaries. He's a wanderer."

With a nod, Lacy resumed her task. More than half the bowls had broken in the crash. Damn bear. In all his travels, Diego had never gotten close to any bear shifters. They kept to themselves. Today's confrontation didn't make him any keener to cross paths with one.

The clearing quieted as shifters ambled into the woods. A petite female wearing the hollow's ceremonial costume walked over.

"I'm so sorry about this," she said. "Can I help?"

Lacy looked up. "It's not your fault, and I think we can manage."

The brown-haired female—Elsie, was it?—chewed on her bottom lip. "The next time I visit Balmar Heights, I will scrounge up as many bowls as I can carry to bring back to Wolf Hollow."

"Thanks," Lacy said. "I guess everyone will have to share for a while."

Diego hid a smile. He wouldn't mind sharing a bowl of food with Lacy.

Sasha walked swiftly over to them. "Thanks for cleaning up this mess, Lacy," the pureblooded female said. She looked at Diego next. "And thank you for helping. It is very nice of you." He shrugged like it was no big deal. Sasha turned to the petite shifter in the fur bikini. "Elsie, I'd like to get you and Zackary settled in the den. Ready?"

Casting one last look at the broken mess of bowls, Elsie lifted her head to face the pureblood and nodded.

After they'd gone, leaving Diego alone with Lacy, he cleared his throat.

"Is there always this much excitement in your pack?"

Lacy chucked a large piece of white porcelain into the basket then pulled her blonde hair over one shoulder.

"This is our first bear attack, but I guess we have been shaking things up lately. There've been a lot of recent claimings." She smiled playfully. "No one said courtship was easy."

Her grin lit his own. "Is that what this is—a courtship? Will you and I have a lot of drama?"

"Not if you behave." She batted her eyelashes then resumed picking up bowl fragments.

Diego chuckled. Damn, she was cute. Stubborn, but sweet. He had to have her for his mate—whatever it took.

It was time to talk to his brother.

NEARLY A WEEK after the bear incident in the glade, the sound of hammering echoed all the way to the den's communal garden where Elsie and Kallie removed bean pods that had been left to dry and brown for seed saving.

"I love that you're living in the den," Kallie said as she pulled another pod from the matured plant.

It had been such a relief to see her friend's happy face the moment Elsie and Zackary made the den their home. Kallie had been bursting with excitement from the start.

"Ever since your return, Wolfrik's been spending more time around here. At this rate, he might finish our shelter before winter." Shooting Elsie a sly smile, Kallie added, "I think he just wants to finish before Zack."

"Well, whatever motivates your wild wolf man," Elsie replied cheerfully. "It shouldn't be too difficult to finish before us since everyone seems to want Zackary's help with repairs." She sighed, but she felt too much contentment to mind. "Maybe one day I'll get my treehouse."

"Something tells me your mate would move mountains

to make you happy," Kallie said with a chuckle.

"He doesn't have to move anything. He makes me happy every day all on his own."

Kallie's smile reached her eyes. "I know exactly what you mean."

After they finished removing pods, Elsie carried the beans in a basket to the community shed where they would spend another couple week's drying out. She really enjoyed the down-to-earth way things were done in the hollow rather transforming things like sand to flour at Balmar Heights. Everyone here was in tune to Mother Earth and the natural order of things. Although she considered herself a decent hunter, she found satisfaction in working the soil—especially when it meant partnering up with her dear friend.

Contentment buoyed her spirits. She felt like she was right where she wanted to be.

Before returning to the garden, she skipped over to a tiny home belonging to the shifter couple Farley and Tanya. Elsie ducked around back where Zackary crouched at the base of the wall, holding up a misshapen plank of wood as he nailed it into a gap between boards. A rotted piece of wood had been tossed aside a few feet away. Farley, burly with a big bushy dark beard, carried over more wood planks. Each one looked pretty rough and uneven, but the den mates shaped them as best they could with the tools they had.

"Hi, guys," Elsie said.

Zackary turned around, grinning up at her. Sweat glistened over his bare muscular chest and on his forehead. Elsie licked her lips.

"It looks like you're getting a lot of work done," she said.

Smiling through his beard, Farley nodded. "Thanks to your mate here. Zackary has been a huge help. There's practically a line forming for his services." Farley winked at Elsie. She chuckled, happy Zackary was keeping busy and appreciated. She could wait for their treehouse.

Farley's mate, Tanya, rounded the home carrying two glasses.

"Water, Zackary?" She handed him a clay cup before he could answer.

"Thank you," he said, tipping it back and swallowing deeply, clearly parched.

That was her mate, too nice to say anything. He'd work through the night if there was lighting.

Elsie was glad for the darkness. The treehouse could wait, but her evenings with her mate weren't to be messed with.

"Water, Elsie?" Tanya asked politely.

"No, thank you. I'm headed back to the garden—just saying hi to my sweetie."

A faint blush entered Zackary's cheeks. Farley and Tanya stared at one another, sharing a tender smile.

That evening, they had dinner with Heidi, Peter, and their kids, Amy and Eric. Den mates were taking turns inviting the newest mated pair over for meals until they had a setup of their own.

After eating, Elsie and Zackary retired to their small tent. Heidi had helped dig it out of the shed, saying new couples used them while working on a more permanent structure. Zackary had erected the tent beneath the tree he and Elsie picked out for their eventual home above the ground.

Elsie looked up wistfully before crawling into their tent for the night. She could already picture their cozy dwelling with its enclosed living area and open deck where she could sit with her legs dangling over the ledge watching den mates go about their day. They'd need a couple of climbing ropes, too—for their kids and their friends. And a swing! They definitely needed swings. All the other children were going to want to come over and play at their treehouse every day.

It was going to be so much fun. Their lives would be filled with laughter.

Smiling wide, Elsie settled onto their shared blanket. Having rinsed off in the river after dinner, Zackary climbed in naked. Elsie changed in the tent knowing her mate preferred other shifters not see her naked. That was fine with her. She didn't mind showing her body to her mate alone. It still felt awkward to her, having grown up always clothed. She liked watching her mate's eyes alight as she pulled her dress over her head and stuffed it along the side of the tent. She especially liked being seized by her legs and pulled to him until their bodies became one. This time and space was theirs without interruptions.

As her mate made love to her in the confines of their tent, Elsie couldn't help a teasing smile.

"You know, as long as we're living in the den, we might as well get started on our own family."

Zackary went still and stared straight ahead. In the lingering silence, Elsie worried that she was pressuring him too soon. She wasn't one to drag things out, but she had already rushed him into the claiming.

"Never mind," she said quickly. "We should build our treehouse first. And I didn't realize how much help these couples needed. How did they even manage before you moved to the den?" Elsie stroked Zackary's arm. He was so toned and fit. They'd make beautiful children . . . one day. *"Nolosha para bos, nolosha para–"*

"Stop," Zackary said, interrupting her protection spell. Elsie squinted up at him.

"No more spells."

"But–"

"Let's have a baby."

Elsie's heart expanded. "Really?"

"Yeah." Zackary rubbed the back of his neck.

"Are you sure?" Elsie pursed her lips, unconvinced.

Caging her head in between his arms, Zackary dipped down and kissed her on the nose.

"Yes," he said. "But you're going to have to be the disciplinarian."

Before she could answer, *"Fine, I'll keep our little rascals in line,"* Zackary was rocking his hips in a rolling motion that made her moan.

Their nearest neighbors, Flynn and Chloe, would be smiling knowingly at them in the morning.

Who knew? If Zackary got her pregnant soon enough, maybe he'd finish building their home before Wolfrik. Nothing like a little friendly competition in the den.

✦ "tail" end ✦

SOUTHEAST OF THE hollow's den, Rafael ran past a cluster of hills that made up part of their host's borders. He had explored all the perimeters several times and taken to short sprints beyond the territory. He always returned for meals. Tonight, as the sun faded, he had half a mind to catch his own dinner rather than join the Wolf Hollow shifters in their routine feast. Spending an evening away would serve Diego right for drooling hopelessly over the dainty blonde shifter.

After he'd put some distance between himself and his brother, Rafael shifted into human form and shook his fist at the half-moon that had appeared in the blue horizon several hours prior to dusk.

Fucking Diego. Rafael wanted to wring his brother's neck. Better yet, knock him on his furry back and take his neck between his jaws. They should shift into beasts first then have it out. Maybe the idiot would be more reasonable in animal form.

Settling down had never been part of the plan.

Wolf Hollow wasn't a bad place, but it wasn't their

pack, and it certainly wasn't their home.

Rafael's grumbles came out as growls through his wolf's lips. He'd shifted several times. In human form he could cuss, which he'd done brashly in both Spanish and English. In wolf form he could snarl, which required no translation, pronunciation, or explanation.

He was all kinds of pissed off.

Rafael had stormed off right after Diego finished sharing his intention of wooing the little blonde she-wolf, claiming her, and settling down with his new mate in Wolf Hollow. Just like that he'd chosen a female over his own brother. They'd spent their entire lives together as a team. No one deserved Diego's loyalty more than Rafael. No one! Certainly not some hussy who knew exactly how to bait his brother. It was the quiet, seemingly sweet ones who were most dangerous.

Finding himself back on two legs, kicking at pebbles, he bellowed. "Damn it, Diego!"

No female would ever pull that shit with Rafael. Hump and haul out. He always made his intentions clear from the start.

"I'm not looking for a mate or to settle down. Take it or leave it," he'd told the two females he'd boned after the welcome celebration.

They'd taken what he had to offer with pleasure. No fighting. No drama. That was how it was done.

But oh no, Diego had gone and picked the one female who liked to play games.

Yep, better to keep away tonight so he didn't run into the glade and bite Diego's head off. Speaking of which,

Rafael was ready to shift again. He dropped onto all fours, relishing his body's metamorphosis into the lean, muscled beast that provided warmth, food, and protection against predators. His wolf had carried him across the continent. What kind of wolf shifter chose to settle down when there was an entire landform to explore?

One who was whipped, that's who.

It was a sad day indeed when Diego would rather curl up at a female's feet and eat scraps from the community cauldron than roam free.

Rafael resumed snarling, snapping at a log that he momentarily mistook for a beast of some sort—an inert bear or mountain lion.

He was projecting onto his poor wolf. In a matter of seconds, his beast form took over propelling him into a jog. Annoyance at his brother turned into a hollowed-out ache of loneliness. Rafael's wolf didn't enjoy running alone. He wanted his family, his best friend . . . his only packmate.

Stopping on a narrow path trampled over time by deer, he lifted his head and howled. When he lowered his muzzle, surprise jolted him at the sight of a beautiful white wolf standing before him. She'd appeared like a spirit, but unlike a phantom, her scent filled his nostrils. She stared straight at him with bright eyes that were like moonbeams. It felt as though the moon had created her especially for him after all these years of wandering without an equal.

Unlike his obstinate human side, Rafael the wolf longed for a resilient female companion to claim as his own.

This one stood proud and fearless. Something else intrigued him. He sniffed the air. What was that enticing aroma?

Moon above, the female was in heat.

Drawn to the scent of her need, Rafael circled around her, closing in on her arousal. He stuck his nose to her butt and breathed in. The female kept her patience as he got up in her business, flicking his tongue for a taste. She glanced back at him, eyes momentarily closing—the essence of serenity.

Was he dreaming? How had he stumbled upon this healthy, yielding female? The moon wasn't full enough to impregnate her, but she permeated the air with her desire. She had the calm, cool stance of an alpha female and a regal air that communicated she was allowing his perusal…for now.

He rubbed his face against her hind flank, testing her. When she didn't move away, he pressed his luck and mounted her. The female swept her bushy white tail to one side, allowing him entry. She bore his weight without moving an inch while he mated her. Hunched over her soft, thick fur, Rafael burrowed into her overpowering heat, pushing the ground with his hind legs.

Howls in the distance had the female breaking away from him much too soon. As she stepped aside, Rafael slid off her back and landed on the front paws that had been wrapped around her lower belly seconds before.

She sprang past him and took off running westward into the hollow. Rafael gave chase, never quite catching up until she reached the shifters who had gathered for dinner in the glade.

Seeing her shift, he quickly did the same. Crouched to the earth, he lifted his head and watched her sublime beauty unfold as she lifted to her feet and straightened her back. She had smooth, fair skin; firm, perky breasts, and short wavy white-blonde hair that didn't quite reach her shoulders. Her face was perfection: a proud jaw beneath smooth, rosy lips, a slender nose neither too long, nor too short, and arresting olive-brown eyes that gazed with calm ease into the group gawking at her. Lips slightly parted, she looked around the gathering as though she'd been there first and everyone else had materialized with the moon.

Rafael got to his feet and tried to catch her eye, but she appeared to be looking at everyone at once and no one in particular. First, he thought he'd imagined her. Now he felt as though he'd dreamed up the whole mating incident. Maybe it had been a wolf's fantasy. It's not like the beast got a whole lot of action—poor guy. Rafael needed to treat his inner animal better.

Two more wolves ran in and began their shift. One of the wolves was massive and looked vaguely familiar as he got to his feet and towered above everyone. The second wolf was a male who looked about twenty years older than the mysterious female. Her father?

The gorgeous blonde nodded briefly at the older male before turning her attention to the shifters who had gathered closer.

"I am Hailey of Glenn Meadows," she announced. "I was told there was a pureblooded male interested in meeting me."

All eyes now turned to Diego who stood beside Lacy. It was almost worth it to see the meddlesome female's deep frown when she took in Hailey.

No comparison. Both females were slender, but whereas Lacy looked docile and delicate, Hailey appeared limber and athletic. The newcomer had legs for days, ones Rafael could imagine running for miles in both human and wolf form—legs he'd gladly wrap around his torso while he took her standing up.

He'd totally hit that … except that she was a pureblood, so he wouldn't. Number one Raphy rule. Except that he already had. His wolf had mounted and pounded her and she'd let him do her without a single snarl of discontent.

What the fuck?

He covered his cock with his hands before shifters noticed him sprouting wood. Right now the attention was on his dumb-ass brother.

Diego forced a smile.

"I am Diego, a pureblood from the south. I am very sorry you traveled all this way, but my interests have landed elsewhere." Diego placed his arm around Lacy.

Murmurs arose from the pack at Diego's declaration.

Hailey looked from Diego to Lacy. She kept her focus on them, saying nothing, as though holding her silence long enough would make Diego alter his answer.

The male who had come in after her grumbled something Rafael couldn't make out. Ignoring the older wolf, Hailey slowly turned her attention to the rest of the shifters present. She passed over the females quickly, while studying the males.

Rafael's heart rate kicked up, thumping heavily against his chest.

"Thank you for coming," Sasha said, pushing her way

through the crowd. She walked up to Hailey and smiled warmly. "I am Sasha."

The male who had grumbled before looked Sasha up and down with a scowl. Both pureblooded females ignored him.

"You are very welcome to stay as long as you like," Sasha continued in a friendly tone. "Diego is not the only pureblooded male visiting our pack. His brother, Rafael, is here as well." Sasha didn't need to point. Her direct gaze provided Hailey with a clear view.

Keen olive-brown eyes fastened on his. He was the only naked male standing around, not counting the travelers who had just arrived. She had to know he'd been the wolf on her back. If she did, she gave nothing away. She just kept looking at him like he was a wild boar she intended to hunt down and devour. The slightest smile appeared on her lips only to vanish a second later.

He had to fight the urge to turn away so she wouldn't see his arousal. This bitch wasn't about to dominate him. Rafael stood his ground, cupping his balls and wooden dick, cursing his brother *and* Sasha.

Fucking Diego. Fucking pureblooded females.

If he didn't get out of there soon, this dangerous beauty was going to fuck him up good.

His greatest fear was he'd enjoy letting her take him down.

Rejoin the Wolf Hollow shifters in Animal Attraction. Turn the page for behind the scenes commentary and what's coming next.

author's note

Elsie and Zackary's love story is one I waited with anticipation to tell for several years. Roadblocks in my own life meant getting to their tale took longer than I would have liked, but we got there! I loved being a part of this couple's star-crossed journey filled with self-discovery, sacrifice, and second chances. It was wonderful catching up with their packmates along the way.

Halfway through writing *Moon Cursed*, my father died of a heart attack. It was devastating. I couldn't function. Going up to Alaska (where my dad had been visiting my sister, Sara) to attend his Celebration of Life helped me to process and heal. When I returned, I tried to jump back into *Moon Cursed* only to find I was emotionally drained. Zack and Elsie had some heavy issues of their own to go through. I felt like I should be able to describe their anguish in detail, going through such raw feelings myself. But I couldn't. I had nothing to give these characters. Rather than fall into a state of panic, I allowed myself time to grieve and find my way back to life. I did a lot of meditating, took long walks, danced in the kitchen to music, and reconnected with family. When I felt ready, I burrowed back into the hollow. It felt cathartic to get back to that place beyond here. The place where stories take us.

I know Zackary wasn't popular in the beginning, or maybe ever, but reading back over the previous books, I was reminded of how hard he worked to redeem himself and how he and Elsie had their eyes on each other from the moment she appeared. Knowing Zackary's history of mental and physical abuse pulled at my heartstrings. I love each of the Wolf Hollow males for different reasons. Zackary has an extra special place inside my heart.

What's next? At one point, I planned to wrap up the series with a fifth and final book: Aden in *Forever Free*. But then Rafael and Diego wandered in and captured my fancy. From the very beginning, when Hector first visited Wolf Hollow in book one, I wanted to introduce his sister Hailey to a future WHS novel. As soon as Rafael spouted off about never wanting to claim a mate, I couldn't resist. Hailey is this badass, sensual yet pragmatic, pureblood I'm excited to show you more of in WHS #5: *Animal Attraction*.

Being the bleeding heart I am, I also have plans for Brutus in WHS #6: *Bear Claimed*. Wizards stole his family's mountain community then tricked him out of a mate. This bear shifter is holding onto a heavy grudge. Skulking on the edges of Wolf Hollow, he never expects a feisty female wolf shifter (holding a grudge of her own) to give him the night of his life. Can you tell which packmate I'm referring to?

"Stop being a tease. When are these books releasing, already?"

Currently, reader interest is with my fantasy romance series: Royal Conquest. Now that the main saga is complete, I am working on shorter follow-up books with second generation characters whose voices are shouting to be heard. I think one character may have even dreamscaped and threatened to blow lust dust over me if I didn't get my mortal booty back to Faerie. That said, I am making a commitment to finish Wolf Hollow Shifters, even if it means squeezing in one book a year. The beauty of this series is that each book is complete on its own. Each new couple gets a chance to go through their story arc and claim a forever mate. I might tease you with hints of what's to come, but I will never leave you hanging from a cliff.

If you would like to see WHS books release sooner, your reviews are a huge help in encouraging new readers to give the hollow a visit. Thank you for supporting Wolf Hollow! I have links at the back of the book on where you can follow me to receive release alerts when new titles are available.

Before I sign off, I want to thank the WHS Team. My editors; Jordan Rosenfeld, Hollie Westring, and Roxanne Willis; cover designer, Najla Qamber; and paperback interior designer, Nada Qamber. Thanks to my publishing coach, Kate Tilton, for keeping me on track; and my PA, Bam Shepherd, for helping me navigate social media and stay organized. And most importantly, thank you, my incredible readers. You motivate me to continue dreaming up new stories. You inspire me to make each one special. I've got a wonderful pack! I appreciate you all so much.

If you would like to hang out with me outside the hollow, I invite you to join my reader group on Facebook: The Fantasy Fix with Nikki Jefford.

Until next time, look for the beauty, take good care, and run forever free.

Nikki Jefford
October 2019

Nikki News!

Sign up for Nikki's spam-free newsletter. Receive cover reveals, excerpts, and new release news before the general public; enter to win prizes; and get the scoop on special offers, contests, and more.

Visit Nikki's website to put your name on the list. Make sure to confirm your email so you won't miss out:

nikkijefford.com

See you on the other side!

MORE PLACES TO FIND NIKKI JEFFORD

Instagram:

www.instagram.com/nikkijefford

Facebook:

www.facebook.com/authornikkijefford

Twitter:

@NikkiJefford

BookBub:

www.bookbub.com/profile/nikki-jefford

GoodReads:

www.goodreads.com/author/show/5424286.Nikki_Jefford

SLAYING, MAGIC MAKING, RUNNING WILD, AND RULING THE WORLD!

Discover your next fantasy fix with these riveting paranormal romance and fantasy titles by Nikki Jefford:

AURORA SKY: VAMPIRE HUNTER

Night Stalker
Aurora Sky: Vampire Hunter
Northern Bites
Stakeout
Evil Red
Bad Blood
Hunting Season
Night of the Living Dante
Whiteout
True North

SPELLBOUND TRILOGY

Entangled
Duplicity
Enchantment
Holiday Magic

WOLF HOLLOW SHIFTERS

Wolf Hollow
Mating Games
Born Wild
Moon Cursed

ROYAL CONQUEST SAGA

Stolen Princess
False Queen
Three Kings
Holiday Crown

about the author

NIKKI JEFFORD is a third-generation Alaskan now living in the Pacific Northwest with her French husband and their Westie, Cosmo. When she's not reading or writing, she enjoys nature, hiking, and motorcycling. Nikki is the author of the *Wolf Hollow Shifters* series, the *Royal Conquest* saga, the *Aurora Sky: Vampire Hunter* series, and the *Spellbound Trilogy*.

To find out more about her books and new releases, check out her website.

Printed in Great Britain
by Amazon